forbidden love in conception ridge

chloe maine

This collection was first published in 2025, from collected works.

Included works have the following copyright dates

Midnight Snack, 2023

Her Wedding Night, 2024

Unwrapping His Naughty Secret, 2024

All rights reserved. Chloe Maine.

www.chloemaine.com

MIDNIGHT *Snack*

from the author of
Before He Was Her Headmaster

CHLOE MAINE

He was my first crush. But he was my dad's best friend, so he pushed me away...

Now I've done what he told me to do. I went and lived my life. I still know what I want (and it's him, no question), so I show up on his doorstep, hoping he won't turn me away. I may only have one night to convince him that we both need to test the wild chemistry between us. So I'm going to make myself the most irresistible, secret midnight snack he's ever been offered. And I'll have to hope that once he has a taste, he won't be able to let me go again.

1
eden

FOG ROLLS OUT, cinematically, from between the rain-soaked trees as I slow my nondescript sedan to a stop at a cabin in the woods just outside Conception Ridge, Oregon.

If this were in a thriller movie, I'd be the plucky young FBI investigator closing in on my prey.

But I'm not in a thriller movie.

I'm a twenty-two-year-old girl with a general liberal arts degree and a year of sailboat crewing experience. The car is a decade old and on its last legs, but it was all I could afford.

And my only training in taking down a criminal is that I've listened to every single episode of my dad's best friend's true crime podcast.

Since he's my prey, though, I think that makes me an expert in him.

This is his cabin I'm looking at. Raindrops dance upon the windshield, forming delicate patterns that distort the view. I speed up the wipers so I can see better. A warm yellow light glows from a window to the right of the door. Did he hear a car approaching? Will he look out that window?

But there's no sign of Nolan Adler. I won't have a chance to glean any additional information before I knock on his door and we're looking at each other, face-to-face, for the first time in four years.

In my pocket is a letter he gave me when I turned eighteen, with a step-by-step guide on how to prove to him that we are meant to be together. Not that he meant it to be that. He meant it to be a gentle redirection for a girl with a misguided crush on a much older man.

And for almost two years, I believed him. I thought I could outgrow my fiery fantasies of what it might be like for us to be together. Hot, explosive, secretive.

Instead, those dreams have haunted me as I've tried to live a… what did he recommend? *A deeply realized, fulsome adult life.*

A phrase so filthy that if he ever said it on his podcast, his fans would spontaneously combust. Even if they have to look up the word fulsome.

I don't think he realizes just how erotic he makes everything sound.

Although, he should, if he ever spends any time in the comments after a new pod episode drops. *I* certainly do. I know exactly how many women out there want a piece of the reclusive criminology professor who stormed to true crime podcast celebrity two years ago.

But they can't have him. He's mine. He just doesn't know it yet.

I ignore the letter burning a hole in my pocket. The letter that says I'm wrong, that he's not mine, that—

He wrote that when he thought I was a child with a foolish crush.

I'm all grown up now.

Get out of the car, Eden.

Before I can chicken out, I shove the car door open. A light mist hangs in the air, with fat raindrops slapping against my cheeks. Everything smells earthy and intense. Like danger and mystery.

You've listened to too many podcasts, Eden.

I have a small duffel bag on the backseat. I grab that, then take a hesitant step forward. My foot immediately lands in a wet puddle. Great. Sucking in a quick breath, I run to the porch before I can get any further into my own head, and I pound on the door.

For a moment, all I can hear is the pounding of my own pulse. My throat goes dry.

But then there are footsteps on the other side of the door, and the deadbolt is thrown. The handle turns, and—

"Eden?" His voice is an electric shock to my soul. And even though his gray eyes lock onto my face—*oh, I've missed your attention*—I only see surprise and confusion in the smoky depths. "What are you doing here?"

Rain drops that had collected in my hair during my dash now slide down my neck. Cold, wet, slithering reminders that I could have stayed in the Caribbean and just…not bothered. That was always an option, and I chose not to take it.

I shouldn't have just shown up like this, I think to myself, miserably. I should have called first. But if I called first, he could have declined to have me visit.

And now that I'm here on his doorstep, my gaze gobbling him up like I've been starved for too long, I know I wouldn't have run that risk.

He looks the same as he did four years ago. No, he looks even better. The same square jaw, but newly covered in a few days of stubble. His hair is longer, with a few streaks of silver threading through the chestnut brown that's verging on shaggy. He's fitter than ever, wearing a simple t-shirt and jeans, and I can see the muscles in his arms and shoulders as he crosses his arms over his chest.

The wind picks up, causing a chill to settle on my damp skin. I shift my weight, my duffle bag cradling in my arms as I feel the rain drip down my spine.

"Eden," he says softly, prompting me again. His voice is like velvet, and I can feel it wrap around me like a blanket, even if he doesn't mean it that way.

"Surprise," I manage to say weakly.

His brows pull tight and he nods harshly. "It is. Yeah."

From behind him, I hear laughter.

There's no other car in the driveway, but my powers of deductive reasoning didn't go so far as to consider that he might live with someone now.

Wouldn't I know that? Wouldn't I have felt some disturbance in the force?

"It's been a long time," I say. "I wasn't sure if I would be welcome."

The furrowed brow pulls even tighter. "You're my goddaughter, Eden. Of course—"

"You're an atheist," I snap.

Those brows shoot up.

"Sorry."

A ghost of a smile tugs at the corner of his mouth, just for a second. "You aren't sorry."

"I should be." For so, so much. For trying to kiss him the night before my eighteenth birthday.

For not letting go of a stupid, girlish crush a long time ago.

For showing up unannounced when he's making dinner, barefoot and in jeans—the stuff of my fantasies—but for someone else.

I glance past him, into the warmth of his cozy cabin. Where something smells amazing, like garlic and tomatoes. And I try to do some mental calculations of where I could head tonight instead of here. Can I make it to Portland before I have a complete meltdown?

A gust of wind carries damp spray against the bare backs of my legs, and I shudder.

Nolan's arm snaps out and hooks around my back, dragging me inside. "Let's get you out of the rain," he sighs, closing the door behind me.

Then he glances down at my bag. His face hardens.

Okay. I've stepped in it. "I'll leave first thing in the morning," I promise. "I'm on my way to Vancouver."

That's not exactly a lie. My back-up plan is to keep driving north on the coast and soothe my broken heart in a winter of working at ski resorts.

"Fun adventure up there?"

Maybe. But I have some things to say before closing this chapter finally. Will I be able to fully immerse myself in the twenty-two-year-old life he wants me to live once I do that?

There's another laugh from deeper in the house, but we're still standing in the cozy darkness of his foyer. I glance past him.

He swears under his breath. "Come on in. I'll— Just, be quiet for a minute, okay?"

2
nolan

ONE MINUTE I'm making dinner and attending a faculty Zoom meeting. And then a knock at the door yanks me back in time to the hardest thing I've ever done.

Delivering the object of all of my off-limit desires, wearing a white sundress and a green canvas cargo jacket that makes her auburn hair look like burnished bronze. From her rain-studded ponytail down to her bare legs shoved into scuffed Converse sneakers, Eden looks improbably real. And she's clutching a duffle bag that says this isn't a drive-by.

My heart leaps—and then plummets.

Four years ago, I told Eden I didn't want her, that she was mistaken in reading anything but paternalistic love in our unique connection.

I lied to her.

Because I *couldn't* want her. There was no justification that would allow me to look my best friend in the eye and say, "Your daughter kissed me, rocked my fucking world, and suddenly I saw her as a grown woman the night before her eighteenth birthday."

I'd have punched myself in the fucking face.

So instead of going to her birthday party the next day, I made my excuses and came back to Conception Ridge. It was the first time in a decade that I was grateful that the only college that wanted to take a chance on a soldier turned criminologist was so fucking far away from my hometown.

Grateful, but not happy.

Leaving her behind felt suspiciously like grief.

There was a part of me that thought I would never see her again. Not in person. Avoiding her online is hard enough, with her bright smile and her auburn waves getting longer and longer with each new adventure, documented in sporadic photographs that her parents literally tag me on. Because they assume I want the occasional updates of her college studies, her travel overseas, and her adventures in sailboat crewing.

Why wouldn't I want to see her curled up under the arm of some hot young man, or sprawled in a co-ed pile, or alone in a picture, wearing nothing more than a skimpy bikini top?

How could they know seeing those images is like a knife to my gut every single time?

There's no way to politely ask them to stop sharing and tagging me, either.

They can never know how those photos make me feel.

And now I'm leading her into my kitchen.

Alone.

I gesture for her to sit anywhere that isn't within camera view of my laptop, which is set up on the island. The faculty meeting has devolved into a gossip session, and I don't feel bad cutting out—but I don't need them knowing I have a visitor.

"Gotta go, all. Mary and Ramesh, I'll see you in the office tomorrow. Alix, send me that proposal to review." And then I slam my laptop shut and turn my full attention back to my unexpected house guest.

It's hard to breathe, having Eden in my space. Having anyone here. I've turned into a God damn hermit.

More to the point, I haven't had a *woman* in here in four years. Since I spent Eden's eighteenth birthday driving like a bat out of hell away from that sizzling spark of desire that was ignited at the base of my spine when she threw her arms around my neck and pressed her—

Here and now, Adler. Focus on the here and fucking now.

This house is my sanctuary. My carefully constructed shrine to doing the right thing. I have poured myself into podcasting and home renovation and cooking, all in an effort to not think about the girl who has just shown up on my doorstep without so much as a whisper of warning.

And sure, she looked nervous when she was standing in the rain, but now she's found some fierce bravado. Her shoulders square off, her chin comes up, and she gets a hard glint in her emerald green eyes.

She pulls an envelope from her pocket. "I'm here to talk about this. I've done everything you said I should."

White hot flames leap in my chest. That's the letter I wrote her.

I circle around the island and take the worn paper from her hand, ignoring the wave of nervous energy radiating off her body that makes me want to yank her against my chest and tell her it's okay.

I can't promise that. I don't fucking know what this is, but it's not *okay.*

Setting the letter on the counter, I take a deep breath, then cock my head and give her what I hope is a welcoming smile. "I'm making pasta. Are you hungry?"

"Pardon?"

I tug her duffle bag away from her and toss it on a nearby chair. "Dinner. It's the third and final big meal of the day. I eat late, so I'm still—"

"Did you hear what I said? I came to talk about—"

"I sure did." I circle around her and set my hands on her shoulders.

She goes still.

Eden's not a small woman. She's shorter than me, but not by much, and her curves and long limbs give her a lot of presence.

But in this moment, as I loom behind her, my big hands curving around her body, she feels little. And not just little, but young and vulnerable. Any of which would be a good reason to step back and give her space.

It is fucking hard to do.

"Let me take your jacket," I manage to say.

She shrugs out of it.

My fingers brush her bare shoulders, sending a dark pulse of need right through my core, then the coat slides into my hands.

Beneath it, she's wearing a slip of a white sundress, spaghetti straps tangling beside bra straps, both pale against her tan skin.

For a redhead, she tans exceptionally well. But there's still a spray of freckles across her bare shoulder, and even as I step back to hang her jacket over the back of the chair, my gaze stays tangled on that lazy constellation of little brown dots.

Those freckles deserve the world.

"Nolan," she starts, turning around.

"Eden—"

We both stop.

She takes a step toward me and my chest threatens to rip itself open to make room for her inside my body.

Fuck.

I step back, and her face falls. Carefully, I find her gaze and hold it, trying to ignore the hurt I see there. "I understand that you have some things you think you want to say to me. But you might change your mind after you have a glass of wine and a bowl of ragu, you know?"

"No." Her face twists in confusion. "I don't, actually. Explain it to me like I'm a child."

I sigh. "You're not a child."

Her expression immediately brightens. "Glad we can agree on that."

That makes me laugh. "But you're still a brat."

"Well, we can't all be perfect," she says lightly. But her gaze doesn't quite meet mine.

Fuck.

Because she is perfect, exactly as she is.

I shove a bunch of feelings into a box deep inside and slam a thousand pound weight on the lid.

"Hey," I say softly. I repeat the entreaty and move toward her. Offering her the hug she tried to just give me, the hug I dodged like a coward.

I might be a lot of things. A pervert, a terrible friend, and a questionable-at-best godfather. But I am not a coward. I can stand in the pain of not being able to have her the way I really want her and give her what she needs, anyway. I hold out my arms, bracing myself.

The first brush of her body against mine is as torturous and wonderful as I feared it would be. She folds in against my chest, her head resting on my shoulder, and I wrap my arms around her tight. "It's…good to see you. Really."

"You've changed," she whispers.

In more ways than I can ever tell her. "It's been a long time. You've changed, too." I tug her ponytail, which falls halfway down her back. "Your hair is longer."

She laughs. Then she leans back and reaches up to tousle my hair. "Same to you. You need a haircut."

"Nobody sees me."

"You were just on a Zoom call!"

"That was a faculty meeting. They don't count."

"What about your classes?"

"My students come to class in pajamas half the time. Me needing a haircut makes me more relatable."

"Your podcast fans?" The pitch of her voice shifts on this question.

And if everything were different, I'd like the hint of jealousy I detect. I like it anyway, even though I need to shut it down. I release my hold on her and separate our bodies.

"Nolan—"

"Eden." This time, I put as much authority as I can muster—which is a lot. I'm a former drill sergeant turned college professor. I've spent a lifetime enforcing rules and order and important limits.

This girl is the only person in the world who could drag me into utter chaos. But I won't let her, because she deserves better.

"Let's eat."

She pouts for a second, then twists away, her sundress spinning around her thighs. She glances back at me, her expression just as carefully chosen as my own. "You're managing me."

I laugh under my breath. "I'm doing my best to manage myself. This isn't how I saw my Tuesday night going. How about some wine? Do you like red or white?"

She hesitates. Then nods. "Either. Whatever works best with dinner?"

"I was going to have red."

"Sounds amazing. Thank you."

I pour us each a glass, then hand her one.

She holds it up. "In vino veritas?"

"Is that a question? Because in my experience, generally not." I have no doubt we'll get to some heartbreaking truth tonight—it seems inevitable—but if her uncertainty can be an out that saves us both, I'll take it.

"Well," she says softly. "To a good meal, then."

We clink our glasses and both take a drink.

Then she turns to the pasta I've carefully laid out. "So what's with the intense cooking show style set up here?"

Also known as the complicated, busy work I'd set out for myself to do during the meeting, but had barely gotten into before Eden showed up. "Short answer is, I like to cook."

"And what's the long answer?"

A muscle twitches in my cheek. The long answer is, I never know when a precocious problem is going to show up in my fantasies—or on my doorstep. "I've found myself in need of distraction lately."

"That's not much longer of an answer. Sounds like you're skipping over some details."

"I'm forty-nine years old, Eden. There's a lot of details we're going to skip in the interest of brevity."

"Ah. Well…" Her eyes get bright and she feigns nonchalance. "Go on, then. Distract me. Put on a cooking show. Did you make all this today?"

"Yep."

"Homemade noodles?" She leans in to inspect the ribbons of pasta that I laid out to dry on a cutting board. "That's impressive."

"Worth the effort."

She flicks that bright gaze up to meet my eyes. "Do you do everything this carefully?"

Heat swirls in a vortex inside me. I change the subject instead of answering her. "How'd you end up on my doorstep? Last week, you were in the Bahamas."

Her eyes go wide. "How did you…?"

I shrug. "Your parents share pretty much every photo you post."

She groans. "That's embarrassing."

"No. I'm happy that you're having adventures." I turn on the stove so the water for the pasta can come up to a boil.

"Mmm." She nods, probably not believing me. But it's true. "Well, my adventures are over. That's what I wanted to talk to you about."

We both look at the letter.

And she takes a big sip of wine.

In vino veritas. Maybe I should have offered her the pineapple juice I have in the fridge instead.

"After dinner." I say it like a command, but when she lifts

her gaze to meet mine, I know that finally she understands. I'm not telling her. I'm asking her for a bit more time. Maybe she had a plan in coming here—I'm sure she's going to tell me what it was, and soon. But I've been blindsided.

And if we talk about what's on her mind too soon, I'm going to do something I'll regret for the rest of my life.

3
eden

WHILE NOLAN COOKS, he asks me more about sailing, and school. I do my best to answer his questions, politely following his lead through this conversation instead of shoving my way between him and the stove and demanding he let me just say it.

I love you. I'm in love with you. I don't know how to get over you. I can't actually continue trying to live my life as fully as you want me to when I'm pretty sure my heart is here, with you.

That would be a lot to dump on him before dinner.

Maybe after.

Definitely before dessert.

"Is there dessert?" I blurt out.

A curiously amused smile tugs at the corner of his mouth. "Nothing specific."

"One fancy course is enough for a Tuesday night." I nod. "Makes sense."

"I have some homemade mango sorbet," he offers.

"Of course you do." Even as I hear it, I'm cringing at myself. Am I being extra lippy because I'm afraid he doesn't love me back? *I swear I'm not like this with anyone else.*

I don't say that either.

And Nolan ignores my attitude. He points to the fridge. "Can you get the pecorino from the fridge? That's a—"

"Cheese." I nod. "I did a lot of crew meal prep in the last year. Pasta was a bit of a staple, and good cheese made it fancy."

"How many people did you crew with at a time?"

"Usually four to six. I spent a month on a big sailing yacht that had a crew of twelve. That was a lot of fun."

"I didn't see any photos of that."

"Had to sign an NDA and our phones got locked up unless we needed them."

He stops stirring his sauce and turns slowly, his expression hard to read. "Really?"

"Yeah." I shrug. "It's not that unusual in the yachtie world. Not really my thing. Worth trying to know that I didn't like it. But it was fine. And that was a month of eating *well*, even the crew."

"But not worth the NDA."

"Not worth not being able to listen to Interrogation Daddy every week." I say it as a joke.

But his eyes blaze pure fire, heating up the space between us. "Eden." My name comes out strained, a low and intense warning.

My breath flutters shallow at the base of my throat. "I listen every week."

"Don't call me that."

"But it's your nickname," I whisper.

"Not for you." Three slow, careful words.

He's so very careful around me, always.

He didn't use to be. For most of my life, he was carefree and easy. And then the summer before college, when I turned eighteen, his visit to my hometown was just…different. I was different, and he picked up on that, and immediately put distance between us.

I'm not going to apologize for growing up, but I miss him.

And since there's no going back to what we once were, there is only rolling the dice and seeing if we can move forward. "Would you rather I call you *Chef* Daddy?"

His whole body visibly tenses. "You should call me Nolan."

"Not Uncle Nolan?" I never called him that when I was younger. He was always simply Nolan. It never felt right to pretend he was a family member. But if it needles him now…

I suck in a breath. God, I want to get under his skin. I want to crack that careful control and discover who he really is when he isn't trying so hard to do the right thing.

Beep. Beep.

The kitchen timer going off cracks the tension between us.

He scoops out a noodle and tests it. His shoulders are stiff, but his attention is swiftly refocused to finishing dinner.

I tip back the last of my wine and grab the bottle to refill my glass.

And then, for good measure, I top up his glass, too.

"Thanks," he mutters. Then he jerks his attention sideways. "More wine?"

"Is that okay?"

He drags in a breath. "Yeah. Of course."

4
nolan

LETTING EDEN GET herself halfway drunk is risky. But I'm not about to infantilize her, so…we'll deal.

And it's a good bottle of red.

It's *very* nice to have someone to share it with, no matter the risky side effects of liquid courage.

I plate up two wide, shallow bowls of pasta, giving them both a generous finishing pile of cheese.

"Island or table?" I ask.

"Where do you usually eat?"

"Island." I give her a rueful smile. "With my laptop open, working on a lecture or podcast notes."

Her smile back is full of temptation. "Then we should sit at the table."

I pick up the bowls. She snags my glass and sweeps around behind me to follow me as if I'm the Pied Piper.

"This is nice," she says as she swirls a noodle around her fork. Then she lifts it to her mouth and slides it onto her tongue, her lips closing around the fork.

Her eyelids flutter shut, and she groans, a happy, earthy sound that I feel in my balls. It reverberates up my spine and makes my fingers itch to grab her, to yank her around the table and push her to her knees. Feed her as she kneels for me, then pet her hair as she thanks me for dinner by taking my cock in her throat.

This is nice.

Fuck.

She shows up looking like sunshine personified, wanting to revisit the topic of her childhood crush on me, and it makes the inner villain inside me want to rip its way out of this civilized shell of a man.

I am not nice.

I am dark and wild, and filled with desires that will only disgust her. I know that revealing myself to her will ruin our special relationship forever, but it may be the only way to deal with the inconvenient but intoxicating chemistry she's reacting to.

Because as terribly wrong as I am for sweet, kind Eden Myers, she is one thousand percent my type. Not even my type. My singularly perfect fantasy woman. Sexually curious and naturally bratty, she makes my blood pump in a way nobody else ever has.

It didn't take long after my podcast, *Interrogation Questions*, launched—and hit some good luck in finding an early audience —that a certain segment of my listeners started referring to me as "Interrogation Daddy".

I get it. It's a funny internet meme. One of my teaching colleagues is a big fan of romance novelist Andie J. Christopher, who apparently coined the term "Stern Brunch Daddies". And then the entire department agreed I would make a decent SBD if I would just go on a godforsaken date.

But the Daddy nickname grates when it's strangers on the internet using it. It always has, and I never understood why until I heard it purred in Eden's voice.

Only one woman should call me Daddy, ever, and it's the innocent girl sitting across from me, who would never want me to bounce her on my lap. Not like that.

Fuck, again.

My cock is hard beneath the table, straining at the confines of my boxers and my jeans. Throbbing to be released and given to my little girl.

A gift from Daddy.

A massive cock to choke on.

And since she appeared on my doorstep, I've known that my polite redirection of four years ago—that she kept, that she carried here in her pocket, and clutched in her tight little fist—won't fly again.

I'm going to have to be more honest with her tonight, and live with the consequences.

Doesn't mean I'm eager for her to turn the conversation there.

But instead of loosening her tongue to talk about the letter, it turns out that second glass of wine makes her sleepy.

"I'm so sorry," she says after yawning again, halfway through dinner.

And I, like the absolute fucker I am, take full advantage of the out.

"Don't be." I hold out the bottle across the table. "Want a bit more? We might as well finish the bottle."

She gives me a soft, crooked smile. "A little bit more."

I give her a generous pour. With any luck, in another half hour, I can similarly pour her into my spare bed, and have one final night of soaking up that she thinks I hung the moon in sky.

"So, are you going to look for another yacht crew position?"

She shakes her head. "Nope." The P pops noisily. "Not sure what I want to do. Some of the experience is transferable to hospitality on land. Know any bespoke inns that might want to hire me around here?"

Jesus Christ. She's not going to want to be in the same state as me in the morning. "I bet you could find work anywhere."

"Fingers crossed!" She lifts her glass in a toast, then takes a big swig.

5
eden

I HAD a plan when I arrived. But then I stepped in a puddle, got tongue-tied, fell right into Nolan's civilized "let's have dinner first" trap, and now I'm three glasses of wine past the point being able to clearly make any good argument about our relationship.

Future relationship.

We don't have a relationship. Yet.

I love you.

It's still on the tip of my tongue.

But the more I drink, the less safe it feels to say it. The less capable I feel to deal with his reaction, which isn't going to be good.

I'm going to have to fight for this man. I know that. *I bet you could find work anywhere.* I don't want to work *anywhere.* I want to work *here.*

But maybe I need some coffee first.

After I scrape the last delicious bite of pasta out of my bowl, I insist on doing the dishes—an insistence that lasts only as long as it takes for me to stand up, and promptly wobble sideways.

"Okay," Nolan says, laughing softly. He jumps to his feet

and catches me by the arms. "How about an early bedtime for you?"

"No!" I pull away from him, but I start to topple backwards, and his arms scoop around my back, holding me even tighter.

"Eden, how far did you drive today?" His voice is low and soft.

I yawn despite myself. "Eight hours."

"Oh, is that all?" He rubs my back. "Come on. Let me show you to the guest room."

"You have a guest room?" I might have hoped that he'd just have one bed, and no other horizontal surface appropriate for sleeping on.

"Right next to mine," he murmurs. "I'll tuck you in if you want."

I nod. I do want, I want that so much. Interrogation Daddy probably tells the best bedtime stories.

"I love your podcast," I tell him as he steers me across the kitchen and scoops up my duffel bag. "And I don't need handling, by the way. I'm fine."

"Is the room spinning?"

"Nope." It's a little extra bright, maybe. And distance is hard to judge. "Did you hear me?"

"You like my podcast. Yes. I did."

"No, I don't like it." I collide with him and spread my fingers wide across his chest. "Nolan. You have to listen to me. I love it." I lick my lips and tighten my fingers in his shirt. "I love your show, because I get to hear your voice in my ear. Do you know how many times I've fallen asleep with you right beside me?"

"That's…" He exhales, and I feel it through my fingers, and feel it against my cheek, and that's when I realize just how close we are. He's cradling me in his arms, and I'm pressed flush against his chest. But I'm looking down, so I didn't realize just how close our faces are until I felt his breath against my cheek.

Warm, soft.

Slowly, I lift my face and he's right there. God, I love his face so much. Slight lines around his eyes. Strong planes. Solid jaw. And soft, off-limit lips. The same mouth that talks so confidently about clues and suspects and investigations gone wrong. Details missed.

It's the little details that matter. The things that are just slightly out of place.

Like the way he's holding me. Still holding me. Not letting me go.

"Nolan," I breathe.

And there's a flicker of something raw and real in his eyes. His hands tighten against my back.

"I'm still in love with you," I whisper.

"Oh, Eden." He presses his forehead against mine. "You're so fucking sweet. But you don't know me. Not like that. You were never in love with *me*."

My heart wants to crack. I can feel it, the pressure. The feelings. But I knew he would say this. I had a plan, I just need to dig deep and— "Kiss me, then."

"No." But there it is again. That raw edge.

Yes. I force myself not to smile. Too soon. Just push that button again, Eden. "If you're so sure that I'm wrong about my feelings for you, then you should kiss me. Show me that we don't have…" I drift off and look at that mouth again.

He groans. "That's not happening."

"Why?"

"Because it's inappropriate."

"Nobody will ever know."

"I'll know."

"Then do it just to embarrass me!" I slide my hands up to his neck, where his pulse jumps against my fingers.

And he doesn't push me away. "It won't be embarrassing."

"You know what I mean."

"Jesus Christ, Eden. You deserve so much more than an old man with—"

I cut him off. "Let me worry about what I deserve."

"I will always worry—"

"I *dare* you to kiss me."

6
nolan

IT'S four years ago all over again. Except this time, she's a grown woman who knows her own mind, even if she is slightly intoxicated.

The night before her eighteenth birthday, there was a big, casual gathering at her parents' house. A good-natured, PG-13 game of Truth or Dare broke out, and carried on for more than an hour. As it wound down, Eden disappeared. I went out to the garage to grab more beer, and found her eating a yellow popsicle by herself.

"Hey, you."

She shrugged.

I pointed to the popsicle. "Banana?"

"Pineapple."

"Nice. Why are you out here?"

Another shrug. "Got bored."

I used the truth or dare construct to make her tell me what was on her mind. Normal teenage melancholy stuff. Then she turned it back on me. "Truth or Dare?"

And I wasn't really prepared to answer just *anything* that a teenage girl might ask me without any witnesses, so I said dare.

I expected her to tell me to eat a popsicle in one giant bite or something like that.

Instead, she carefully hopped off the bench she was sitting on, got rid of the wrapper in her hand, then she crossed to stand in front of me. She nudged her way between my thighs and leaned in. "I dare you to kiss me," she whispered against my mouth.

And my brain short-circuited.

I didn't.

I didn't fucking kiss her.

But in that split second that felt like a lifetime, I saw how it would start. Her mouth, sweet and ripe and inexperienced. Soft lips and warm breath, and then I'd taste the seam of her mouth, and find her pineapple-popsicle flavored tongue.

And fuck me, I saw how it would end. Her up on my lap, riding against my cock.

I didn't fucking kiss her.

But I got hard as rocks just fucking thinking about it. And that's just as bad.

Four years ago, I pushed her away. I kissed her forehead and told her it was past her bedtime.

Now...

Now.

Well, I haven't pushed her away. But it is past her bedtime.

I'd hope we wouldn't do this tonight. But here we are. Time to end this once and for all. I drop her duffle bag to the floor and turn her, pressing her against the nearest edge of the counter. Trapping her.

Not pushing her away at all. Pulling her tighter against me. "Why do you want me to kiss you?"

"To *know*, Nolan." Her eyes are deep, endless pools of green. Guileless. She doesn't have any idea what she's asking me to reveal. "To know," she repeats breathlessly. "If we have chemistry. Or not. If we don't, maybe that will put my silly crush to bed."

"It's not silly. It's just innocent."

"So cure me of that innocence. *Show me that—*" She stops.

Because now she can feel my cock throbbing between us. Because *now*, I'm not hiding how much I do want her. She exhales sharply. Against her belly, she has to feel exactly how hard I am.

"I can't kiss you," I growl. "Because if I do, you will *know* it's not silly. If I kiss you, it will be hard and punishing, and I will get harder if you squirm and get nervous. And God help me, Eden, but if you protested. If you changed your mind. If you *cried—*"

"You would like that?"

I would hate it. "I would enjoy it more than anything else, ever."

Her breath jags out of her in shocked little bursts. "Oh."

"Now go to bed like a good girl, and we can talk in the morning."

"Wait, do you mean—"

"God damn it, Eden, stop talking. We cannot have this conversation while you are intoxicated."

"I get that. I'm just confused."

"You aren't. You're tired and full of wine. When you are sober, you are the most clever girl in the entire world, and you see right through me. Now *go to bed.*"

7

eden

I DON'T EVEN REMEMBER FALLING asleep. One minute I was crawling into bed, confused and turned on and full of questions, and the next I'm staring at the ceiling, suddenly wide awake again.

It's pitch black out, so…middle of the night?

Where did I put my phone?

I roll onto my side.

Red numbers stare back at me. It's quarter to midnight.

I haven't been asleep that long—

And then the rest of what happened earlier comes to me in a rush. Nolan sending me to bed with a curt, "It's the first door at the top of the stairs."

Me slamming the door, and then bursting into tears.

Heat and confusion swirl through me.

I do a quick head to stomach check, but I don't feel drunk. Or sick. Just embarrassed, and a little heartsick. Maybe it was just the long drive followed by a heavy dinner—and yes, a little too much wine—that made me crash, but I'm fine now.

Physically fine.

Emotionally…Oof.

I pat the bedside table until I find the switch for a lamp. As soon as the light flickers on, I see a glass of water has been placed next to the lamp on a coaster and my duffle bag is sitting on a chair in the corner. He must have brought them up after I passed out.

He came in here, where the girl who keeps trying to kiss him was passed out, probably snoring, and he must have thought to himself, *why did I ever put my address on the Christmas cards?*

I sit up, grab the glass of water, and down it. I make a face. My mouth tastes like ass, which isn't helping my weird midnight mood. Getting up, I dig out my toothbrush and go to the attached bathroom to freshen up.

After I wash my face, I brush my teeth and poke around in the bathroom cupboards to be nosy. This bathroom is a cheater, attached to both my little bedroom and the hallway, and it has a big cupboard in it where he keeps his towels and other supplies. Q-tips, soap that smells like him, and a box of expired condoms.

I laugh because it feels better than crying, and move back to the sink to rinse my mouth out.

Getting scrubbed up does make me feel better. Still thirsty, though, so I quietly open the bedroom door.

The whole house is quiet and dark.

Leaving my bedroom door open to cast light down the hallway, I make my way down the stairs. There's a single light on in the kitchen, under the cabinets, enough for me to find my way around.

Earlier, I spied pineapple juice in the fridge, and it's my favorite. I pull that out and half-fill my glass.

Then I lean against the counter where Nolan pinned me just a few hours ago, where he pressed his erection into my belly and told me if he kissed me, it would be hard and punishing. I press my thighs together at the mental image. *And if you cried...I would enjoy it more than anything else, ever.*

I know he meant it as a warning, but it makes my clit throb.

He really doesn't understand just how much I want him. If that means he needs to see me cry as part of…whatever we do, that's fine by me. It wouldn't be the first time I've combined pleasure and pain.

Not with another person, but I was saving that for him.

I take another long sip of juice and glance around. It's a beautiful kitchen. So is the room upstairs that I'm sleeping in, with a bathroom that looks brand-new, too. I wonder if he's renovating this cabin to sell it, because it's a lot of house for one person. Bigger on the inside than it looks on the outside.

A single creaking floorboard is all the warning I get before Nolan appears out of the dark hallway.

His gaze is hooded, his head tilted forward just enough to cast shadows that make it hard to read his expression. "Can't sleep?"

"Thirsty," I say carefully.

"I was looking for a midnight snack myself." He shoves his hand through his hair. "Listen, Eden, about earlier—"

"I've slept off the wine," I say calmly. "I'm not drunk. And I stand by what I said earlier. I have feelings for you that won't go away, no matter what I try. When I read your letter—and I read it often, pouring over every single word—I think you revealed more of yourself in it than you intended. I think—"

"Eden," he snaps, my name exploding out of him. He lifts his head more fully and pins me with a desperate glare. "You had a crush on what I represented. It's very normal for teen girls to idolize older men in their lives. It's well-documented."

Oh my God. He thinks I'm some kind of statistic. "You said that I don't know you."

He winces. "There are parts of me that would shock you."

I shrug. "I know you need a haircut. I know you like that I'm a brat, despite yourself. I know your idea of a hot Tuesday night is making yourself homemade pasta, Nolan. Are you doing that for anyone else? When was the last time you went on a date?"

"What if I tell you that it was last weekend?"

"I'll know you're lying," I say softly.

"How?" He plants his hands on his hips. He's still in the jeans and t-shirt he was wearing earlier.

I hold my fingers up in the air, ticking off the evidence one by one. "Other than a few married colleagues, you haven't added any female friends on social media in…years. A guy who likes to make home-cooked, from-scratch dinners isn't just getting his back scratched in a dark alley. If you dated, you'd be friends with your exes—something I know used to be true, from hearing my parents discuss you. And the condoms in your bathroom are two years out of date."

He's gone stock still.

I finish my glass of juice, cross to the sink, and rinse it out.

Then I grab the letter I brought with me, all the way to this sleepy little coastal college town, and I walk straight up to him. Stop in front of him. "You told me I should follow my dreams, even if they're scary. *It's important that you live as much of life as you can, little one. Spread your wings and leave the nest. Follow your dreams, even if they're scary. It's a big, beautiful world out there, and it will be better with you in it.*" I recite some of the letter from memory.

He swallows hard. "Exactly. You cannot…we cannot… You should live your life as fully as you can. I stand by that advice."

"Four years ago, my dreams told me to come here and find you. I knew, deep down, that if I could go anywhere I wanted in the world…it would be here. I thought about coming to Ridge College."

He blanches.

Yeah, he would have hated that.

"But I read every word of your letter, Nolan. I *heard* you. I didn't come here, because I knew you would turn me away. I went to school. I studied hard. I traveled and dreamed and then followed those dreams in new directions. I trusted myself, even when it was scary. And now I'm old enough to know my dreams of you aren't going to stop. This is where I'm always going to want to be. Even if you try to show me the worst parts of you, they aren't going to scare me off. Because you taught me that scary isn't bad. Scary is a challenge."

"That's not what I meant." His voice is low and full of gravel.

"Is this scary?" I press myself up on my toes so we can look at each other, eye-to-eye. I wind my arms around his neck, and his hands land heavy on my thighs. His fingers curl in, just under the hem of my rumpled, slept-in sundress, and the callouses on his fingertips scrape against my bare legs.

He exhales roughly. "Yes."

I bring my mouth right against his. An almost-kiss. Our breath intermingles, and his grip on the backs of my thighs tightens.

"What do you dream of, Nolan?"

"You," he says hoarsely.

As far as midnight confessions go, this is absolutely top tier. Might never be beat. And he might regret it in the morning, so I'm going to remember every second of my father's best friend closing the gap between our lips and finally—*finally*—him kissing me.

His mouth is warm as he slants his lips over mine and takes control. One of his hands slides up under my dress to cup my ass and pull my hips in against his. The other tracks all the way up to my neck, then slides into my hair, where he makes a fist and tugs me gently to where he wants me.

I gasp into his kiss and his whole body reacts, a taut wire being snapped even tighter. His tongue slides against my lower lip and he groans. Between us, I feel his cock pulse.

"Pineapple," he whispers before kissing me again, deeper now. Long, slow stroking tastes of my mouth. Thrusts of his tongue that feel like what I've dreamed sex will be—dirty, all-consuming, brain-scrambling. And then he turns his head the other way, and this time when our mouths come together, his licks are shallow. Tasting my lips, then pulling on them. Sucking, savoring. "God damn it, Eden, you shouldn't taste this good."

"Makes you want to do bad things?"

"You have no idea." He groans again and picks me up, slapping my ass. "Wrap your legs around me."

I'm already doing it. Oh my *God*.

He carries me with ease to the living room, then tumbles me onto my back on the couch. He kisses me again as he stretches my arms over my head, pinning my wrists down with one of his hands.

Hot.

But I need to—

He drags his mouth to my jaw, then my neck. He exhales roughly against my skin, then scrapes his teeth against a soft spot he found. "I won't hurt you," he whispers. "But the urge to bite you is overwhelming."

I laugh. "Do it."

"I'm serious." He sucks on that spot instead and fits his body tighter between my legs. My dress is up around my waist, only panties and his jeans between us, and this, too, is very hot.

But I really do need to tell him some things.

Like, biting is fine. Good, even.

"Nolan, wait."

He freezes immediately.

I smile and kiss him. "God, you're so hot. And see? You won't hurt me. You just told me, and showed me, that."

"We're just getting started." His chest expands as he takes a deep breath, pushing me into the couch. Trapping me between his body and a part of his house for the second time.

Interrogation Daddy's techniques are amazing.

"I want to tell you something," I say.

He waits.

I was expecting an argument, so the silence pulses for a beat. My heart races. But I've thought this conversation over a million times. I know what to say. I just didn't expect to be saying it flat on my back, with his cock wedged against my panties. Very distracting in a very good way.

"I tried to fall out of love with you. I think it's important that you know I'm not exactly innocent. I tried to fall into lust with a lot of other people, and it never worked. In college...there's a lot of opportunity. It's not neck biting or anything like that, but there were people, and I tried. It never went anywhere. And then on boats... There's no privacy. I heard and saw a lot of things. Biting, for example. That's not shocking to me. Spanking. Dirty talk. And—"

He cuts me off with a gentle finger against my lips. He shifts, bracing himself on one arm, and looks down at me with a quizzical look on his face. "Are you trying to tell me that you haven't been pining for me for the last four years?"

My heart squeezes. "The exact opposite, actually. I have pined for you, endlessly. Even when I tried really hard not to. I promise I *did* try. But I couldn't be with anyone else. So I got my sexual education in other ways."

"Oh!" His gaze searches my face. "Hearing and seeing a lot of things?"

"And thinking..." I squirm against him, rocking my hips. That feels better than I imagined it would. "Touching myself and thinking about you."

"For four years?"

I nod.

"That's a long time to be alone." He traces my lips, his gaze going pensive. "I should know. It's been that long for me, too."

My heart stops.

"Fucking pineapple juice." He laughs quietly, his gray eyes warming. "Should have offered you a glass of that when you showed up instead of wine. It might have sped up a few pieces in my head fitting together differently."

I'm not following, but I love the look on his face. "Why?"

He lowers his mouth to hover just above mine. "Because, little one. I've been stroking myself to a memory just like this, the sweet scent of pineapple on your lips, for four long, lonely years. And my imagination had to work feverishly to fill in the gaps because I didn't let myself have a taste."

8
nolan

THIS TIME, it's Eden who kisses me. Open mouthed and hungry. Giving and eager.

I cannot get over how good she feels beneath me. Strong limbs, soft skin. Her legs wind around my hips, pulling me against her.

"Let me taste all of you," I rasp.

She trembles as I move down her neck again, this time not stopping, not returning to her mouth. I yank down the front of her dress, revealing a simple cotton bra. Her nipples are tight peaks, even through the fabric. I drop my mouth to one and then the other, making her cry out my name. Her hands go into my hair as I bare her breasts fully, yanking the bra cups down as well. I plump them in my hands, speechless and in wonder.

Eden's breasts in my hands. Fucking beautiful little tits. And God damn, her nipples. God *damn*. She whines as I descend on them again, kissing and licking. Sucking. Pulling. Biting, gently.

Jesus.

I suck hard, pulling as much of her flesh against my tongue as I can. Making her writhe and grind against me.

She has a unique incredible taste here, sweet earthy flesh.

But it's just an appetizer. I didn't lie in the kitchen when I said I needed a midnight snack.

Daddy's hungry.

Starved, in fact. I've waited a long time to feast on my little girl.

Swiftly, I move off the couch to kneel between her thighs, angling her sideways. Her dress tangles up around her waist. Only a skimpy pair of white cotton panties stands between me and what she tried to give me four years ago. *Four years.* I deprived us both of so much pleasure, so many pineapple kisses.

I bow my head, as if in prayer, and kiss her pussy through the panties. Breathing in the scent of her, nuzzling my face into the cotton. I lick at her seam and pull at her soft cunt lips, and even through the fabric they swell with my attention. Her clit rises, throbbing through the cotton. I push against that thickening nub with my tongue and she says my name now with more urgency.

She's said my name a few times, breathlessly, but this is sharp.

"Nolan! I need to tell you—"

And then I feel it. A hard metal bead just above her clit, that rocks beneath my tongue.

She exhales, her whole body shuddering. "I told you. I'm not innocent."

She lifts herself up, pushing onto her elbows. She looks down at me with a slightly embarrassed, beautiful expression. Sexy and bold, absolutely, but still shy and yes, innocent, no matter what fun little experiments she's done with her body.

"Eden Myers," I mock-scold. "Are you pierced?"

She bites her lower lip and nods. "Yes."

I yank the cotton aside. Her pussy is beautiful, puffy and tan, with dark lips parking to reveal pink, slick folds. And just above her clit, a curved metal bar with beads on either end pierces her clitoral hood. "Who did this to you?"

"A girl on one of the boats."

"Does it feel good?"

"Mm-hmm."

"Did it hurt?"

She squirms, and in front of my eyes, her clit trembles. "Yes," she whispers. "But I liked it."

"Good girl," I groan. "That's what Daddy likes to hear."

I lean in and and pull her pierced little secret into my mouth. I had all sorts of plans to go slow, but Jesus Christ, my little girl got her clit pieced and I wasn't there to hold her hand.

I wasn't there to see the wave of pleasure and pain twist across her face.

That's my punishment for not kissing her properly four years ago.

And now I'll give her a reward for being brave and going through that on her own. I slide my tongue around her clit, teasing the piercing. With each wiggle, she lets out a shocked little gasp.

I yank the panties even more to the side, needing more of her skin bare for me. I lick down her slit to her glistening entrance, slick and tight for me, then pull that arousal back up to her clit.

She pushes at her panties, baring her mound, and I break away from kissing her cunt long enough to scrape them down her lush thighs. They fling across the room to God knows where.

Good.

She should never wear panties in this house anyway.

Her pink entrance peeks at me again as her legs tumble wide, and I taste her there next, burrowing my tongue into her hole. She shoots off the couch, her hips snapping up against my face.

God damn it, she's eager to get fucked.

She came here for this.

My best friend's daughter came to my house in the middle

of the woods so I would pin her down and fuck her. With my tongue, and my fingers, and my cock.

And the only condoms in the house expired two years ago. My little detective has already figured that out.

I replace my tongue with a finger, working into her up to my first knuckle. Her walls are hot and soft and snug, and she's so fucking responsive, one finger is all she needs. I lick my way back to her clit, glancing up to catch another glimpse of that shy-sexy-boldness that is uniquely Eden.

"Has anyone ever done this for you?" I growl the question. Selfishly wanting the answer to be no.

And when she shakes her head side to side, her eyes wide, I rear up and lever myself forward to kiss her mouth. Giving her a taste of herself off my lips.

"Nobody else ever will," I promise, my voice fierce. "Daddy will give you what you need. You're mine, you understand?"

"Yes." She pauses, and her pussy clenches around my fingertip. "Yes, Daddy."

A quiet groan rips out of me so fiercely it might as well be a roar. "Say that again."

She licks her lips. "Yes, *Daddy*."

"Nobody else calls me that like this. Ever. Only you."

"Yes, Daddy," she repeats, and now she sounds joyous. "Nolan, I want more."

"I'll give it to you, baby. Anything you want."

"I want everything. I want you inside me."

"We need to talk—"

"I know." She kisses me again, rocking her pussy against my hand. "But please, Nolan. Please, Daddy. I've wanted you so long. We've both waited so long."

9
eden

"YOU ARE A LITTLE TEMPTRESS," he growls. "Do you like surprising me? Little Miss Sunshine on the outside, and all this delicious need on the inside?"

"Yes." I'm panting now, riding his hand. His thumb finds my clit, and oh God, *yes*.

"We can't rush this," says the man working my clit in a way that is going to make me come all over his fingers.

"Four years," I manage to get out.

"Four years," he repeats. "But not four years of understanding, Eden. Four years of fantasy. What if we don't want the same thing?"

"I want to…" I rock against him. "I want…"

"Tell me." He flicks my piercing. "Be bold, little one."

"I want to be yours. I hate all the women who lust after you and call you Interrogation Daddy." The words spill, fast and furious. "I want you to be *mine*."

"I am. Oh Eden, I am. Do you want to know how you make me feel? I never want to let you leave this house again. I want to hold you here, my curious, dangerous little captive, until we exercise four years of filthy fantasies."

"Okay."

He laughs. "Jesus Christ, how are you this eager?"

"Four years of filthy fantasies," I repeat. "Of you taking my virginity, the way I wanted you to all along. Hard and fast. Having to be quiet."

"No way would I have taken you that night. No matter how much I wanted to. Your beautiful moans shouldn't be stifled." He kisses me again. "I want to hear you come for me, Eden. I want to hear you scream as I lick you to pieces."

He drags himself back down to the floor and lifts my ass in his hands. I stare down my body in disbelief as he buries his head between my thighs. His tongue slides exactly where I'm most sensitive, dragging against my skin, up to my piercing. And then he pulls my clit into his mouth, and a jolt of *oh, this is different* zaps through me.

Before, he was kissing me. Before, he was warming me up.

Now...

Oh.

This is sex.

He's using his mouth to get me off, and it's working. Tension coils inside me, winding tight and fast from the pull of his mouth and the thrust of his tongue. It yanks and drags me out of myself, separating me into distinct parts. Eden, the person, floating in a haze of wonder. And Eden, the body, ramping hard and fast toward something better and bigger than anything I've ever done with my fingers.

"Oh God oh God oh God," I cry out. "You're making me..."

Come.

I don't say the last word, because I can't speak, I'm gone. It's a blinding white snap that sends pleasure to every inch of my body, a powerful electric sizzle kind of shockwave. My hips jerk and my pussy spasms, flooding Nolan's face.

He groans and licks harder. "Yes, baby, give it to me."

I whimper as his tongue pulls against my sensitive clit. "Nolan..."

"So fucking good." He growls and hauls me off the couch,

pulling me onto his lap on the floor. His arms wrap around me as I shake in his embrace. "I've got you. That was perfect. You're perfect. You taste so good, you know that? Love the way your clit pulses when you come. Your whole pussy clamped down."

I wriggle in his lap, rubbing against his erection. "Want you inside me for the next one."

"Are you on any birth control?" His voice sounds strained.

I lift my head to look at him. "No."

He groans. "Baby..."

I squirm against him. "The condoms I found upstairs...were they the only ones you have?"

"Yes."

"We could still use them." But we aren't going to. I know that now. My heart is pounding so fast. I'm giving him an out I don't want him to take. "Expired is better than nothing, right?"

"Wrong." His gaze flashes possessively. "Nothing is better. We don't have to do it tonight, but when I claim you, Eden, I want it to be skin on skin. I want to feel every inch of your perfect pussy sliding down my cock, and I want to bury myself deep inside your body. My body inside yours. Nothing between us. *That's* better. And I will wait until you're ready for that."

"I'm ready now." I scramble between us, trying to unzip his jeans while sitting on his lap, which isn't actually feasible.

He rolls me onto my back, stretching me out on his very soft rug. "We don't need to do this."

I spread my legs around him and tilt my hips up. "But actually, we do. I need you. I've needed you for a very long time. I waited, Nolan. I waited and touched myself and listened to your podcast. Are you telling me *you* don't need to do this?"

He growls a string of curse words and frees his cock. He slaps it down on my clit, thrusting it up and over my clit. "You sure you want to know what I need?"

Finally.

I suck in an excited breath and nod.

10
nolan

"I…" I trace her trembling flesh with my fingers. "I need to claim you. I want to bite you and bruise you in places where only a lover could be. I want to bury my seed deep inside you, so fucking much, but I want to paint it across your flesh, too. I want every inch of your body to be baptized with my come."

"Dirty Daddy," she breathes. Her eyes sparkle. "Yes, please."

"It might hurt," I strain between gritted teeth. Fuck me, I don't hate that idea. Not a brief little sharp pain. Something she will remember forever.

I'll make it so good after that. Make her fly.

"I want it to hurt," she whispers, and it sounds like a confession.

Is it wrong to feel like that makes us some kind of kindred spirits?

"I want it to be you that makes it hurt," she adds. "Because I know you'll soothe the pain after."

It was always going to be me. I just needed to get out of my own way. I gather her beneath me and kiss her fiercely. "Then it'll be me."

My cock is hard and heavy against her, where she's wet and

warm, and it doesn't take much to fit us together. That part is easy.

What happens next is not easy. There's a long pause, as I look down at my virgin love and see all of her desire, clear and constant in her bright gaze. The tip of my cock is straining at her slippery entrance, so fucking eager to get into her body, but she's already tight, her body having no idea of what's about to happen.

And that only makes me bigger. Harder. Needier.

What do I need?

I need to steal her innocence.

"You're such a good girl," I growl as I press my hips, stealing the first inch. All I can get before her eyes flare wide, panic clawing it's way past the desire.

"Daddy," she pleads.

"I know it hurts. You can take it."

She whimpers and clutches her hands around my arms, up onto my back. Clinging and trembling.

Her pussy flutters around my cock in protest, but then a rush of arousal floods around my erection and I steal another inch. She's unbelievably hot and tight and soft. Velvet perfection, squeezing me to death.

"That's my girl," I praise her, even as tears pool in her eyes. "You can do it. Every inch is for you. I've waited for you so long. Nothing between us. God, you're so tight."

I snap my hips back, giving her a moment of relief, then thrust in again. I groan her name, and she chokes on a sob, her body tearing itself apart to make room for me, and her hot little cunt fucking loves it. She's so wet, so slick and welcoming, even when it feels like too much for her and impossibly tight for me. Her body makes exactly what we need to make everything fit together, and then I'm all the way inside her.

I groan with soul-completing satisfaction of finally being where I've wanted to be for four long, lonely years. "Eden."

She hiccups on a sob, but then presses her mouth to mine. A

little desperate, a lot reassuring. *She's* reassuring *me*. Fuck no. That's my job.

"The hard part is over," I promise her. "You feel so good for me, and it's going to feel good for you soon. Just stay still for Daddy."

"I can't." She's shaking and rocking against me. "Please keep moving. I need it."

"Keep moving your hot little pussy up and down me like that, and you'll make me come."

Her eyes light up.

"Eden," I warn.

"You like it when I'm a brat," she whispers. "Do brats make their Daddies come?"

Jesus. "Yes. And then they get spanked for it."

A wide, excited smile spreads across her face, chasing the last bit of panic from her eyes. "Okay."

I laugh.

Laughing while I'm buried deep inside my best friend's daughter was not on my bingo card for tonight.

"Tell you what," I murmur before catching her lower lip between my teeth. I growl happily. "If you come on my dick, then all will be forgiven, and there won't be any spanks on your perfect ass for making Daddy come too fast."

"If I come, and you come, then how can it be too fast?"

Impeccable logic. I plant one hand on the floor beside her and rock us together. I can't hold her and rub her clit at the same time in this position, but I'm not ready to pull out yet, either, so I give in to how good it feels and just fuck her on my living room floor.

When she starts begging me for more, I drag her off my cock and slap her ass. "Up onto the couch again."

She scrambles up and I grab her hips, roughly putting her where I want her. Legs spread, pussy glistening.

I rub my cock through her wetness, then thrust deep again.

The little steel balls above her clit beg for my thumb, and I might want to see her hurt, but I never want to see her deprived. I give her clit the pad of my thumb, and immediately her pussy starts clutching at me.

"Needy little pussy wants to get bred," I growl.

She gasps. "Yes."

"Want Daddy to put a baby in you?"

"Oh God."

I thrust harder, telling her over and over again how I'm going to fill her up. And when she comes, I follow her hard and fast myself. "Here it comes. Daddy's gonna breed you." I groan and slam into her, my fists squeezing her hips. "That's a good girl. Take all Daddy's seed."

With a roar, I unload inside her, my cock punching as deep as it can get, spending right at the entrance of her untouched womb.

I didn't even strip her down fully. We're both still half dressed.

Blood rushes back to my head as my pulse pounds erratically.

"Jesus, that was…" I was too rough. Too hard, too thick.

But I couldn't have held back. I needed to take her like that, to show her everything I am. She has to know what she's getting into. I slip out of her, my cock still half-hard. I drop my head to her belly and exhale. "I should run you a bath."

"Together," she whispers.

First I peel her out of her clothes, and discard my own as well. Then I scoop her up and carry her upstairs. I set her down so I can get the water going before I grab a washcloth and nudge her thighs apart.

"Let's get you cleaned up," I tell her, my heart still pounding hard in my chest. "And then we'll climb into Daddy's bed for the night, yes?"

She catches my face in her hands. "For the night?" Her right eyebrow curves up in a challenge, and her gorgeous mouth gives me a soft smirk. "Nolan, I'm climbing into your bed for life."

11
eden

I WAKE up in the cradle of Nolan's arms. We're both naked, and his hands are…everywhere.

"Please tell me I'm not dreaming," I whisper.

He chuckles into my hair as he squeezes my breast. "Feels like a dream, doesn't it?"

"You're okay?" I try to twist around, which is hard when your dad's best friend has a firm grip on your pussy.

He bites down on my shoulder, stilling me. "You're the one who lost her virginity last night. That should be my line."

"Yeah, but you were full of…reluctant feelings."

"Was. Past tense. I'm more than okay." He drags in a deep breath, gives my sex a final squeeze, then turns me in his arms. "Eden, I love you. I am *in love* with you. I have been longer than I wanted to admit, but that's done. I am yours. You are in this bed for life."

"Do I get to wander around barefoot and pregnant sometimes, too?" I tease.

He growls. "Maybe occasionally."

I kiss him, a soft brush against his lips.

"That's the kind of innocent kiss that makes me want to do

terrible things to you," he says, but it doesn't sound like a complaint. It sounds like a promise.

"Is that how last night escalated so quickly?"

He gives me a slow, wicked smile. "Yes. From that first kiss, I needed to be inside your body." He searches my face as he talks. "I didn't care if you were a virgin. I didn't care if it would hurt. I knew I would make it feel better."

"Didn't care?" I prop myself up more, and the sheet falls away from my breasts.

He traces a circle around my nipple. "What kind of debrief are you looking for here, Eden?" He finds my gaze again. "I'll tell you anything. We won't have any secrets between us. But do you want to know everything right now?"

"I want to know how much you like it when it hurts me," I admit. "What is it about that?"

He rolls his lower lip between his teeth, his gaze going thoughtful. "I've considered this for a long, long time. Before you were…you…I just had very generic fantasies. And I could put them in a box, but…I mean, there's a reason I went into criminology. I'm good at it. Maybe that's because it takes a terrible mind to understand the horrible thing people do."

Suddenly, so many things that he has said on his podcast are cast in a different light. My breath gets yanked out of my body. "You think you're a monster?"

"Living inside my head, I know I'm capable of monstrous desires."

I push at his chest. "It's not monstrous to walk away from temptation. That's what you did. I wanted you so, so much, and you didn't cross that line. I bet you never even thought about crossing it."

"I thought about it in great detail," he growls.

"But did you actually consider it?" I challenge.

He pauses. Then he smiles. "No. Not until last night."

"Ooh, such a monster," I tease. "You would never have hurt me, not until I told you that I might like it if you did."

"You brat. Don't psychoanalyze me."

"But I learned from the best! Interrogation Daddy."

"That's just Daddy to you," he murmurs as he rolls me onto my belly and pins me down to the bed.

"Okay, Daddy." I giggle and twist my head to the side. "I missed you, you know."

"I missed you, too. You drive me crazy in the best way." He hitches my hips up and slides his fingers between my legs from behind. "Is this wet little slit for me?"

"Yes, Daddy."

"So fucking ready. Don't even give me a chance to beg for your pussy."

I laugh. "You don't need to beg."

"Maybe I want to. Maybe I want you to know just how much I crave being inside you."

He tells me, in great detail.

And when he sinks inside me—one hand clamped on my hip, the other tangled in my hair, pushing me into the mattress and pulling me back against him at the same time—he narrates what I can't see.

"I love how you take me. Your pink little pussy stretched so wide around my big cock, Eden."

"You're fucking incredible. So wet. Jesus, look at you."

"Who's my best girl? Who's gonna take all my come? Who wants Daddy's baby?"

With each hard thrust in my still-tender pussy, my clit rubs against the bed. It's erotic overload, and once again he takes me from zero to can't-speak-getting-fucked in less than sixty seconds.

I moan into the sheets and let that mind/body separation happen again. I let him fuck me, use me, fill me up, and he sends me flying twice before he growls that he's going to come, too.

And when he does, it feels so good, so right, I know it's always going to be like this, for the rest of our lives.

But then.

After the sex, after the orgasms and the joyous mostly naked late brunch, and more sex (because we have four years to make up for), then comes the serious talk.

We're in the shower. Nolan exhales roughly against my shoulder, his head bowed, his whole body heaving from the way I just made his body explode.

I'm feeling so confident for a girl—woman, twenty-two years old, fully capable—who was a virgin just yesterday.

And he says, "We need to tell your parents about this."

A lump forms in my throat, so I play it as a joke. I lean into where we are, what I just did, and I repeat the one word I can handle. "This?"

He won't be tricked. "Not this," he says gently, using his podcast voice. Interrogation Daddy, teaching the world about how to keep an interview subject focused on the point. "Us."

"I know." But my voice sounds small.

"Not this weekend."

"Good." I step back into the spray of the shower and lean my head back, knowing it puts my tits on display.

My off-limits tits. The tits of his best friend's daughter.

Let him look at me and crave me and want me to be his secret, just for a little bit longer.

I'm not ready.

I'm not a fool. I know that loving Nolan means having hard conversations with my family about what my future will look like. And worse, maybe some very awkward conversations about the past. Did he ever…? No. Did I want him to? … Yes.

That's a secret I'll keep from my parents forever.

But the conversation itself? Not sure I can avoid that. Not when Nolan is already bringing it up on day two of our forever.

12
nolan

THE NEXT DAY—THE third day I get to call Eden my lover
—I need to go in to work at Ridge College. I'm a professor of
criminology. That's my day job. The true crime podcast I host is
a side gig, although it's exploded in popularity and turned into
a somewhat unexpected second career for me in my late forties.

Eden comes with me, because we've got New Relationship
Energy zinging like we're at the center of a lightning storm. I'm
her Daddy, she's my little one, and if I could somehow attend
the meeting with my cock inside her (and not violate any rules
of academia), I would.

I'm also hoping that being open about our relationship to
my colleagues will help her see that it's okay for us to tell her
parents that we're dating.

Dating.

Such a simple word for what this really feels like.

And that intensity is part of the problem. I know it's too
soon to push Eden. I'm not going to see her parents until the
holidays, probably.

God damn it, I want to claim her already.

She showed up on my doorstep with a plan to make me see

her, really see her, as a woman, and I did. I do. I'm never going to deny the tug between us ever again.

I should have acted on it way sooner.

Could have had her panting *Daddy, Daddy, Daddy* beneath me sooner...

Which is not a thought I need to have as I usher her into the criminology department hallway.

I greet the department administrator. "This is my girlfriend, Eden."

Eden blushes as she holds out her hand. "Nice to meet you."

"And you." There's a pause.

"I'm not a student here," she blurts out.

The admin's eyebrows go up. They pause. Then they grin. "Well, I'm glad I didn't have to ask."

I grunt, but otherwise stand in the moment, being soft to the reality of that question. It won't be the last time we have to answer it.

"You could be a student," I tell Eden softly after two more introductions, once we're safely behind the heavy door of my office at the end of the hall. "There's a family discount on tuition."

"I'm not family, either," she points out.

"You will be soon." I tug her against me. "Mrs. Nolan Adler."

She snorts. "That's so old-fashioned."

"I'm practically a dinosaur, it comes naturally to me. But I know what kids these days like. I'll be Mr. Eden—"

She cuts me off with the soft press of her mouth against mine. "I want to be Mrs. Adler," she whispers once she pulls back, her lips swollen and wet. "And have little Adler babies."

Now my grunt is entirely different.

We make out against the back of my office door, until I'm hard and aching.

"I should make you suck Daddy's cock for that tease," I growl.

"Okay," she gasps breathlessly against my mouth.

Fuck me. "I don't actually have time for that."

"But it was a hot idea." She licks her lips. *Licks* her beautiful *lips*.

I kiss her again, harder this time, then point her toward my desk. "Go. Sit. Poke through my stuff and be bratty."

She smirks. "Is that what you're going to think about while you're in your meeting? Wondering if I'm doodling dicks on your papers?"

"You can doodle whatever you want on anything podcast related. Keep it PG-13 on the academic stuff."

"Okay, Daddy." She slides away from me, batting her eyelashes.

I pause, something twigging at the back of my mind, but then it's gone, replaced by the very real, very mundane reality of a meeting that starts in five minutes.

I scoop up the folder I need for that, then stop and give her a serious look. "Was that all right? Meeting people?"

She nods. "I like seeing where you work."

"You can come and go from here as much as you want."

She chews on her bottom lip. "Maybe I'll try to find a job on campus? I like that idea more than going back to school."

She finished a degree a year ago, then went to work on sailboats and yachts in the Caribbean.

If nothing else reassured me that what we have is real, even though it's happening really quickly, the fact that she would trade the Caribbean for the dreary rain of the Pacific Northwest is a sure sign.

"Whatever makes you happy. If you want to just laze around my house and make it your own, that's okay, too."

She sticks out her tongue at me, and I force myself to go to my meeting before I do something better with that mouth.

When I return an hour later, need still humming in my veins, she's still in the big chair behind my desk. One of my legal notepads is in front of her. Her head is down, and she's intently scribbling. Her auburn waves spill over her shoulder, curtaining her work.

I knock on the door I've just pushed open. She makes an acknowledging sound but doesn't lift her head. I smile to myself as I round the desk and sweep her hair up in my hands. The way she goes still, a blush creeping up the back of her neck, is perfect.

My Eden is perfect.

Everything I've always wanted in a partner. Bratty but obedient. Eager, willful, curious.

I drop a kiss on the back of her neck. Her skin is warm where the blush is rising. "What are you working on?"

"A letter to my parents. It's not good." She shivers beneath my questing lips. "Did you lock the door? Feel free to distract me."

"Can't do that. Not when you're being such a good, brave girl. Can I look at what you've written?"

She squirms, but nods.

I replace my lips with my hand, cupping the nape of her neck so I can squeeze her there while I read.

"It's not really a letter," she adds. "More of a set of talking points."

This might take you by surprise, but I've fallen in love with someone you know. Someone unexpected… to you. Not me. Someone who shares these feelings.

Then there are a few blank lines, and it looks like she's started over again.

I want to tell you something very important, but before I do, I want you to know it's not up for debate. It's about me, and my feelings. My _grown-up, well-thought-out feelings._

Grown-up is crossed out, but it's low enough that it could be underlined, and that makes my cock twitch.

The page is covered in similar thoughts.

"Any of these would work," I tell her honestly. "Do you want to tell them starting with this framework?"

She turns her head a little to look at me. "I like it when you say smart, sexy things like framework."

"Brat," I growl.

"What else were you thinking?" she asks.

"I thought I might do more of the talking. I've spent a lot of time imagining this conversation."

Her eyes flare wide in surprise. "Really?"

I clear my throat. "I should warn you, most of the iterations in my head end with your dad punching me."

She gasps. "He won't."

He might. It's fine. I'll survive. And it would be worth it. "I'm not afraid of standing in the fire for you."

She twists all the way around, pushing herself up out of my chair and throws hers arms around my neck. "I don't want you to get burned," she protests. "Maybe we shouldn't tell them."

"We're telling them." I squeeze her tight and look down at her notes. Below the pad of paper is my podcasting schedule, and sure enough, there's a dick doodled in the margins.

But there are also flowers and a little house and a lot of hearts. It looks like she used every different color of highlighter that I have in my big mug of pens.

I reach out and nudge her pad out of the way so I can see the full extent of her art.

She twists to look at what has caught my attention. "Sorry, I got carried away."

I squeeze her hips. "It's okay. I like to see you play. I'm glad you weren't worried the whole time I was gone. Is that a sailboat?"

She giggles. "Because you…" She leans over, too, and now both of our fingers are tracing her drawings. "Right here. It says, *kinky boat trip / can you murder someone at sea*, and I had to illustrate that, even if it didn't make any sense to me. What a good hook for an episode. I mean, it'll give your fans more ammunition to call you Interrogation Daddy, and I thought we agreed that was just for me, but…"

I laugh, hard, and sit down in my chair, tugging her into my lap. "Come here, you minx. It's not an episode for me. And I'm not going to be—" I take her face in my free hand and draw her in for a long, deep kiss. "It's someone else's podcast. I'm just a guest and only there to answer the murder question."

"Okay," she whispers, before kissing me back.

13
eden

A WEEK GOES BY. We make incremental plans on telling my parents—definitely before Christmas. Probably before Thanksgiving. We'll drive out to see them, but book a hotel so we aren't stuck staying at their place if it doesn't go well.

But when Nolan wants to pick a weekend, I hedge on asking them if it's a good time for a visit.

He asks me if I need him to threaten to do it himself. (He doesn't, I'll find out if they're home, I swear it.)

I distract him with kisses, which he tells me isn't going to work forever, but he'll let it work today. Tomorrow. A week of kisses, and it's working, it's working, we'll put that off—

Until he comes out of his soundproof recording studio with a very… bossy look on his face.

"What?" I ask, scrambling to my feet.

His expression says he's going to fuck me, and growl in my ear, and call me his good little girl, and I can't wait.

I'm practically panting.

He grins, and it's feral. "I think I've found the right incentive for you to pick a date for us to talk to your parents."

My stomach goes into free fall. "Oh?"

"I just recorded a guest spot on a kink-positive podcast. To celebrate hitting a subscriber milestone—and the host turning forty—they've chartered a yacht for a week. They've been talking about it for months, with different guests. I was invited on to talk about the laws of the high seas."

"Is that something you're an expert on?" I tease.

"I'm an expert on how you're a brat," he growls. "Come here."

I leap into his arms and he carries me into the living room.

"After we finished recording, they happened to mention that one of their guests had to cancel on the charter. So they have an extra stateroom."

A tremor of excitement ripples through me. "Oh?"

"How would you like to show me a bit of your yacht life?"

"I've never been a guest," I breathe. "Only crew."

"Would that motivate you to let me tell your father how much I love you?"

I nod. It's nervous, and my palms are sweating, but yes. That would motivate me. The truth is, I *want* Nolan to talk to my parents. I'm just not sure *I* want to, and I'm embarrassed by that. It feels... childish.

"Eden..."

"I just wish we didn't have to tell them at all," I blurt out.

He raises one eyebrow. "Say more about that."

"No." And I pout for good measure.

He waits.

I slump in his arms. "Sorry."

"For what?"

"Being bratty."

"I don't mind bratty. Especially if it's a productive kind of pout that gets you through your feelings to where we need to be on the other side."

"Which is telling my parents?"

"It'll be quite the shock to them to show up at your wedding and discover I'm the groom," he points out.

"I love that you're so logical," I mutter under my breath.

"I can tell from your tone."

"When is the yacht charter?"

"In two weeks."

"So soon."

"No time like the present." His eyes glitter as his gaze doesn't waver. "You're tough, Eden. Be strong with me."

"I don't want to be tough."

"I know." But he says it with a firmness that promises he's going to ask me to be strong, anyway.

I change the conversation to the carrot he's dangling. "Just how kinky is this charter going to be?"

His gaze turns to pure fire. "The host is a Daddy Dom. His wife has been his Little one for more than a decade. The other guests are kinky podcasters or content creators."

An unexpected flair of jealousy spikes inside me. "How do you know them?"

"Through podcasting." One eyebrow quirks higher than the other. "Do you have another question there?"

"Have you ever... Are any of the people on this trip an ex?"

"No. I wouldn't do that to you."

"I know the kink community can be a little... familiar."

He growls. "And how would you know that?"

"These aren't the first kinky people to charter a yacht. I've seen some things. Things that made me dream of you wanting to spank me and be in charge of me." I blush, but I hold his gaze.

His growl deepens into a lusty rumble. "I want to know everything."

I lean in and kiss him. "Right back at you, Daddy."

"After we call your parents."

I squeak and nod. "Okay. You call them."

He keeps me in his lap as he dials my parents' home number. When someone—it sounds like my mom—answers, his face breaks into an easy smile. "Hey, it's Nolan. Is this a good time?"

A murmur.

The smile widens, and he winks at me. "I was thinking of driving out to see you guys this weekend. Will you be around? Eden said she was thinking of coming for a visit, hmm?" His eyebrows curve high in surprise. Yeah, I started to make a plan, I just didn't follow through completely. But I tried, and he likes that, I can tell from the look on his face. "Maybe she wants to drive with me. We'll see you in a few days."

14
nolan

THE GOOD NEWS IS, Eden's father doesn't punch me.

The bad news is, it might be easier if he did.

He knows what's going on from the second she hops out of the passenger seat of my vehicle. He's doing yard work when we pull up, and maybe it's the way I help Eden out of the vehicle, or how she looks at me and her gaze lingers for a long beat before she turns fully to greet him. But whatever tips him off, his expression goes from a flare of surprised recognition to stunned, wary concern in the blink of an eye.

"Dad," she says softly.

"I'll get your mother," he says sharply.

It goes downhill from there.

Once we're all sitting in their living room, it's Eden's mother who starts the real conversation. "I don't understand. When was the last time you two even saw each other?"

The night before Eden's eighteenth birthday is the answer. But it's the wrong answer to say out loud. Pointing out that nothing happened wouldn't help. It would reveal that something could have happened.

That there was a reason for four long years of carefully not seeing each other, until she showed up on my doorstep.

"The internet is a magical thing," Eden says sarcastically. "You might be aware that Nolan has a podcast."

"He's never been one for commitment," her father rumbles, not looking at me.

He's not wrong.

I never was—until now. Until her. Almost as if I were waiting my whole life for this woman to reveal herself, to show me she'd been hiding in plain sight.

Eden starts to protest. But she shouldn't have to defend me. That wouldn't make me worthy of her. I take her hand in mine, ignoring the sizzle of tension that sparks through the room at the tight, claiming squeeze of fingers.

"We don't expect you to understand today or tomorrow. But you know your daughter. You know how strong-willed and clear-headed she is. So lean on that while I show you over time just how much I love her and how committed I am to her happiness."

"Our happiness," Eden says firmly. "I love Nolan. And honestly? If it were up to me, we wouldn't have told you yet. We're here because this is important to him."

Her mother snaps her gaze to me, then. She doesn't say anything. Just looks at me with that searing, assessing stare.

I don't blink. We've known each other for a long time. She's fussed over my dating life, and the long periods of being single. I know she never wanted me to land on her daughter as my soulmate.

"That's right," I say. "This *is* important to me. Even if you need time, we don't. Nothing has ever felt as right as Eden showing up on my doorstep and making me see her as a woman who knows her own mind. I hope that in time, you'll come to see this as the same kind of thing. I love your daughter—"

"You were her uncle," my best friend of twenty-nine years spits out. "We trusted you—"

"I never violated that trust. I swear to you. But she's not a child anymore, and I don't see her as a child. I am going to put her first for the rest of my life. I'm going to make her my wife. That's already how I feel about her, and it doesn't matter if it's new to you. In time, it won't be."

"We should go." Eden tugs my hand and together we stand up.

Her mother frowns. "No. Wait." Her father mutters something under his breath, but her mother shakes her head. "You drove all this way. You'll stay for dinner. And we will talk about football and the weather. Nothing else, understood?"

I'd rather be punched in the face. But I nod, and Eden nods, and finally, her father nods.

It's not the best outcome, and it's not the worst. It's somewhere in the middle, and it's hard for Eden. By the time we leave, she's exhausted. I drive just far enough away to know we aren't being watched, then I pull over on the side of the road and haul her into my lap. "You were a very brave girl today," I reassure her. "And you've earned that reward trip."

She makes a small, wounded sound and wraps her arms tight around my neck.

Fuck.

The trip wasn't the carrot she wanted, after all. She'd dragged her feet in reluctance because she wanted this to go better, and she knew it wouldn't, and there's no reward in that.

I kiss her temple, then her nose, then her lips. Softly. Gently. "They'll come around," I promise her. "They'll see. In time."

And maybe the trip can be a distraction, then, if not a reward.

15
eden

A WEEK LATER, we fly to Los Angeles to meet Nolan's podcasting friends. On the flight, Nolan goes over the dizzying array of rules for the charter one more time. Safewords and nudity guidelines. How I don't have to do or see anything I don't want, but I also need to be careful not to accidentally yuck someone else's yum.

"I know, I know, boundaries are for me to maintain about myself and my own behavior," I repeat.

He smiles and kisses my mouth softly. "And me. You can ask me to stay inside your boundaries this week, too."

"And vice versa," I whisper back. "But I'm excited about all of it."

Once we land, a town car takes us to a marina where we are greeted by the captain of the yacht they have chartered.

I was expecting a small boat with a captain and a chef as the only crew.

This is… bigger than that.

This is a super yacht, bigger than any I worked on in the Caribbean, and stepping aboard it with Nolan's hand firmly in the small of my back feels fancy.

It feels like a fantasy, like something out of a dream.

The captain introduces us to the purser and the chief stewardess.

"Welcome aboard, sir," the purser says to Nolan. "You're the second guests to arrive. Come this way."

She leads us up a set of stairs to the next deck, and I recognize the couple who rise to greet us from a sprawling sun lounger. This is the podcast host and his wife.

"Nolan, it's so good to see you again. And this must be Eden," he says. "I'm Vince, and this is my little one, Kaydie."

Vince, who is a young and fit-looking forty, is wearing shorts and an open birthday-themed Hawaiian shirt. "Nice to meet you," I say, shaking his hand. "Happy birthday."

Kaydie holds out her hand, too. "It's not until Monday," she says with a warm smile. "So I'm still older than him for a few days."

He wraps his arm around her, his hand curving possessively on her hip, and nuzzles her temple. "Or until you put on your favorite tutu for dinner tonight, mmm?"

She giggles and nods. "Touché."

Nolan shakes her hand, too. "Nice to meet you in person, Kaydie."

She leans in toward me. "They've met at podcasting conferences before, but I always stay home with our kids."

"No kids this week, though," Vince says, his eyes bright.

"Until I put on my tutu," Kaydie finishes the joke, both of them laughing. She gives me an appraising look. "Do you like a playroom? I brought a lot of toys."

"Sex toys?" I burst out.

They all laugh.

I look at Nolan in confusion, and he stops laughing immediately. "I think she means literal toys. But I imagine Vince has some sex toys, too."

"Oh."

Kaydie takes my hand and leads me down an interior corridor away from the outside lounge area.

"This is my first time doing anything like this," I tell her.

She smiles and nods. "Vince said that. Don't worry, we won't be too weird."

"I like weird."

Her smile widens. "You know there's no pressure here, right? This is a trip where we can all be ourselves. What happens on the cruise, stays on the cruise."

"Right."

She pushes open a door, and we step into a cabin with two twin beds, clearly designed for children. "Since everyone on this trip wanted cabins with larger beds, Daddy gave me this room as a playroom. Because one of the joys of this week is being able to be as little as I want to be, whenever I want to be."

I think about what Nolan has told me about who else will be on this cruise. Vince and Kaydie have a Daddy/Little dynamic. Their friend Grace is a Domme, and she's bringing "one of her pets", but Nolan doesn't know who that is. Then there will be Aaron and Dylan, who have a Daddy/Little Boy dynamic, and Sean and Rayna, who Nolan doesn't know, but he thinks they are a classic Dom/sub relationship.

I can't wait to meet them all, even though I'm pretty sure I'm going to keep making newbie blunders like the sex toys question.

Kaydie's voice softens as she shows me what she's brought with her. "Stuffies, of course, and some coloring supplies. A couple of my favorite movies. And a pile of fidget toys. But also, check this out." She throws open a cabinet. "They have so many games!"

Having worked onboard yachts—although none this big—this doesn't surprise me. This whole industry pivots on top-tier customer service.

Stocking cabins with everything the guests might want, for example. And giving guests space to be as kinky as they want.

My gaze is pulled back to the art supplies. Escaping to this space to doodle might be a good plan to have in my back pocket. "Thank you for showing me this space," I say to Kaydie.

"Of course." She tilts her head back in the direction we came from. "Do you think we've lost them to podcasting talk? Do you want to see your cabin?"

I laugh and nod. "I'd love to."

But when she leads me down the hall, we find Vince and Nolan on the same mission.

I slide up against Nolan, and he wraps his arm around my waist. "Find anything you like in the playroom?"

"Art supplies."

"Sounds fun."

Vince opens our cabin door. "This is where you two will stay for the week, unless you make other arrangements."

Nolan's hold on me tightens, and he growls, "There won't be any sharing this week."

Vince holds up his hands. "Got it."

From the back of the boat, there's a call of greeting.

"Ah, more guests." Vince and Kaydie leave us to get settled on our own.

As soon as we're through our cabin door, Nolan tumbles me onto the bed. "How are you doing?" His grin flashes at me before he buries his face in my neck and inhales. "You don't smell nervous."

I laugh and push at him.

He lifts up, just a little, and his gaze softens as it locks on my face. "Seriously… I want you to check in with me frequently. If anything gets too intense, we can retreat."

"Or I can go to the playroom," I say.

A little spark of recognition flares in his eyes. "You like that?"

"I dunno. Maybe. Having a safe space is always good."

"One filled with art supplies…" He traces his fingers over my collarbone, to the edge of my shirt. "Good to know."

I shiver under his touch. "Daddy…"

He growls and his fingers tighten against my skin. "Yes, little one?"

"Do we need to go meet people?"

"Not immediately." His thumb rubs down onto my chest, under my loose t-shirt. "Do you—"

There's a quiet knock at the door. "Your bags, sir," someone says on the other side, their voice muffled.

Nolan leaps off the bed. For all the years between us, he has the energy of a much younger man. His body is lean and tightly muscled, and watching him move always stirs something hot and needy inside me.

He opens the door, accepts our bags from the deckhand, then snaps the cabin door closed again.

The look he gives me when he turns back makes me shiver.

"Do you think you can be a quiet girl for me?"

My breath catches in my throat, and I nod eagerly. This is one of my fantasies that I've told him about, but in our short relationship, we haven't been in the same space as anyone else when we fuck. The closest we've come is making out in his office.

He locks the cabin door and comes to join me on the bed.

His eyes glitter as he presses a finger to my lips and leans in, bringing his lips to my ear. "I want you full of my seed when we meet the rest of the guests."

My breath catches in my throat and I nod, suddenly hot and achy, needing that, too.

"Let me see you…" He tugs off my t-shirt. I didn't bother to wear a bra under it, and my little bumps jiggle into view as he lays me down again once I'm bare.

He cups them both in his strong hands, his tan flesh dark against my pale freckled skin. His lips part and his eyelids hood his lusty gaze. "Let Daddy feast on you, baby. Let me love your little breasts. That's it. You're such a good girl, holding still for me."

I am. I'm holding very, very still and wondering if Daddy can feel how fast my heart is beating.

He licks up the bottom of my breast to my nipple, his tongue warm and soft and wet, and then he closes his mouth around my peaked tip and tugs. A long, hard suck that makes me squeal, making me a liar—just for a second—before I remember to be quiet.

I clamp my hand over my mouth as my back arches, and he does it again, and again. And then the other side. Hot, wet licks. Heavy pulls. My little tits throbbing as he gives them attention, so much attention.

And then his hand falls between my legs.

Even through my shorts, that's the pressure I need. His big, strong hand cupping my pussy and pressing against my piercing. I go wild, grinding against him, my body pulling like a bow, like he's an archer, and he knows exactly how to pull me taut.

To make an arrow fly.

I start begging, quietly, so quietly. "Daddy, Daddy, Daddy..."

His hand shoves down the front of my shorts, into my panties.

He swears under his breath when he finds out how slick I am, my arousal coating my pussy lips already.

A messy little girl.

"Eden." My name is a groan and a prayer. "How long have you been this wet?"

I shake my head. I don't know. I just need him.

He strips me bare and pushes his own shorts down enough to free his cock, then he's on top of me and inside me.

Thick, hard. Rough.

Now I'm quiet because he's stolen my breath, because he's so deep inside me it feels like he's pushing up into my lungs, but in a good way. Such a good way.

I'm so full it makes my brain go fuzzy, and then there's the *no, no, noooo* feeling when he drags himself out of me, but then he snaps his hips forward and *yessss* I'm full again. The drag of his heavy cock through my sensitive folds is still a revelation, like *of course* people like sex, this is *amazing*, and I can't believe I waited this long, but also, I'm so glad I did.

I'm so glad I'm his.

He drives into me again, his breath hitching, then his growl sliding out of him again.

I love that he's affected just as much as I am. Both of us covered in a sheen of sweat, both of us altered by this hard-and-fast coming together.

He covers my mouth with his hand and sinks his weight onto my body more heavily, his mouth dropping to my ear. "Shhh," he manages to get out between heavy breaths. "You're going to make Daddy come, Eden."

My brain flatlines, all my body's energy shooting to the center of me where he is thick and hard and throbbing now, on the edge. My clit pulses, too, and I wiggle my hand between us.

"Yeah?" He snarls the word in my ear. "You want to come, too, don't you? Horny little girl, aching to get off on Daddy's cock, hmm?"

I whimper behind his hand and nod as much as the heavy press allows me.

"Yeah, good. Come for me. Milk my cock." He pushes my thighs up and out, stretching me again. The archer at work.

And this time, my fingers are the arrow, maybe, because all it takes is one perfectly timed rub and I'm gone, I'm flying, and he thunders into me with a growly, animalistic rutting that goes on and on and only ends when his cock slides out of me.

So. Messy.

I drag in a happy breath as he pushes off me. His gaze drops to between my legs and I blush, my thighs trying to fold up.

He stops them.

"Look at this well-bred cunt," he says, his voice ragged but proud. "All swollen and pink."

And then he brings his hand down on my flesh with a wet slap.

I gasp, my hips snapping up off the bed.

His eyes glitter. "You weren't quiet at all."

"Oh my God." I laugh.

He smirks. "God didn't make you come like that."

I scamper off the bed before I leave a mess. I stop in the doorway to our attached bathroom and glance back at him. "Nope. My Daddy did."

"Start the shower." He flops backward on the bed again. "I'll be there after I catch my breath."

It doesn't take him long. I've just soaped up when he steps in behind me and wraps his arms around my waist. "We're going to have so much fun this week," he murmurs, his voice fully recovered now. He kisses my wet shoulder. "And nobody needs to know that Daddy filled you up, mmm?"

I take his fingers in mine and squeeze. "Our secret."

"Good girl." He lazily smacks my ass. "Now hurry up. We have new friends to meet."

16
nolan

BY THE TIME we're both dressed in swimsuits and head back to the outside deck, everyone else has arrived.

I start to make the introductions. "Everyone, this is Eden. We've known each other for a long time—"

"He's my dad's best friend," she interjects. Then she winks at me. "They were going to find out sooner or later, Daddy."

The name rolls off her tongue, even though it's the first time she's called me that in front of anyone else.

I forget where I was going with the introductions, and gather her in my arms. "You little minx."

She smiles, but twists her face away from my kiss at the very last second. "Wait, I didn't get their names."

"They'll wait." I catch her chin with my fingers and pull her back so I can kiss her sweet, sassy mouth.

Everyone cheers, which earns them all proper introductions once I'm done.

"This is Eden's first kink-oriented event, but she's an eager girl, so don't feel like you need to hold back. Not that any of you would. Eden, these are my friends Grace..."

The elegant San Diego-based Domme—who I know from her excellent YouTube channel—curves an eyebrow in acknowledgement, then tugs on the leash around the neck of the younger man beside her. "A pleasure, Eden. This is my new pet, Jaden. His pronouns are he/him, and as soon as we're away from the marina, he'll be naked for most of the trip. You are welcome to stare at his cock. I'm very proud of it."

"I bet," Eden breathes.

I yank her into my side, and she giggles.

"And this is Sean."

The younger-than-me, New-York-based Dom introduces his submissive, Rayna, who looks about Eden's age.

"Last but not least, our third Daddy on board, Aaron."

He gives Eden a big, broad grin. "So you're the girl who finally dragged Nolan out of the Daddy Dom closet, hmmm?"

She bites her lip and glances sideways at me. I nod, telling her to say whatever she wants. "I guess so," she breathes. "It just feels natural for us."

He wraps his arm around his Boy. "I get that. This is Dylan."

Eden looks almost shy as she gives Dylan a smile. "Nice to meet you."

The captain comes down the stairs from the bridge deck and tells us we're about to depart. A stewardess appears behind him with a tray of champagne flutes, and the trip is officially underway.

By the time we're cruising up the coast toward Malibu, where we'll anchor for the night, everyone has changed into swimwear—except Grace's new pet, Jaden, who is wearing nothing at all.

Well, he's still wearing his collar.

But as promised, nothing covers his erect cock, and Eden can't help but look at it every few minutes.

Her sneaky glances amuse both me and Grace.

She's not the only one. Kaydie is openly impressed, too.

The other two couples are more laissez-faire about the nudity, for whatever reason. Perhaps by later in the week,

Rayna and Dylan will be naked, too. Their swimsuits are small enough.

I slide my gaze over Eden's black bikini. More conservative in comparison, but still very, very tempting.

When Grace breaks out a bottle of sunscreen, Eden's eyes go even wider. I let her watch breathlessly as every inch of Jaden's skin is carefully protected from the sun.

But when she leans over and snags the bottle herself, I snatch it from her hands.

"Sunscreen is a Daddy job," I growl.

I take my time rubbing it in, starting with her back and arms, then her tits. Cleavage. Side boob. Under boob. My fingers snake under the triangles of her bikini top in all directions, and then finally skim down to her belly.

She leans back against me as I make sure every inch of her front is covered, then I tip her over my lap, ass in the air, and do her bottom and the backs of her legs as she giggles.

Only once I'm sure it's all absorbed in do I let her go play.

Aaron waves at me from the bar. "Beer?"

"Sounds good."

He grabs two, then sits next to me. "Here you go, man."

"Cheers." We clink glasses.

"It's good to see you happy."

I smile as I take a good, long sip. "Mmhmm."

"It's even better to be happy, hmm?"

I chuckle. "Indeed."

"I'm getting serious vibes. With your best friend's daughter? Brave man."

"She's worth it. And I resisted. For four years. I told her to let herself grow up and live her life. Forget about me. She did all but the last instruction, and finally came to find me."

"God damn, that's something."

"Yeah." My chest tightens up at the thought of it going any other way. Of her finding someone out there, and choosing a path that never included showing up on my doorstep. "It feels like a near miss in some ways. So… yeah. It's serious."

"And your kinks align, that's great." His gaze drifts to where she's sprawled next to Dylan and Kaydie. "How little is she?"

I don't want to tell him that I don't know if she even is, exactly. Two days ago, I'd have laughed at the question. What we have is something more like… I dunno. Nolan and Eden kink. Not some externally defined Daddy/Little age thing.

But watching her curl up with two very sure-of-their-littleness Littles, and be drawn to them over anyone else on the boat (except me, of course) … I'm not sure at all.

"Ah," Aaron says quietly. "Still early days?"

"She's new to kink," I finally say. "And new to me. We'll figure it out."

And new to sex, although she's a fucking natural at it. A virgin until twenty-two, she never wanted to be that intimate with anyone else.

Could that have been another possible flag that she has a Little side, too? Not a question I'm going to ask anyone other than Eden.

"There's no rush. I was just making conversation." He leans back and tips his face up to the sky, to the sun. "This is the good life."

———

When we gather at the table for dinner—after anchoring and swimming, and a whole afternoon of the good life—I tug Eden into my lap. She winds her arms around my neck and brings her cheek to mine.

"Hi," she whispers.

"You good?"

"Mm-hmm."

"You look good in my lap."

She giggles.

"I'm serious. You want to eat dinner like this?"

She glances around.

Jaden will eat dinner on a pillow at Grace's feet. Kaydie has a sippy cup and a unicorn plate instead of the china settings the rest of us have. The social rules are clearly different on this trip, if she needs any convincing.

Eden nods quickly. "Is that okay?"

My heartbeat slows down and my grip on her tightens. "It's more than okay. I want to hold you."

When the stewardess brings the first course, a chilled gazpacho that is very easily shared by two people with only one of us using the spoon, Eden relaxes all the way into my lap and lets me feed her.

Then come oysters, and I'm not sure what's hotter—watching them slide over her lips or kissing her throat and feeling her swallow.

She slides over to her own chair for the main course, steak and lobster that really does require both arms.

But she crawls back onto my lap for dessert, and stays there until she starts yawning, and I have the absolute honor of telling everyone that my little girl needs to be tucked into bed.

17
eden

I WAKE UP AT DAWN, because I practically passed out in Nolan's arms after dinner last night. He's still asleep, so I creep out of bed and go in search of coffee.

There's a quiet crackle of a radio ahead as I pad down the corridor, then a stewardess appears and says a cheery but quiet, "Good morning!"

Since it's just the two of us, I tell her I was working on yachts myself until a little over a month ago. "You can shove a cup of coffee in my hand and then get back to what you were doing."

"You're not the first one up," she says. "Aaron and Dylan are doing yoga on the upper deck. And I think Kaydie is in her playroom."

"I will go find her, then."

The stew smiles. "I'll bring you some coffee there."

I reverse direction and head to the playroom. The door is propped open, and when I push it open, Kaydie looks up from where she's reading on a tablet.

"Morning," she says softly.

"I thought I might be the first one awake."

She shook her head. "I'm up at six every day with the kids. Daddy can sleep in like a champ, but I cannot. Do you want a first breakfast? They'll bring us snacks here."

"I ran into someone in the hallway. She's bringing me coffee." I glance at the pile of art supplies. "Do you mind if I draw?"

A smile spreads across her face. "Not at all. I sort of hoped someone would. I like art. I don't love to make it."

I grab some markers. "What are you reading?"

"A monster romance." Her eyes sparkle.

"Demon? Minotaur?"

"Orc."

"Oooh." That needs a green marker. "Tall?"

"Of course. And he has tusks."

I giggle. "Of course."

I draw a giant, muscle-bound green dude, then a tiny Kaydie hanging from his biceps. Curves and wild blonde hair, and the rainbow t-shirt she's wearing this morning.

Just panties on the bottom, which I'm sure the orc will make short work of.

"What do you think?" I show her, and she shrieks.

"Oh my *God*, you are *good!*"

"Thanks."

She asks me to add glasses like Vince wears, which I do with a black marker, and then she takes it and races down the hall to show him.

She doesn't come back before the breakfast tray is delivered.

I keep drawing, and then there's a knock at the door, and Nolan pokes his head in.

My breath catches in my throat as he steps inside, and his gaze slides over me in this space. "Here you are," he says softly. "You snuck out of bed."

"I didn't know if you stayed up late last night after I passed out."

He shakes his head. "I was tired, too." His gaze drops to the notebook I'm drawing in. "What's that?"

"Monsters." I show him another Vince and Kaydie sketch, and in this one, Kaydie is holding a sippy cup.

"That's cute." He sits beside me, all big and warm and muscular in this decidedly girly space. "How come I didn't know you could really draw?"

"We've been busy learning other things about each other," I manage to get out, but my voice is shaking.

His hand has settled on my back, and it's all I can feel.

Oh, and his leg. His thigh shifts sideways, and now it's pressed against mine, and I can feel *that*, too.

His hand skates up to the nape of my neck, and his thumb teases a circle there before he squeezes.

I shiver.

"What is it?" he murmurs.

I close my eyes and let myself remember, for a second, another time, a long time ago, when I first became aware of his body in a similar position. He had no idea, and I kept my crush on him a secret for years.

Then there's a sound in the hallway, and Kaydie bounds back in, her cheeks flushed.

She's wearing a different outfit. She's put on a swimsuit and a pair of jean shorts.

"People are waking up so we're going to have second breakfast," she says. "Or first breakfast for you," she adds for Nolan's benefit.

He nods. "We'll be there soon."

I jump up, hand her the notepad, then escape to our cabin, where I see that Nolan has laid out a swimsuit for me. It's a bright pink-and-red-floral bikini with tiny, cheeky bottoms.

"Oh, that one is my…" I blush. "Smallest suit."

"How do you feel about wearing something skimpier today?" He asks it like he doesn't care one way or another, like he's really just checking.

But I still pause. "Do you want me to wear this one?"

"I picked it because it's girly." He pauses. "But I like that it's tiny."

I bite my lower lip and quickly change.

He growls as soon as I turn around and wiggle my bum at him. They are extra cheeky bottoms.

Nolan growls. "Mmhmm. We're going to need a safeword today."

I squeak. "Why?"

He circles around me, his eyes flashing. "How do you feel about Daddy getting you off in front of the others?"

"Mmm…a little shy." Heat swirls low in my belly.

"Do you not want me to?" His voice is dangerously silky. I'm pretty sure he knows my answer.

I suck in a quick breath. "No. I want you to." Let it out. *Whoosh.*

He makes a satisfied sound I feel right to my core. "Do you want to be shy about it?"

Yes. That's it.

"Then we need a safeword." Everyone on board has been asked to respect the universal color system of *green* means go, *yellow* is caution, and *red* is stop. Personalized safewords are optional.

"I thought we agreed we didn't need one?"

"That was yesterday." He takes me by the shoulders and I shiver. "But maybe things have changed since yesterday."

Has it only been one day since we arrived?

A lot has changed.

I've changed. And Nolan sees that. Of course he does, but… still. "I'm still me," I whisper.

"I know. And a safeword makes sure that no matter what we explore, we always come back to us."

"Correspondence," I say.

The night before my eighteenth birthday, I tried to kiss

Nolan and he stopped me. Then he wrote me a letter, that I've kept this whole time, telling me to live my life to the fullest, but also learn more about the world, basically.

I never wrote him back.

If I had, maybe we'd have found our way together sooner.

18
nolan

OUR FIRST FULL day at sea is a fucking delight. Sunscreen application, safeword practice usage, and a sizzling energy that just feels *right*.

And late in the afternoon, Eden, Dylan, and Kaydie disappear to the playroom when Sean and Grace take their submissives to their respective rooms for naps.

Aaron, Vince, and I play a few hands of poker, but after some time loud giggles and shrieks interrupt us.

Vince sighs. "They're going to wake the others up."

As one, we all rise, but I'm closest to the corridor, so I lead the way.

The shrieking stops as soon as I push open the door to the playroom and see Dylan lying flat on his back on the floor, Kaydie jumping on the furthest twin bed, and Eden sitting on the other, a beach ball in her hands—like she's about to toss it over Dylan to Kaydie.

The silence only lasts for a beat, then they all take one look at me and dissolve into giggles.

"What is this, three little monkeys jumping on the bed?" I ask, my eyebrows raised.

Behind me, Vince laughs. "Oh, are they doing that?"

Kaydie squeaks and slides off the bed.

Eden freezes, her eyes big. "Uh…"

"Come on, monkey," I growl, crossing to her as she scrambles up to her feet. Not sure where she's going. There are three big Daddies blocking her exit path and we're out on the open ocean.

She squeaks as I flip her over my shoulder.

"Kaydie…" she calls out, pleading. "Help me!"

Vince chuckles darkly. "She can't help you, little girl. She's going to be busy getting a paddling in three, two, one…"

I leave him to discipline his Little the way he sees fit. Aaron steps out of my way as I carry Eden down the corridor to our cabin, and the last thing I hear before I set her down and nudge her through the door is him sighing and saying, "Dylan, you know better."

They all do, which makes me wonder if they were deliberately trying to get a certain kind of attention.

"Having fun with your friends?" I ask Eden dryly.

"Yes?"

"Is that a question?"

"Depends." Her eyes sparkle. "How much trouble am I in?"

"How much trouble do you want to be in?"

"I don't know." She laughs. "Oh my God. I might want to be in trouble? I just got carried away, but…"

I advance on her.

Her eyes get big and wide, her pupils dilating. Her lips flush and part. She's never been prettier than in this moment, I think, in a distant kind of way that I'm only partially aware of over the pounding of my pulse.

Nerves look good on her.

Panic looks good, too…

Adorable, adorable panic.

I pounce and pin her down. "We need to be good guests on this trip." The stern bark comes naturally. Too fucking naturally.

"We can't be having such a good time that we forget our manners."

"But Kaydie—"

"Right now, Kaydie is getting her ass turned neon red. And probably loving every second. Did you want her to make that choice for you, too?"

Eden's eyes have never been this wide. "Uhh…"

"Who gets spanked, Eden?"

"Bad girls?"

"Little girls," I say with silky menace. "Kaydie is a very little girl sometimes, who craves correction from her Daddy. Are you that little?"

"No…" Eden's protest is a thin whisper.

"What kind of punishment would be more appropriate for you, then?" I release her wrists just long enough to bare her tits, then I pin her again and rock down her body, sucking at her nipples with enough aggression that this could be it. A hard, fast tease of my mouth, working her into a lather that I will do nothing about.

Let her sit in a squirmy haze of arousal and think about what she's done—which is, most importantly, fib to me about being little.

But I'm going to work my way up to calling her on that.

Give her time to get comfortable with all the possibilities.

Beneath me, Eden squirms. "You should punish me with your cock. Be rough and just use me."

The first rule of doling out Daddy punishment is probably, don't give the eager brat what she suggests. But we'll be saving that one for another time. Like tonight, maybe. Fuck. "Why do you suggest that?"

"It feels like a good Big-girl punishment."

I nip her rib cage just below her breast. "Mmm. Sounds more like a Big-girl reward, and you weren't acting like a Big girl in the playroom with your friends."

She goes still.

I wait.

When she doesn't say anything, I ask, "Correspondence?"

"No," she whispers.

"Hey..." I surge back up, covering her body with mine. She kisses me, and I let her.

Nothing is more important than this.

And then she's stripping my clothes off, and I'm helping.

Because getting inside her is as natural as breathing now. As essential, too.

She trembles beneath me when I stroke between her legs and find her swollen and slick.

Her tight little cunt takes my cock with ease, and her cheeks are pink by the time I bottom out. She tips her head back, crying out.

Fuck.

Yes.

I cover her soft mouth, muffling her beautiful sounds. She writhes beneath me and my fingers slip over her lips, into her mouth.

"Suck," I demand.

And she does.

I groan at how good the pull of her tongue is. Wet, eager, perfect.

I brace my other arm on the bed and start to move.

As I drag my length out of her, inch by inch, she sucks harder on my thumb. Her gaze turns liquid, needy, until I snap my hips and thrust deep again.

Her lips part in a silent gasp.

"Suck," I growl, and her lips close again around my glistening thumb.

I reward her with another drag and thrust.

Glancing down between our bodies, I purr with satisfaction at the glistening skin where my hips are pressed into her. "You take me so well, Eden. Hungry little cunt."

She whimpers and nods, her mouth pulling hard on my hand. Hungry little mouth, too.

All I want to do is fill her up with come, over and over again.

Maybe later tonight we'll talk about whether she really needs sterner boundaries or corrective instruction.

Maybe tonight I'll be more of a Daddy. Right now, she's got Nolan, the man, wrapped around her little finger—or, more accurately, she's wrapped herself around *my* finger, and my cock, and she's going to drain me of my entire soul.

But not before she comes first. A few times. Maybe more than a few times.

"Your punishment," I decide, "is an orgasm every hour between now and bedtime."

"What?"

"You heard me." I pull my thumb from the lovely cradle of her mouth and shove it between our bodies, finding the beads on either side of her throbbing clit. "You're going to come now. And in one hour, you're going to excuse yourself from whatever you're doing and say you need to find Daddy for a punishment."

A low, whining groan starts deep inside her. She pants, trying to regain control, but that's not what we're doing this week.

She has her safeword.

She can use it any time she wants.

"Come for me, Eden," I whisper as I thunder toward my own climax. "Come on Daddy's cock, and then start the countdown until you get to do it again instead of playing with your friends."

19
eden

BY THE TIME we get back to the group, I only have forty-five minutes. First I crawl onto the extra-wide sunbed next to where Vince has Kaydie wrapped in a towel on his lap. "I'm sorry for being loud while others were sleeping," I say to him.

He smiles. "Thank you. Maybe you can be a better example for this naughty little girl later today, mmm?"

I swallow hard. "Maybe. But I might need to excuse myself often."

His eyebrows curve up in interest. "Oh?"

I blush.

From the bar, Nolan chuckles. "Don't make her explain, Vince. Just trust that it's a good one." Then he crosses the deck and hands me a large glass of water. "Stay hydrated, baby."

My blush deepens.

Thirty-five minutes.

I down the glass of water, then Nolan tells me it's time for more sunscreen. I sit in front of him.

"Did you see that Kaylie's naked under that towel?" he asks quietly in my ear.

I did. "Not completely naked," I whisper back. "She's wearing bikini bottoms."

"Maybe her Daddy said that little girls don't need to wear swim tops." Nolan murmurs. And he tugs on the strings of my own bikini, loosening the top.

I squeak and press my hands to my breasts, keeping the fabric against me. "I'm not that little yet."

"Yet?"

"Maybe?"

"Okay." He gives me a kiss on my temple, then carefully applies sunscreen all over my back and around to the sides of my breasts before he reties my top. "Scoot back and I'll do your front."

I relax into his chest and he smoothes the sunscreen down my tummy, to the waistband of my bottoms.

I hold my breath, but he just rubs his fingers there for a bit before carrying on to my hips.

"We'll do your legs after," he says quietly.

After.

Right.

Because it's almost that time. "Since you're right here, do I have to say that I'm going to find you?"

He laughs. Low and happy. "You can just say you need a punishment."

Oh God.

My pulse is racing when I push to my feet and clear my voice.

Nolan is looking at me with ridiculous pride on his face, which I love, even as I feel silly. "Excuse me," I say, a little louder than is strictly necessary. "I need to excuse myself because I need a punishment."

Everyone nods like this is normal, and then Nolan follows me down the corridor to our cabin.

Once we're inside, he presses me against the door and slides his hand into my bottoms, his fingers going straight to my folds. He pulls some slick arousal to my clit and sets his fingers in a position he's already learned I like a lot. Love, in fact. Two of his fingers, one on either side of my clit piercing. A hard press, and then slow circles.

"Thank you for being prompt for your hourly punishment," he says, a smile in his voice—and when I hear it, that's when I realize I've closed my eyes and thunked my head back against the door.

"Uh huh."

"It's up to you how long it takes to come. If you take a half hour, though, you'll only have thirty minutes to recover before we do it again. And in an hour or two, you'll need to manage dinner around these orgasms."

He says *orgasms*, plural, with a sharp kind of joy that makes it very clear why this will feel like a punishment by the end of the day, but right now, it feels amazing.

Good news for me, I'm already pretty close.

His fingers push lower than my clit, picking up more slick, then slide back to where I'm most sensitive.

"I want to tell you something," he murmurs.

"Yes?" My voice shakes.

His fingers press harder, making that shaky feeling worse (which is better, in a way, oh my God). "I love it when you're little. It makes the part of me that just wants to take care of you very, very happy."

I shatter, jerking off the door and into his hard chest. His other arm scoops around me, a steel band holding me up as I hump his fingers shamelessly.

"Good girl," he says. "You came so fast. You have fifty minutes until the next one."

———

The next orgasm happens as he changes me for dinner. He takes off my bikini, pinching my nipples and softly stroking my pussy, but he doesn't give me anything that's enough to make me come until I'm dressed—so to speak.

"No panties?" I squeak.

He smooths his hands down my short sundress to my bare thighs. "No. I want you to feel like the messy girl you are. God, you're pretty like this." He crouches in front of me and looks up. "Hold your skirt up for Daddy."

Hands trembling, I lift my skirt, and he dives into my pussy face-first.

This time, there's no door to lean back against, I'm in the middle of the cabin, so I hold on to his head and his hands come around my thighs.

Maybe that will keep me from collapsing when I come on his tongue in three, two, one…

————

Dinner is actually served when we return.

Everyone looks innocent about this fact, cheerily agreeing that it's fine if we wait another hour, but that feels like a specific length of time for a delay.

Nolan gives me another glass of water, because—

"Stay hydrated," I say numbly.

My legs are sticky, and we're not even sitting at the table yet. One stiff breeze off the ocean and my dress will fly up, showing everyone my glistening shame.

Nolan's hand curves around my waist, coming to rest low on my hip, as if he can read my mind and will be on skirt duty.

And punishment duty, too, in less than forty minutes.

Thirty.

Twenty.

Ten minutes.

When it's time, my head feels like it's detached from my body. Such an alien feeling as I rise on unsteady feet.

"Excuse me, I need another punishment," I say breathlessly.

The stewardesses arrive at exactly that moment with the first course, and mortification races through me, even though everyone looks understanding.

I run down the corridor, and by the time Nolan calmly walks into our cabin, I'm on the bed, on all fours, my hand between my legs. Waiting.

"Please, can I help?" I choke out.

He smoothes his hands over my hips. "Of course. You're beautiful like this, you know." One hand trails over the wetness on the inside of my thighs, and then higher, where it's coming from. "Fuck, I need to be inside you."

I nod feverishly.

He unzips, and then he's at my entrance, his cock thick as he pushes into my cunt without any preparation other than the orgasms I've already had and the anticipation over the last hour.

I sob and my fingertips find my clit. I'm coming by his third thrust. The orgasm wrenches through me, a tighter, more complicated sensation than the earlier ones, and it doesn't stop, it keeps rippling through me as he tightens his grip on my hips and fucks me harder.

But just when I think he's going to unload in me, he comes to an abrupt stop.

I twist my head around in shock. "Daddy, please come in me."

"No." His chest is heaving. He pulls out and puts his cock away. "You're making us late for dinner."

Fuck.

I scramble to my feet, but I can't stand. I plunk my butt back down on the bed.

He disappears into the bathroom and washes his hands, then returns and goes straight to the cabin door. Holds it open.

And I force myself up on my feet.

We don't even make it back to the cabin the next hour. He finger-fucks me in the corridor while everyone finishes up their main course, and I'm still catching my breath when the stewardesses appear with dessert.

"Nolan," I gasp. "We almost—"

He braces one forearm on the wall beside my head and ducks his mouth next to my ear. "You can always safeword."

"I don't want to, but—"

"Then trust that it's my job to know what's appropriate and not." He sighs happily. "Or we can continue this tomorrow, too?"

"I trust you," I say immediately. And then I laugh.

He chuckles, too, and then kisses me, his mouth soft and warm and hungry.

Someone shouts from the table that our dessert is melting, and we race back to our seats.

Rayna, who is sitting next to me, leans over and whispers, "You look radiant, you know."

We haven't spoken much, although I like her quiet presence, and this blows me away.

Tears prick at my eyelids, and I nod. "Thank you. I, uh, feel radiant."

A sudden smile blooms across her face. "Good. I'm sure that makes your Daddy very happy."

Nolan wraps his arm around my shoulders and squeezes, as if to say, *yes, it does.*

20
nolan

THE NEXT DAY, Eden sleeps in until almost noon, a well-deserved rest after a long night of being tortured by me.

And when she wakes up, she's on her best behavior, listening very carefully to Aaron and Vince so she knows the rules for their Littles. All afternoon, she's like a little mother in the playroom and down on the beach deck when we're at anchor, making sure they behave.

I reward her with orgasms, which looks a lot like the punishment routine, but she gets to set the schedule—and when she begs me to come inside her, I do.

That's how the next few days go, too. It's fucking heaven. And we find our own brand of Daddy kink that works for us, but there's still something that sits at the back of my mind when she's drawing. It's in the way she says *little*, with a bit of wistfulness, even as she clearly sets herself apart from Kaydie and Dylan. Each time I hear it, I pick up on it, and add it to the tally. I feel like there have been moments in the past, opportunities that I missed by not taking control and being the strong Daddy that she needs. I won't make that mistake again.

It comes on the second last day of our cruise, once we've turned around at Monterey and we're heading south again.

She's filled a whole notebook with drawings, with a lot of sketches of the coastline and sunsets. But when she thinks I'm not watching, she flips to a blank page and draws something more childish, with thick black lines that she colors in.

Everyone is somewhere else on the yacht. It's just the two of us up on a forward deck, so I put down the book I was reading and cross to where she's sprawled out against a table, her chin in her hand, her notebook closed beside her.

I tap it. "Show me what you've been drawing."

She jumps. "Oh!"

"Were you daydreaming?"

"I guess." She gives me a warm smile. "I thought you were reading."

"I was. And watching you draw." I lean in, trapping her in her chair. "I want to see your drawings."

"I show them to you."

"You mostly show me the sunsets."

"And the coastlines."

"I want to see the unicorn."

She blushes.

"Am I right? Is that what it was?"

"It's a narwhal," she mutters. "Unicorns of the sea."

"Show Daddy."

There's enough of a pause that I wonder if she might safeword over showing me inside her notebook—which would be fine, if not perplexing—but then she flips it open and finds the page I saw her drawing a little earlier.

It's a narwhal with attitude, and it's adorable. "I love it," I tell her honestly. "What else have you done?"

She turns the pages, slowing down before she gets to the next page that feels more private. Here there's a little girl octopus on a boat, alone on a sea, and below the water is a big old octopus with eyes that look a lot like mine—if I'm reading cartoons properly.

"What's her story?"

Eden shrugs. Then she stops herself. "She's a girl who was forced to go on an adventure by herself," she says softly.

Oh.

Fuck.

"Did the grizzly old octopus tell her to go off on her own?"

"I guess so."

"And she felt pretty little having to do that." I drop my forehead down to gently bump against hers. "I see you."

"It's okay," she whispers. "It's in the past now."

"But we're out on the ocean together, and it's okay if that brings up some resentment about me rejecting you."

Her hands come up and cup my face. "As much as I might fantasize about it going differently, I know I was too young for you then."

"You want to tell me about those fantasies?"

She giggles.

"I'm serious."

She sucks in a sharp breath and her hands drop back to her lap. "Yeah. Okay. Maybe."

"I'm just going to say something that might need to be stated clearly between us, okay?"

She nods.

"Little girls who like to color can also be Big girls who like to ride Daddy's cock."

She worries her bottom lip before saying, "Those two things don't feel the same to me."

"Fair enough."

"Do they to you?"

How do I explain that she can be whoever she wants to be, and I'll still want to be inside her? Still have a hard, thuddy pulse of desperate need driving me in a way I've never experienced before? "It's never not *you*, Eden. So if you're very little, like Dylan, or sometimes little, like Kaydie… I don't think that would be strange to me. If you got something out of sitting on my lap, sucking your thumb, and being a Baby? I'd still get hard for you because you are you."

"Do you want me to do that?"

I sink down to squat in front of her. It's important that I not loom over her as I say this. "I want you to be the most raw and authentic you. What turns me on is the vulnerability. The idea that nobody else gets to see the soft underbelly of tough Eden. There's no age I want you to be. Only a depth of realness nobody else has ever seen."

She leans over and kisses me, and then she pushes me gently and I tumble to my back, and she sprawls on top of me.

"I love you," she says against my mouth.

I kiss her back, then tell her I love her, too.

We make out on the deck, and hold each other, and I don't push her any further.

I've said what needed to be said as the Daddy. The next step is up to her.

———

"Can I make a toast?" Eden grabs a bottle of champagne—the third the crew has opened for us tonight, I think—and hoists it in the air.

"Can you use a glass?" I ask dryly.

She squeaks and hands it over. I top up her glass, then make sure everyone else has what they want, too, before she continues.

"First of all, I want to say thank you for including me on this trip," she says. "You made this baby kinkster feel very welcome."

"I already miss you," Kaydie says wistfully.

"We'll visit again," I promise.

Eden smiles. "But my toast is actually to… love. To vulnerable, honest love." She holds my gaze as she takes a sip of bubbly.

I tip my glass in her direction, too, then drink as well.

We've finished dinner, and we're under the stars with friends. It was already a perfect night, but now my girl is toasting honest vulnerability.

A month ago, I had none of this. I was a tightly wound, lonely bachelor professor.

"Come here," I growl, and she flies across the deck to me, to give me a champagne-flavored kiss. "I love you."

She nods. "I know. But I've loved you longer."

I go still.

Her smile is fearless and sweet at the same time. "It's true." She shrugs one shoulder. "Like, way too long."

"Baby…"

She twirls out of my arms. "More champagne!"

Most of the trip, we've been some of the earliest to bed, but tonight we stay up with everyone—until Eden reaches the zenith of beautifully drunk, perfectly horny, and zero filter.

"Nolan…" she slurs as she spins into my arms sometime on the far side of midnight. "I used to think about your cock. I think you should know how often—"

I grin. "All right, time for bed."

"I wanted to give you a blow—"

I cover her mouth with my hand, and she licks me. I deserve a medal for directing her inside instead of unleashing my erection and ordering her to her knees.

She pouts at me over her shoulder. "Can't unzip my dress."

"I'll get it once we're in the cabin."

"Here, Daddy…"

"Not here. Sober Eden doesn't want people to see her tits."

"Drunk Eden *doesn't care*."

"I'm aware." I catch her in my arms and kiss her. "Come on. Your tits are for Daddy and Daddy alone."

"Ooookay." She twirls around, and her skirt lifts up around her hips, showing almost the entire length of her bare legs.

That's fine. She has spectacular legs and everyone has seen them all week already.

I get her in our cabin and close the door. "You used to think about my cock?"

"I still do."

"I'm a lucky man."

"Mmmm." She sighs happily. "I dream of you undressing me, Daddy."

"I dream of you, too. I did before, too."

She smiles softly. "Undressing me?"

My own grin is more wicked. "In my dreams, you're already naked."

Her eyes go wide. "Oh."

"I follow you to bed and find you already touching yourself." I close the gap between us and put my hands on her shoulders. "Do you touch yourself, baby?"

"Yes, Daddy."

"Good girl." I grasp the zipper gently and draw it down, revealing the long, smooth stretch of her back. My finger trails down her spine, too, following the parting zipper.

All the way down to the small of her back, and then a little lower. To where her hips flared, and now the dress is fully loose.

It catches between her body and her arms for a second, then falls to her feet.

All she's wearing under it is a skimpy pair of black panties.

I put them on her before dinner.

And now I take them off her with a nudge, letting them fall to the ground, too.

"On the bed, kitten. Show Daddy how you touch yourself."

She crawls onto her back, her legs falling apart, and my cock throbs at the sight in front of me.

Beautiful.

Her gaze tangles with mine as she starts to circle her clit, but it doesn't take long for her attention to drop to my cock, stretching my fly obscenely.

"I want to see it." And in her breathy request, I hear an echo of a younger Eden, who I once denied.

Tonight, she gets whatever she wants.

I unzip.

My cock bulges against the soft cotton of my boxer-briefs, wanting to be free. Wanting her young, innocent, curious gaze.

I don't pull it out yet. I cup myself through the cotton, knowing that once he's bare, it won't be long before I fall on her and get inside her.

It's our way right now. We're still full of *can't quite believe this is real*, new- relationship energy.

After a week of seeing my friends in their longer-term relationships, I know we'll find a different balance down the road. More patience with kink. More history we can lean on.

Right now, the only history we have together is one of painful denial, so the present is charged with a desperate need to not deny ourselves anything.

Fuck.

I shove my briefs down, freeing my cock. No more denial.

Her eyes light up and her fingers fly faster on her clit.

"Love watching you love yourself," I growl as I strip off my clothes.

Then I'm on the bed and shoving my way between her legs. My fingers press into her thighs, probably leaving marks, but I can't let go of her.

My cock is leaking already, wet at the tip. I ignore it and work my fingers into her first. Her fingers on her clit, mine in her tight, clutching pussy.

Her ripe, lush body quivering beneath me.

I take hold of her waist and guide her up, lifting her hips and bringing her sweet wet slit to meet my cock. The warm, soft slick of her body giving way for me is incredible.

She breathes my name. First Nolan, then Daddy.

"I've got you."

"I need you deep…"

With a groan, I thrust my hips, working us together. "You're tight, baby. Gotta go slow or you'll make me explode."

"Yes, Daddy… Want you to explode in me. Fill me up."

I change the angle, sliding my hand over her mound so I can work her clit with my thumb. "I want to fill you up, too."

"Want to have your babies."

"Want that too, beautiful." I can feel my balls churning, seed desperate to get inside her now.

My hips snap forward, and I hook an arm under hips, holding her up. She moans low and long, a sexy cry, and then her whole body seizes. Out of nowhere, she's caught by an orgasm, and I can feel it from the inside out.

Now it's her name on my lips, *Eden, oh fuck, yes, Eden*… and then I explode, my come pouring of me, deep inside her.

I bow my head forward, putting my face between her small breasts, and she puts her hands in my hair, holding me against her as my cock twitches in her belly.

My pulse slowly returns to normal, and still I'm inside her.

"Worth the wait," she whispers. "And better than my dreams."

21
eden

ADJUSTING BACK to real life is a slight challenge after a week on a luxury yacht. But it's not like my real life isn't still a fantasy dream.

I get a job in Conception Ridge, an assistant production editor position at the town newspaper that doesn't pay much, but does give me an opportunity to do some graphic design and illustration, because all five people who work for the paper each wear at least three different hats.

And I get to come home every day to a man who loves me for just being myself. Who gives me the most spectacular orgasms—sometimes as a punishment—and has infinite patience for me figuring my shit out.

So I shouldn't be nervous about finally wanting to talk about our past. He's expressly asked me to think about it, and share my thoughts with him.

But I'm nervous for my own reasons. Because I'd rather be in the present, where I'm deliriously happy.

There are some thoughts that keep coming up in my art and my dreams, though, that I'm finally ready to say out loud.

When I tell Nolan I want to talk, he wraps me in a blanket

on the living room coach, where he took my virginity less than two months ago, and he waits.

On the wall, in a frame, is a letter he gave me for my eighteenth birthday.

It's fitting that we're having this conversation in front of it, I realize.

I point to it. "So… that."

He glances up at it. "Yes. That."

"I didn't want to go out into the world and do all those things." It tears out of me.

He nods slowly. "I'm sorry."

"You aren't. You'd do it again. Tell me I need to go and experience everything."

"I would," he says calmly. "Because I couldn't take advantage of an eighteen-year-old."

"It would have been hot," I chirp back, because I can't resist.

He doesn't take the bait. "Don't be a brat."

"You said you don't mind bratty."

"When it's real. When it's raw. Don't use that to manipulate me, though."

"Or what?" If he's going to make me come every hour on the hour, I'll keep pushing.

"Or I'll make you write me an ethics essay before you get another orgasm."

"What?" An essay?

He nods slowly, then leans in and kisses me softly. "Five hundred words on the value of personal boundaries."

"What?"

"You heard me."

"I don't want to do that! Can't you give me a punishment that is more… climax related?"

"No, the point is that you don't want to. I can see that you need to. And you will feel better when it's done. Humor me. If you go away and feel better not doing it, let me know that you have another plan. I'm always open to honest communication with my love."

"That feels manipulative," I mutter. "Calling me your love."

"Damn it," he says mildly. "I was going for deeply open and vulnerable."

I throw my arms around his neck and kiss his cheek. "You're too smart for me. I feel like a stupid kid sometimes."

"I never ever see you that way. I swear. But I think we're getting sidetracked already. You really hated all of your solo life experiences before you came back to me?"

"Not all of them," I whisper. "But I was lonely for those four years. And as the days turn into weeks, and now months for us... don't get me wrong. I'm so happy with you. But I'm starting to realize just how lonely I was."

"Like a girl all alone on a boat in the ocean."

"Yeah."

He nuzzles his nose into my cheek. "What if we frame that picture you drew? And any others you want to draw. A visual reminder, just like the letter, of what we gave up before? Because baby, I'm never sending you away again. I'm never going to give you up. You are *mine*, you hear?"

I nod hurriedly. I know I am.

"Say it."

"I'm yours." But my voice is shaky.

"Say, *Daddy will never send me away*."

"Daddy will never send me away."

"That's right." He kisses me hard now. "Even if you're little. Even if you're bratty. You're old enough now that you can be those things *and* be mine."

"I don't know how often I want to be little."

He smiles.

"But can we go back on the group trip next year?"

"Fuck yes. Unless..." His hand drops to my belly. Two months together, and we've never used protection, and my period is about to be late. "That depends on a few external factors."

"Oh, right." I blush. "The next available opportunity, then."

"We can play like that at home sometimes. Just sometimes. Or as often as you want."

"I'm still a bit in my head about it."

"Can Daddy help with that?" His hand pushes lower from my belly, into my yoga pants. Into my panties, where I'm already slick.

He groans. "How am I supposed to fucking resist when you're this fucking wet? This fucking needy?"

He's not. He's not supposed to resist. He's supposed to make me feel good, so good, in secret, over and over again. And he always does.

"Be as little you want," he whispers.

"Too little," I whisper back.

His hand tightens on my pussy. A shudder ripples through him. And he nods. "Okay."

My mouth finds his, and I let my kiss be what it would have been the night before eighteenth birthday. Clumsy, horny, confused. Inexperienced.

He groans into my mouth and deepens it, his tongue stroking against mine.

I push his t-shirt up, wanting my hands on his bare skin. I love the hard planes of his chest, the warm skin pulled taut over wiry muscles. I want to be naked with him. I want to itemize all the ways our bodies are different and have him teach me how good they work together, though, to make me feel good.

With one hand, he yanks his shirt off and tosses it to the floor. With the other, he spins me around so I'm flat on my back on the couch.

He peels off my yoga pants and panties. They go flying in the other direction, to the corner of the room. He stares down at my cleft. "Perfect grown-up little girl pussy."

I release a desperate gasp, and he shoves my thighs apart.

Yes.

His breath is warm on my hip, then my mound, and finally, *finally*, right up the center of my seam. His tongue teases me open, then slowly makes me bloom, and squirm, and beg.

"Nolan, please…" I'm humping his face, my hands in his hair. "I want you to fuck me."

He pushes up, his face glistening from me. Tension wars across his face, and then he's off the couch, off me. His gaze stays locked on my face as he strips his pants off, then he's looming over me in only his boxer-briefs.

There's something wicked in his expression that matches the new tension in the air. It's radiating from him, I realize.

"Please," I beg again.

He slowly strips off the final piece of clothing between us, then climbs on top of me again.

Slow, slow, slow. Everything is moving like we're in a dream.

His gaze glitters down at me as he rubs his cock between my legs, then up onto my mound toward my belly.

I squirm against him, my clit straining for better contact against the throbbing length of his cock.

"No, baby," he finally says, his voice tight. "You're too little for Daddy to be inside you."

I sob. But the steel in his denial also makes my core tighten up.

"Shhh…" he smoothes his hand over my cheek. His thumb drags across my lips, then pushes into my mouth. "Suck."

I suck, just like I did on the yacht, with hungry, gulping little swallows.

He exhales happily. "Your needy little noises are music to my ears. Good girl. Your mouth knows what it's doing. Daddy's going to teach you how to suck his cock just like that."

I nod and whimper, and he slowly starts working his cock back and forth along the seam of my pussy, so the tip of his erection teases my clit, then the full length of him pushes against it on each thrust.

"Too little to get fucked, but not too little to be loved, hmm?" His voice is hypnotic. It's his podcaster voice, I realize. What I used to listen to while I rubbed myself to sleep. "You're never going to be lonely again, Eden. I've got you. You're mine. And I'm yours."

Tears prick at my eyelids and I nod harder.

"Come for Daddy," he whispers, his hips working faster. "If I feel that sweet pussy flutter against my balls, I'll come, too. Would you like that?"

So much. Another nod.

His thumb tugs out of my mouth, leaving me panting, searching for it hungrily.

"Say it," he whispers, his voice catching on a rough note. "Tell Daddy you want him to come on your belly."

"I want you to come inside me," I say, because it's the truth.

He groans. "Can't do that."

I tilt my hips up, trying to catch the tip of him. He plants a hand firmly on my hip and stops me with a groan. It's rough and deep. I tremble beneath him, my legs spread wide, my pussy aching.

And then, ever so slowly, he fits us together.

Both of us are breathing hard as he breaches me with just the tip. His gaze locks onto mine and the whole world disappears.

He feels big, and he feels right.

He sinks into me, inch by inch, and once he's all the way buried, he gives me his weight, too. His mouth comes to my cheek and I realize I'm crying when he kisses away my tears.

Then he starts moving.

It's slow. It's careful.

It's the opposite of the fast fucks we often have, all eager energy. This is deeply loving, which isn't what younger me wanted. She wanted her off-limits crush to fuck her the way he would fuck a grown-up Eden.

But this is better. This is everything. This is *my* Nolan, loving *me*.

I wrap my legs around him and he cups my breast, both of us moving in unison now.

"Daddy," I breathe.

"Yes…"

I repeat it a dozen times, moaning for him, and then I'm coming, and it's bright and powerful and contagious. He groans on top of me, a drawn-out, ragged grunt that is one of the most satisfying sounds I have ever heard.

And then his whole body curls over mine, and we're kissing again.

When we pull apart, I realize my phone is ringing in the distance. Nolan drags himself off me. "I'll go find it in a minute."

"I'm good, I'm getting up…" I swipe his t-shirt off the floor on my way back to the kitchen, where I think I left my phone.

He follows, collecting the rest of our clothes.

Once I find my phone, I see it was a call from my mom. We've had some polite, short phone calls, but sometimes I dodge her to avoid the slight awkwardness of it all, and she must think this is one of those times, because she's followed up with a text message. "It's a text from my mom." I read it out loud. "*Your father thinks there should be a ring if he's serious about wanting to marry you.*" I roll my eyes. "Can you believe him? How deeply old-fashioned."

Behind me, Nolan says, "I agree with him."

"What?" I turn, laughing, but the surprise at his reaction drops—and turns to surprise of a completely different sort—when I see him down on one knee. A ring is in his outstretched hand. "Nolan, you don't need—"

"Oh, I need. Very much. I need to make you promises, and I need to make you mine. I need to show you in every way, on every level, that I adore you. I adore your little side, and I adore your bratty side, and I adore your everyday Eden side." He pauses, and his voice goes from firmly bossy to silky soft. "I love you. I want you to be my wife. I want you to wear my ring and carry my name and be *mine*. Will you marry me?"

"Where did the ring come from?" He's wearing boxer-briefs and nothing else. The logistics of him being ready for this moment are impressive.

He chokes out a laugh. "My pants pocket, Eden. Come on, don't leave me hanging here."

"Did you coordinate the text—"

"It's been in my pocket since we got back from the trip, all right?" He gives me an exasperated but adoring look. "I love you so much, you curious little thing. Please fucking marry me."

"Of course I'll marry you," I tease back. "That's a given. I just wanted to know—"

"It's not a given." He takes my hand in his and slides the ring onto my finger. "I will never take what we have for granted. And you can satisfy all of your questions later."

"Later?"

"After."

"After..."

"After your punishment for asking too many questions."

"Is that an essay, or..."

He hauls me down to the floor and rolls on top of me. "It's *or*, baby. Now be quiet for Daddy."

epilogue

Nolan

Five years later

"ARE you sure you guys are done having kids?"

Eden slides a wicked glance my way.

"Troublemaker," I growl at her, squeezing her hand. "We're done if you're done."

"He'd keep making babies forever," she breezily confides in the piercing artist who is currently prepping sterile needles on a stainless steel tray. "But I'm ready for these to be mine again."

Eden gestures at her bare tits, which have nursed two babies and given me endless pleasure over the last five years.

The piercing artist nods like this is a totally normal, every day conversation.

Eden turns to me and mouths, *Mine and Daddy's.*

And for at least the next six weeks, nobody's, because she's going to have to let her nipples heal before I can play with her new decorations. It will feel like a lifetime, but it'll be worth it if my little girl is happy.

"Ready?"

"Yes," Eden whispers. But she's not looking at the needle. She's got her gaze locked on my face.

"Take some deep breaths…"

I hold her attention, pouring all of my love to her, as her eyes go wide and tears spring forward.

She gasps silently, her mouth falling open, and then her eyes lose focus as her body reacts to the unexpected pain. Pink heat slashes across her cheeks, and her pupils dilate, as if the sharp spike of pain has spilled impossibly black ink in those glittering green pools.

"All done," the artist murmurs. "You're doing great. Catch your breath, and then we'll do the other side."

Panic pinches the space between Eden's eyebrows, and I lean in to kiss her there. "You're such a good girl," I whisper, and she shudders.

I glance down. "It's pretty."

"Yeah?" She beams, as if the praise is all she needs to get through this. "I'm not looking yet. Not until the second one is done."

The piercer laughs. "Fair. Okay. Deep breaths…"

This one is even hotter. Eden anticipates the flare of pain, and the look on her face is incredible. Going in my special memory bank right alongside the night I took her virginity.

And when it's done, and she looks down, she loves them. "Oh, Nolan. Look at them."

"Hard not to," I admit.

We get a knowing look from the artist, who gives Eden some brief care instructions, and then we race out of there.

I get her as far as the car before I'm yanking her sundress up and shoving my hand in her panties.

She comes on my fingers in record time, her clit twitching and pussy pulsing hard. "That's just to take the edge off," I promise. We have the rest of the day to take very good care of her before we have to pick the kids up from daycare. "Give me one more, and then we're going home. Daddy needs your hot mouth on his cock."

She whimpers and throws her head back, arching as I thrust my fingers into her cunt.

We might be done having kids. But I'm never going to stop wanting to breed her, my wild little sex goddess.

"Look at me," I demand. "Look at Daddy as you come."

Her eyes flare open, her gaze bright.

And she comes on my hand, proving for the ten-thousandth time that she's Daddy's best girl.

———

brunch date

eden

For weeks, Nolan's hand has crept up my midsection while we sleep, and just before he cups my breast, he yanks it away. Even while he's asleep.

And every morning that passes since I got my nipples pierced, we both wake up aching and more aroused than the day before.

It's agony.

Nolan loves it. He's so disciplined. *Even while he's asleep.* I think he likes denying me.

And he gets so rough with the rest of my body that isn't off-limits. He yanks my panties down and shoves his fingers into my still-waking-up pussy. Which only makes me ache even more.

My husband knows exactly how to play my body. But the parts of me that want to be played with the most are being ignored.

With a quiet grunt, he frees his cock behind me and hitches my thigh up. All he needs to do is fit us together and slide inside me, and then I'll tell him—

Bang. Bang.

That's the crib on the other side of the wall.

"Daddy," a little voice calls out. "Good morning!"

I squint at the clock as Nolan chuckles and rolls out of bed, tucking his cock away.

Seven in the morning. Okay, it's time to get up.

I race into the shower, needing not to be a squirmy, wet little mess before we start the day.

By the time I race downstairs, tucking my t-shirt into the front of my jean shorts, Nolan has the kids eating breakfast, and an extra big mug of coffee for me. "Morning," he murmurs as he kisses me. "Sorry we got interrupted there."

"Mm-hmm." I flick my gaze to the clock, then the giant wall calendar. "What does your day look like?"

"Class at nine, then office hours in the afternoon." His eyes darken, glittering as he picks up on my idea. "Brunch?"

"Brunch," I whisper breathlessly. My heart races. "I can take the kids to the drop-in center for the morning."

His hands tighten on my hips. "You are a smart little girl. And you will be rewarded for this very good idea."

I whimper into my coffee mug, because Nolan's idea of a reward can go in a lot of different directions. Some of them make sitting down later a…challenge.

~

I text my friend Summer to see if her kids also want to go to the Ridge College drop-in center this morning. She's a part-time student—she jokes that she'll be studying forever, because she's also a full-time mom a little younger than me. Her husband is a barber on Main Street.

After our kids toddle off together, we grab a coffee from a cute little cart on the quad and find a shady spot to sit.

"What are you doing with your free morning?" she asks.

Warmth floods my cheeks. "Brunch date with Nolan."

Her eyes sparkle. "Nice."

We aren't the kind of friends who talk about sex, exactly. That's private, between us and our husbands. But Henry is almost as old as Nolan. That we're both in obviously large age gap relationships is something that we've talked about. And she's not the only one. In a weird twist of fate, a girl I met in the Caribbean is actually from Conception Ridge, and she fell head over heels in love with her boyfriend's dad.

There's something in the water here, I swear.

Which makes it feel safe to lean in and confess, "I got some...piercings...a few months ago and they're finally all healed up. We're both excited about some alone time."

Summer's gaze drops to my tits, where my barbells are hidden behind a protective padded bra. "You mean..."

"Mm-hmm."

"Wow." She shivers. "I don't know if Henry would want those to be off-limits for that long."

I giggle. "Yeah, it was hard."

She snorts. "I bet."

"Summer!"

She takes a sip of her iced coffee and smiles.

Nolan finds us there after his class lets out. He strides across the quad, the sun glinting off the silver in his hair. And he looks...hungry. Summer takes one look at his expression and mumbles something about needing to go to the library.

Her blush gives away that we weren't talking about childcare.

He gives me his best stern professor glare once we're alone. "Sharing secrets with your friends about what you're going to do with Daddy this morning?"

"Not in any great detail," I protest. But then I'm grinning in a naughty way. "I just told her about my piercings."

His mouth curves into very satisfied smile. "And what did she say?"

I blush.

He draws me close and kisses my temple. His voice is a sexy burr against my skin. "Little one…"

"She said Henry wouldn't want to have her breasts be off-limits that long," I say.

"No, I imagine he wouldn't. It's been quite a challenge for me."

"But now they're all healed up."

"Finally." His hand squeezes around my shoulder. "Then I know exactly what I want for brunch."

"Me?"

"You." I will never tire of how he says that, with so much layered intent. "Your lovely tits as my starter. The rest of your lovely body as the main course."

I whimper. "I can't wait until we get home."

"I have pineapple juice and some granola bars in my office," he says. "Coffee. Maybe an apple?"

I suck in a relieved breath. "Brunch of champions."

I manage to look cool as a cucumber, just a regular wife drop-in visit as we stroll past his colleagues, to the end of the hall, where his office overlooks a ravine.

And most importantly, the big, heavy door has a solid lock on it.

nolan

I've never appreciated having the seniority to have this office more than I do in this moment. It's private, with thick walls protecting my little wife's beautiful noises.

Because those sounds are mine, and only mine.

I tug her shirt off as soon as I throw that latch, then back her up so I can hoist her onto the counter in the little kitchenette in the corner. I have a couch, too, which we've used before—and I will bend her over the arm of before this morning is out.

But right now, I want—no, need—her tits at mouth level.

I palm her cheek and kiss her, deep and thorough, then trace my fingers down her neck and her soft, smooth chest.

I pause at the edge of her bra cup. "Was it worth it? Making Daddy wait to suck on your nipples again?"

She trembles. "I hope so."

I slide my fingers into the padded bra and find her nipple already hard, a tight, plump raspberry—with two hard steel beads on either side of it.

I tug, feeling the bar that runs through the tender flesh beneath my fingers.

She whimpers. "Oh God, oh God."

"Not God," I say.

She nods and shakes her head. "No. Yes. Daddy."

"What do you think now, little one? Worth it?"

"Yes, Daddy."

"Fucking brat. Three *months* I haven't been able to do this."

"I'm sorry."

"I should spank you for that."

"You should." She nods rapidly. Then she glances down my body, where my cock is jutting at the front of my jeans. "But we're both hungry…"

I twist her nipple. "We didn't wait twelve weeks just for you to lick your slutty little lips and trick me into a mind-blowing blow job. We can do that tomorrow."

"Right. We can do that tomorrow." She's babbling already, repeating what I say, and I haven't even gotten to the other nipple.

"What are we going to do today?"

"Nipple stuff?"

"And spanking," I say smoothly.

"Oh." She trembles. Then she smiles. "Thank you, Daddy."

Fuck. Yes.

"I love you," I say softly as I move to the other breast.

I grip her hair with my free hand and tug her head back, arching her back so her breasts—and those barbell-pinched nipples—point up toward me. I suck one tip into my mouth, tonguing at the barbell in a way that makes her keen a wild sound, like I've made her toes curl.

Even better.

And holy fuck, do the piercings make her tits even sexier. Her nipples have never been harder or as swollen.

I make a feast of her peaks, back and forth, back and forth. She braces herself against the shelf behind her, and my hand slides out of her hair and down to encircle her neck.

Her pulse flutters against my thumb, her breath heaving in shallow little gulps.

I lift my gaze, checking her face. She looks blissed out, even as her body feels on the edge of freaking out.

Slowly, I rise up and kiss her again, cupping her wet nipples with my hands.

"You're such a good girl," I tell her. "So fucking sexy for Daddy."

"Am I?" She gives me a wide-eyed look and for a second, I'm taken back almost ten years now, to a time when she wanted me to be her first, her only, and her forever...and I had no clue.

But I do now, and sometimes, Eden pushes that button in a way that makes me crazy.

She's fire in my veins, this girl. This lush *woman* who has given me babies and adventures and a second chance at this incredible life. But it's when she goes all soft and innocent, crawling inside herself and letting out the little girl I once rejected, giving her a chance to have what I refused that first time, when she's maybe the sexiest ever.

Because by showing me that side of her, she is also the woman who taught me to say yes. Yes to secrets. Yes to adventure. Yes to naughty role-plays, and do-overs.

"You know how hard you make Daddy," I say, my voice husky and low. "Even when he shouldn't have those feelings about you."

She jolts against me. "Nobody needs to know," she whispers.

I glance to the door. "Can you be quiet?"

"Mm-hmm."

I flick open the button on her jean shorts. "Good girl."

Then I latch on to one of her nipples again. When she murmurs a confused, questioning *Daddy?*, I just groan and suck harder. Shove my hand down the front of her shorts, and find her panties sticky and wet.

"Daddy, I need..." She whispers the words, trying so hard to be quiet, but her body feels electrified.

"I know, baby. I need it too." I yank my hand out of her shorts, pick her up again, and pivot us to the couch. I tumble her onto her back and peel off her shorts, then her underwear.

Ten years ago, she thought about coming here to be a fucking co-ed, and tempt me with her soft curves and bare pussy.

Would I have been able to resist if she was showing up here all the time to talk to her dad's best friend about school and boys and private, secret needs?

I would have fucking caved halfway through her first year, let's be fucking honest.

Now she's my wife and I can drop to my knees to lick her swollen, needy cunt without any guilt.

I am a lucky, lucky man.

I nose against her mound, then lick down her slit, flicking her clit ring before pulling her pussy lips against my tongue. Both of them at the same time, a hungry pull with my whole mouth.

She whimpers, and I push one arm up to cup her cheek and feed her my thumb to suck on.

My other hand finds her nipples and tugs on one, then the other, back and forth. I need more hands. I need another mouth. I want to consume every inch of my wife, all the time. Forever.

I'm breathing hard when I lift my head and grab my t-shirt with one hand, pulling it off.

Eden wriggles out of her bra, which had worked its way down to her waist.

I unzip.

And then I surge up, and I'm on top of her, cradling her in my arms. Whispering for her to be quiet, shhhh, quiet for Daddy.

Her eyes glitter up at me as she nods wordlessly, and I fit my throbbing cock tip against her sweet pussy.

She's tighter now, after having kids, then she was when I first dragged her into my bed and did my level best to breed her. She always needs me to take my time, which is a gift.

Going slow. Savoring how tight and hot her cunt is. Watching her reactions spill across her face as she gets use to the fat length of my cock inside her.

She squeezes me. In the best way, she's *just* slick enough to make resistance impossible. She has to take my thick intrusion. She couldn't stop me if she tried as I push my hips, gaining ground inside her. Deeper, deeper, and once I'm buried all the way, both of us are breathing hard.

I pause and just gaze down at her face. Her beautiful, expressive green eyes.

Carefully, I cup and squeeze her breast, pinching the tip between my thumb and my forefinger. "I love you," I say.

This is so much more love than I ever thought I would have.

She gasps, her pupils dilating.

My cock grows even bigger as I feel the ripple of sensation move through her body. That little zap of pain I can give her now, any time I want.

And then I skate my hand down her side, to grip her hip, then cup her ass. I lift her body against mine as I begin to move.

"God damn it, I love the way your pussy clutches at the tip of Daddy's cock," I rasp as I drag myself out of her body, and her body clutches to my erection, not letting it go. "Needy little cunt."

"Yes. Yours."

"I'm always going to want you like this. Off-limits, in my office. Pierced little body. Gotta prove to me that you're all grown up, hmm?"

She whimpers.

I'll take that as a yes.

"Went and got these little tempting tug points in your tits, like that will stop me from breeding you again."

She throws her head back and silently moans, her mouth wide open and her eyes wide shut.

That makes my wife come every fucking time.

I pound into her, my cock sawing in and out, thick and full and primed to flood her tight channel.

Flood her womb, her lovely, sexy, off-limits womb.

Mmmm.

I think about putting another baby in her and I lose it. I hunch over her and kiss her hard, too hard, and I snap my hips home, burying my cock and my seed right where it belongs.

Where it has always belonged.

Inside my Eden.

Inside my wife.

When the darkness recedes from the edges of my vision, I'm curved on top of Eden, and she's kissing my mouth softly.

I taste her lips back, savoring our connection before I pull out and make a mess everywhere that I didn't really prepare for.

"Your gym bag has a towel," she whispers, reading my mind.

And then we both laugh.

I grab it and clean us both up, then she stretches out naked on my couch.

"Coffee for my lovely wife?" I ask as I zip up my jeans.

"Mmm yes, definitely. And were you serious about the pineapple juice?"

"Of course."

"Because it reminds you of that almost kiss," she says. Teasing me.

"God, woman, you just got fucked. You trying to get me to rail you again?"

She giggles. "Maybe. I like it when you get all…growly. And you haven't spanked me yet."

I abandon the coffee and stride back to the couch. "Asking for a spanking is a good way to not get one."

She scrunches up her face. "Meanie."

I sink my fingers into her long, silky hair and tug her up, then over the arm of the couch. I kneel behind her and give her one hard swat to the ass, then leave my hand there and squeeze the stinging flesh. "If you wanted a proper spanking, we should have gone home to eat."

"There's still time."

I give her another swat. "Tomorrow."

"Definitely tomorrow," she pants, her thighs drifting apart.

I slide my fingers down the cleft of her ass and into her fluttering pussy. Two of them, thrust hard and deep. Not letting her adjust. Taking up that space because I need to be inside her again, one way or another.

"You want to know why I always have pineapple juice here, little one? It's not just because it reminds me of the almost kiss. It's because it makes me think of what would come next. How I'd still be licking the taste of pineapple from *my* lips as you took my cock between yours. How it would be all I would smell if you climbed onto my lap and took my cock inside you. Bare. I didn't have any condoms that night. You weren't on any birth control. I'd have put a baby in you that night. That's what I fucking think about when I drink pineapple juice."

She squeaks, and I snake my other hand around to her tits. Those little metal barbells are addictive. They make me want to pinch and tug and twist and— Yes. That sound. I want to make her make that sound over and over again. That desperate, needy little whine.

I yank her up so she's plastered against my front, caught against my body and being forced to ride my hand. "Come like this, Eden. Come on my fingers as I tell you just how bad I wanted to be with you. How I burned for you. How I started drinking pineapple juice just to torture myself about what I couldn't have. For four long years, the only pleasure I got was jacking off with the taste of it on my lips."

Her body snaps like a live wire, her cunt clutching my fingers hard.

"That's it," I say, lust thickening my voice. "Oh, fuck yeah, come for me. Break my fingers."

She shakes in my arms, and I bury my face in her hair, holding her and breathing her in as she comes again for the second time this morning.

This time, I don't rush to make us coffee. I ease her down and hold her on my lap. Hold her tight, because even after five years, there's a part of me that can't quite believe we have this.

"Thank you for being mine," I whisper.

"You're welcome for being such a stubborn tease," she whispers back.

I laugh.

"I love it when you tell me how I drove you crazy with that kiss attempt," she says.

"So fucking crazy."

"I'm sorry."

"Don't be sorry. Fuck, you're so sexy. It's not your fault. You can't help it. And now I get to fuck you every chance I get."

Across the room, my cell phone vibrates. I ignore it, but when hers goes next, we both scramble to our feet. It could be the childcare center.

Of course when she gets to her phone, she makes a face.

Okay, not kid care. "What is it?"

"My parents want to come for a visit. They want grandkid time."

When we first told her parents we were together—and I made it clear their opinion wasn't necessary, or welcome—there was a long stretch of silent treatment.

Eden getting pregnant changed that.

Sort of—they always stay at an inn in town. Which is for the best, of course. We don't need them listening to us at night. Nobody needs that.

I pull on my t-shirt. "Okay."

"How do they always seem to text us when we're having sex?"

"It's just a statistical thing. The probability of anyone texting us when we're sex-adjacent is high because we're always sex-adjacent." I flex my chest. "Because you can't get enough of this old man."

She giggles. "I can't, it's true."

I gather up her clothes and help her restore herself to still-sexy-but-respectably-dressed. Then I finally dig out that cold bottle of pineapple juice, which she takes instead of a coffee, and we share a granola bar and an apple.

When it's time for her to go, she catches my t-shirt in her hand, holding on. Her face is flushed and her eyes sparkle. "What do you want to have for dinner tonight?"

Her, again, but we have kids to feed, too. "Pasta?"

She smiles, her eyes so bright they almost hurt to look at. I would never look anywhere else, though. "Home made?"

"Always."

She nods and leans in, ghosting her lips just above mine. She smells like pineapple juice and my heart squeezes. "Always," she repeats.

And on so many levels, that's just how it fucking is with us.

We always have been. We always will be. And there are subtle little reminders of how fucking special that is in food and drink and the barest brush of lips against lips.

I catch her in my arms and press her against the door. "A proper kiss goodbye," I demand. "Show me that you love me."

She laughs and does exactly that. And then she does it again, and again, until I'm hard and aching, and she waggles her fingers goodbye at the horny professor who just wants to drag her back to his couch for another round of off-limits slap and tickle.

Tomorrow, maybe.

No. Tomorrow, definitely.

And every day after that, until the end of time.

———

her wedding night

CHLOE MAINE

For all the smut loving readers who want stalkers and primal chase through a forest, but not too scary!

I didn't choose tonight to be my wedding night. And no matter what, a stalker will get to claim my innocence…

I'm tricked onto a luxury yacht and taken out to sea. The boat party I was invited to? Turns out, the boy who sits beside me in class has an obsession with my purity, and his friends all want to see him take me as his bride.

But my classmates aren't the only ones on board.

When Gabriel Rudd steps from the shadows and gives me the choice of who will strip me out of this translucent white bridal gown—father or son—I pick the grown man with the frightening, flashing gaze.

And I have to hope the mountain man, with his whispered, urgent words that fill me with an unexpected heat, will protect me when the rest of them want a turn…

Her Wedding Night is an over-the-top spicy instalove romance with a reclusive former Navy SEAL who will stop at nothing to protect the innocent, unknowing girl he's been watching from afar.

1
lucy

OH MY GOD, *that's my stalker.*

Which is a weird thought to have as I wait in line for coffee before my Thursday morning Anthropology class.

He's three people in front of me at the coffee shop just off campus, Brewed Awakening. He's half a head taller and half a body broader than the people in between us. Plus, he's probably twice the age of my classmates. But even if he weren't a big, thick silver-templed giant, I'd recognize the tattoos crawling up the back of his neck.

I've seen those tattoos a lot.

The first time I noticed him watching me was about a month ago.

Lately, I'm seeing him almost every day. A couple of times we've made eye contact, and it makes me shiver.

But the two times I tried to take his photo—so I'd have something to take to the campus police to identify him—he disappeared as I was digging out my phone.

My pulse bounces at the base of my throat as I scramble for it now. Can they identify people by neck tattoos? Probably. Maybe he's in a gang or something.

Fingers shaking, I lift my hand, thumb on the button to snap a pic…and he turns around.

His gaze catches mine, his eyes piercing blue. His chest lifts, like he's pulling in a deep breath, then he squares his shoulders and holds still.

A wild, terrifying feeling I don't recognize spikes inside me. I feel locked in place, as if someone slammed pause on the world.

This is my stalker? This man with eyes like the ocean?

It's as if he's cast a spell on me, because I feel an unholy tug, low in my belly, that is keeping me tethered here. Tethered to him.

And then he sucks in another breath, breaking that spell.

I turn on my heel and run.

———

I'm a few minutes early for Anthro, since I didn't wait for coffee, and most of my classmates aren't there yet. A frat guy who I tutored last term, Ethan, gives me a familiar wave.

He's kind of awkward and intense, but he's one of the few people on campus I'd call a friend. Between my need to keep my grades up for my scholarship and my tutoring work, I haven't had any time for a social life.

Ethan pushes out of the seat he'd already gotten settled in and crosses to sit in my row, two seats over from me. "Hey."

I give him my brightest, *I'm fine, not being stalked or anything* smile. "Hey."

"I, uh, wanted to invite you to a party Theta Zeta Alpha is having tomorrow night. I've wanted to ask you all week, but I haven't seen you around." He gives me the same soft puppy dog look he used when he didn't do the studying work between tutoring sessions. "You haven't started dating anyone, have you?"

I laugh nervously. "Me? Dating? No."

"Oh, good." He licks his lips. "Do you like boats? Gilly's parents are away for the weekend, so he can use the yacht."

My eyebrows shoot up. *Yacht?*

He glances past me. I twist to follow his gaze and see three of the most popular girls on campus. Alyssa, Hannah, and Gracie. "You're all coming tomorrow night, right?"

Gracie smirks. "We wouldn't miss it for the world."

Alyssa skims her assessing gaze over me. "Are you coming?"

Something in the challenging way she looks at me gets my back up. And what am I going to do if I say no? Stay home and hide from a man who looks like Reacher?

"Maybe," I say.

Hannah gives me a once over that makes me blush. "She might even be a real one, Ethan."

Behind me, Ethan exhales so loudly I can hear it. "Of course she is. Don't be a bitch."

Before I can look back and ask what he means by that, our Anthro prof arrives and we all have to focus on the lesson.

———

When I get back to my dorm after class, there's an envelope shoved under my door.

Inside is a polaroid photo, and a note.

I'm not a threat to you, I promise.

The words scald my fingers, and I almost drop the simple white piece of paper.

What kind of stalker gives his prey an incriminating selfie and a note that practically reads as a confession?

Why is the only person who sees me, who reads my panicked mind and offers up an answer, albeit deranged, also a psycho who is probably lying to himself about his intentions?

He saw me try to take a picture of him and he gave me a picture.

What. The. Fuck.

What did I do to attract his attention? My chest aches, and I crush the note against my skin.

Maybe he thinks I'm lonely? If he wants to give me what I want, maybe I need to show him I just want to be left alone with my friends.

Friends. That's a stretch.

And I wish I had better options in front of me, but I don't.

Hot, frustrated tears scald my eyelids.

I came to Ridge College a complete loner. After bouncing through a couple of foster homes over the last five years, I focused all of my energy on getting a scholarship to a good school on the other side of the country.

When I got here, the last thing I wanted was to make connections with people that would only be yanked away. People are always yanked away from me.

But in the last few weeks, I've started to crave something new. I don't recognize this strange, unfamiliar desire… To be seen, to be touched, to be held. It started with dreams, and now I'm starting to have thoughts about random people I see on campus. Would I like to be close to that person? So far, the answer is always no, but the question still pricks at me. How about them?

There's no way that Ethan or his posse of popular girls are my true people.

But the stalker dude doesn't know that.

And just in case something happens between now and the party tomorrow night, I feel like I need to do something with this small crack in the mystery.

Before I can chicken out, I shove the photo back in the envelope and head across campus to the ivy-covered building that houses the Criminology department.

"Is Dr. Adler in today?" I ask the department secretary.

"Not today, dear. His office hours are posted on his door, and in the online classroom as well."

"I know." I chew on my bottom lip for a second. "Would you be able to take a photocopy of something for me? It's, uh, for a cold case project."

The lie rolls off my tongue with alarming ease.

When I first arrived in Conception Ridge, I was an innocent hayseed. Then I took Dr. Adler's Criminology 101 and fell in love with crime. Solving it, I mean.

And Dr. Adler says sometimes solving a crime means being devious. Meeting criminals where they are at to outsmart them.

"Here's Dr. Adler's copier code. You can use it today only."

"Got it." I snatch the paper she hands over and dash to the photocopier, making a copy of the photo.

Then I scrawl a note at the top of the paper.

Dr. Adler,
If I disappear, find this man.
Lucy Martin

I stare at it. *What are you doing, Lucy?*

I can't give that to my professor.

So I fold it in half, then in half again, and then wrap that in another piece of paper, and write on the front of that, *From Lucy Martin, for safekeeping. Don't open just yet.*

And then, before I soften and protect an absolute stranger for misguided politeness reasons, I shove it in Dr. Adler's mail cubby.

On my way back to the dorm, I look for the guy everywhere, but there's no sign of him. My heart pounds in my chest and I clutch my keys in my fist until I'm safely behind my dorm room door.

Who is this guy?

What does he want with me?

A spark of inspiration hits me, and I carefully take a close-up photo of the image in good light, then upload that to my computer.

But when I do a reverse image search, I get nothing. Whoever my stalker is, his face isn't on the internet.

And I'm back to being confused.

———

On Friday, Ethan texts me twice, asking if he can pick me up. But I don't want him to think this is a date. I'm going to a frat party by myself, that's it.

I arrive at the marina by myself, on foot, wearing a t-shirt and jeans, with Chucks on my feet and a *we're just friends but thanks for the invite* expression on my face.

White lights twinkle off every line of the yacht, and water laps at the side of the dock as I climb aboard, following the sound of laughter and the clinking of glasses in the air.

I knew some of my classmates were rich, but I didn't know any of them were *my parents have a yacht* rich.

And as I climb up to the next deck and follow the party sounds, it gets even better. Or worse, depending on the viewpoint. This yacht is big enough to have a pool.

A pool. On a boat!

I recognize Hannah, Gracie, and Alyssa. They're all wearing matching diaphanous bikini cover-ups in various shades of pastel colours. Pink, green, peach.

I didn't get the memo.

I'm wearing a bright blue math equation t-shirt. And I didn't bring a bathing suit.

"There's my something blue," Ethan says, coming up beside me from out of nowhere.

"What?" I spin around, confused.

He pushes a red Solo cup into my hand. "This way to the bar."

"Ummm…" I take a deep breath. "Okay."

There's a pitcher of something fizzy and pink on the bar, but there's also beer and wine and soda. It's self-serve, so I dodge the offer of whatever is in the pitcher and go for a weak rum and Coke that I pour myself.

Ethan watches me take a big sip of it. He's more confident tonight than he usually is. I guess he's a party animal.

Someone calls his name, and he frowns before he excuses himself.

Even though I made my drink pretty weak, it still makes me head spin. Or maybe that's the extravagant wealth everywhere I look.

"Hey, Lucy." One of the frat guys on the other side of the bar lifts his cup in my direction, then strides over. "Tonight's going to be fun. Glad you decided to join us."

"Back off, Forrest," Ethan growls, reappearing at my side. "Sorry, Lucy."

"It's okay." I take another drink, this time a bigger gulp.

Ethan shoves at Forrest's shoulder. "Go tell Gilly to get the captain to fire this thing up and let's take it out."

"Out?" My stomach quivers.

Ethan grins. "A little night cruise."

"There's a captain?" I glance up at the top deck of the gleaming white boat.

Forrest smirks. "And a cook, but it's the cook's night off."

"Oh wow."

Ethan leans in, his breath warm against my cheek, and then my ear. "The captain can be bribed."

My heart goes into free fall for reasons I can't name. That doesn't sound good. "Why…do you need to bribe him?"

"We're going to be gambling tonight." His voice is low and private. "There are so many things that are legal out on the ocean that we can't do here."

My head swims trying to guess at the possibilities. I take another sip of my drink, as if the answers to anything ever lay at the bottom of a red Solo cup. Then I try to ignore the way he watches my tongue, his gaze hot and lingering, when I lick the boozy sweetness off my lower lip.

No, this is not a good idea.

"Where is a bathroom?" I ask.

"There's a cabin for you." Ethan tries to guide me deeper into the boat, but I don't want that.

"Sort of urgent," I say.

Hannah smirks lazily at me from a nearby sun bed. "There's a head right through there."

Ignoring the way Ethan glowers at her—not my problem—I dart in that direction.

Whatever feelings of loneliness drove me to accept the invitation to this party, they aren't nearly as strong as my feelings of self-reservation.

On one level, none of this feels real. It's like playing dress up, but with an undercurrent of very real, grown up danger.

I don't need that in my life.

That burning, desperate ache that has been growing inside me won't be satisfied tonight. Not here, not with any of these people.

I do need something. But it's not this. And it's not here.

As soon as I'm sure they're not looking, I head for the gangway.

But I stop short at the bottom of the stairs, because across the dock, in the shadows of the boat across the way, is a man.

Taller than anyone else in town.

Broader than anyone else in town.

Moonlight glinting off the hint of silver at his temples. If he didn't have tattoos all over his body, he'd look like what I imagine a concerned father would look like. Except I've never needed a concerned father before, and I don't want one now. Especially not one who might kidnap me and turn me into his plaything.

He steps forward, and the shift makes some reflecting light from somewhere catch his eyes.

My breath freezes in my throat.

My legs feel like lead.

I'm not sure I'm safe on this boat, but I know I'm not safe on land either. What is going on and what have I gotten myself into?

"Lucy?"

In the blink of an eye, my stalker fades back into the shadows.

I turn around.

Ethan's looking at me, his brows tightly furrowed, his mouth pulling down.

My throat tightens up, my voice coming out tight as I explain, "I thought I saw someone." I give him a bright smile. "It was nobody, though."

He holds out his hand, and I hesitantly climb the steps to join him. I don't give him my fingers. Instead, I brush past him with a boldness I don't actually feel. "Let's get this party started."

2
gabriel

WHEN THEY HEAD FORWARD, a lumbering man in a white uniform comes down from the bridge. He pulls in the gangway, then unmoors the yacht.

I cross the dock and quietly leap aboard as soon as he heads back up to the bridge. I take off my shoes so my footsteps won't make any noise, then stash them in a compartment under a cushion. I don't want anyone finding them should they come down to the swim platform level.

Then I silently creep up the stairs.

Time for me to get familiar with this fucking boat.

3
lucy

AS THE YACHT motors out to sea, Ethan takes me below deck to a cabin where he almost shyly gives me a large white box wrapped in a blue ribbon.

"What is this?" I don't take it, not exactly.

So now we're both holding it, me very gingerly.

He gives me a slow, frightening smile. "It's time for you to put on something that matches the others."

"Why?"

"It's part of the fun. Go on, open it."

When I don't open it, he sets it on the bed for me and fingers the blue ribbon. Glancing sideways, he drags his gaze down my dress. "I knew this would be your color."

I expect a pastel blue diaphanous gown inside after that, but when he lifts the lid, all I see is a big cloud of gauzy white fabric.

But there, at the edge, is a peek of blue. The same ribbon that tied the box up is also stitched to the gown's waist.

And when he lifts the white gauze out of the box, I see a matching blue bikini beneath it.

A very small bikini.

"Oh," I say.

He gives me a look that clearly says he'd like to see me in it, a look that sends a violent feeling through my core.

"I..."

"Don't worry," he says. "That will be underneath."

I frown and touch the billowy, transparent material. I'm not sure it'll actually disguise much.

"It's beautiful," I say, trying to find the right words to say *I'm not sure what's going on.*

"You are beautiful," he says solemnly.

"I don't understand. Why would you buy me this outfit?"

And how did he organize it so quickly?

"I've wanted you to come to one of these parties for months. I wasn't sure how to ask you." His gaze softens. "I knew it was right to wait. I'll let you get dressed in privacy."

Great. It'll just be after I put on a bikini that I'lll be paraded in front of his friends. As he goes to leave the cabin, I stop him. "Ethan..."

He looks at me expectantly.

"I don't want to lead you on. I'm not like Alyssa and Gracie. You know, I've never done anything."

His expression turns almost proud. "I know. You're a virgin. You're a good girl. That's okay, Lucy. That's what I love about you."

Shock ripples through me.

Before I can respond to that, he turns and leaves the cabin, the door clicking shut behind him.

Oh my God.

Lucy Martin, what have you done?

And are we too far out to sea now to swim for shore? Maybe I should have rolled the dice with the stalked dude.

But now I've clearly told Ethan that I'm not going to do anything tonight. And his weird crush aside, he seems to understand that. So there's no harm in trying to fit in.

I haven't had to play this part so far this year at Ridge College, but I had some wild rebellious moments in high school.

When you have been alone your entire life, any attention is good attention.

And I know. I *know* that's a trap. I'm smarter than that. But yet here I am, soaking up the twinkling lights and the fancy drinks and the hungry eyes, in the same way I went to house parties in high school.

Because I'm tired of being alone.

But for all their stupid games and expensive gifts, this is the exact same as a dorm or house party. It just smells better.

You aren't alone tonight, Lucy.

4
gabriel

I LOVE RICH PEOPLE. They buy a lot of easy-to-use shit that makes spying on them a breeze. I'm in the engine room, familiarizing myself with the security system on board. I'll do a physical room by room sweep next, but there are enough cameras wired into the servers here that I've already done a complete digital sweep and I'm pretty sure there's only one crew person on board—the captain.

The galley is completely clean and quiet. There's nobody down here on the crew level.

I flip to the passenger cabins to be sure I didn't miss anyone there, and I've nearly completed that pass through the cameras when I see Ethan and Lucy on the screen.

My body snaps to attention, tension coiling inside me.

There's no audio, this is a video only feed. She says something to him, then he leaves, and she turns toward the bed.

With a visible sigh, she picks up a scrap of blue from a box and turns it over in her hands.

Then she sets it down, crosses her arms over her body, and pulls her dress up in a single, fluid motion.

I stop breathing.

Look away, Gabe.

I should. I will.

The first time I saw Lucy Martin, it was in a photograph on my son's bedroom wall. She was studying, her dark reddish shoulder-length waves spilling forward over her face. Her lower lip was caught between her teeth as she hunched over a textbook, figuring something out for him.

It was the most innocent photo of a tutor, illicitly captured by her tutee.

My heart had crawled out of my body and pressed itself against that photo, wanting her neat little row of teeth to be pressed into my flesh instead.

Fuck. Me.

Watching her strip down to nothing, baring every inch of her small, curvy body, is that moment all over again, times a thousand.

Her ass is more of a handful than I expected, jiggling as she fits that scrap of blue—a bikini bottom, apparently—over her most intimate parts.

And not much else gets covered.

Her back is to the camera, so I only catch a bit of her breast from the side as she puts on the top.

She twists around, her face cringing. The suit is clearly too much for her. Too much and not enough. Not enough by a long shot.

My cock tightens, lengthening down my pant leg, as she loops her fingers under the fabric again, adjusting the small triangles over her small breasts.

I would give anything and everything to do that for her, carefully ensuring that she was covered up.

As much as I appreciate how stunning she is in the too-small suit, it's not what I would put her in. Lucy deserves something more comfortable, a modest one-piece that she could swim comfortably in.

A mental image of her racing down a dock and leaping into the water, cannon balling with joy, slashes through my mind.

She's so sweet, so small and fragile and perfect and innocent. And completely wrong for this night, this place, these people.

What the fuck is my son doing with her?

On the screen, she wraps herself in something white and see-through, the fabric so light it floats around her as she ties a ribbon around her waist.

She looks like a bride about to be stretched out on her marital bed for the first time, and I have to shove a fist in my mouth to keep myself from groaning out loud at how indecently perfect that image is.

Hot seed slicks the tip of my cock, not caring that she's not mine to claim.

She's young enough to be my daughter and terrified of me.

She will never be mine. Not in all the ways I crave.

But she will always be mine in the most important ways, the only ways that matter at the end of the day.

Mine to protect.

Mine to keep safe.

5
lucy

ETHAN SWEEPS his arm around me as I rejoin the group. His hand, curling over my hip, makes my stomach jolt. I try to edge away, try to get some space, but he clamps down hard.

"You look beautiful," he murmurs.

Words I've always wondered if anyone would ever say to me. But now that I'm hearing them, they don't make me feel beautiful. My skin crawls.

And when someone shoves another plastic cup into my hand, I gulp at it, grateful for an excuse to "accidentally" jam my elbow purposely into Ethan's side.

"Sorry," I say brightly. "Hard to drink when you're holding me so tight."

His friends laugh as he releases me.

Alyssa grabs my hand and tugs me to the lounge bed where Hannah and Gracie are sprawled.

"You look pretty," Hannah says in a sing-song voice that makes me think she does not think I'm pretty at all, but more like a threat. Some sort of competition for Ethan's attention.

She can have him, I don't care.

"This all feels very over the top," I say under my breath, as much to myself as them.

Alyssa laughs. "Right? They're so extra." She takes a long sip of her drink. "But like, free booze and the *Eyes Wide Shut* vibe is fun, you know?"

Is it? Is it fun? And I only vaguely get the movie reference.

"I guess," I say.

She rolls her eyes. "Look, they want us all to be virgins so they can do their little auction, but it's—"

"Their what?" I can't keep the alarm out of my voice.

Gracie giggles. "I know, right? As if any of us are still virgins."

Hannah snorts. "Uh, like, they've all put their dicks in us."

"Oh, so it's like, uh…" I'm trying to find the right words. Because I, an actual virgin, have never done the whole *have someone put their dick in me* thing. "Like a game?"

Hannah's eyes narrow and she rakes her gaze over me. "Yes, like a game. Of course, it gets kind of intense when they bring a new girl. And then Ethan went way over the top and dressed you up like his pretty little bride."

The bottom of my stomach goes into free fall. The rocking of the waves as we turn out to sea doesn't help, either.

Fuck me.

What have I got myself into?

"Okay…" I'm desperate to stay cool here, even though I know this is bad, very bad. "So they…"

But I was specific with Ethan, wasn't I? Maybe I should find him and be more blunt with him. When I was his tutor, sometimes I had to get stern with him and have a "come to Jesus" talk about his study habits.

Keeping his dick out of my vagina might need the same bossiness.

But before I can say anything, Gilly announces that it's time for the first round of poker.

Okay, well, that's at least not some sort of faux virgin auction.

"All right, boys, what did you bring to wager with tonight?" Forrest rubs his hands together, his eyes bright.

Gilly flashes some bling on his wrist. "My dad's Rolex."

Another guy whose name I missed smirks and lifts his hand, showing off a gem on his pinky finger. "My step-mom's ring. It's too small for her now. She never wears it."

The casual way they've stolen from their parents takes my breath away. If my family was still alive...

But they aren't.

"We're up," Gracie says.

Hannah and Alyssa push me toward the poker game.

"What are we expected to do?" I ask.

"Look pretty. Create curiosity." Alyssa lowers her voice. "You get to keep whatever is bid on you, by the way."

Hannah's watching me. Waiting for me to react, but react to what? What am I going to do with someone's stolen watch?

"There are six of them," I whisper. "And only four of us."

"Ethan said you were good at math." She shrugs. "Sometimes they share. Sometimes they just watch. Sometimes they have more girls and they each get two. It's different every time."

My head is spinning from the fact they've done this repeatedly.

I will never step foot on this boat ever again. But until we return to shore, I need to do whatever it takes to keep ahead of this madness.

6
gabriel

I GRIND the heel of my hand into my eye socket as I watch Ethan and his frat buddies finish their first hand of poker.

As far as I can tell, everyone is here willingly. And it also seems like with one singular exception, everyone knows what is expected for the evening—which makes me very fucking concerned about why Ethan kept Lucy in the dark about what is essentially a costume sex party. But if I call in the Coast Guard too soon, and they don't find anything other than rich kids drinking, I'll have burned my nascent relationship with Ethan for no reason—and Lucy won't be any safer.

Because no matter what happens tonight, I know he's obsessed with her.

That's how I fucking became obsessed with her, too. The apple doesn't fall far from the tree.

On the security monitor, the inconvenient object of our shared secret obsession crosses to the bar and pours herself another drink. I note with interest that the splash of booze is barely anything. She waves the bottle in the air, asking the others if they'd like drinks, too.

She has the right approach. Get them drunk, and outsmart them. The drinks she makes for them are much heavier on the alcohol, as if she's figured out that she needs to keep her wits about her—and dull theirs at the same time.

"Good girl," I mutter under my breath.

Fuck, I can't believe I let her get on the boat. I should have tossed her over my shoulder and dealt with her outrage once I had her alone, in a safe space.

I'd take her little fists pummelling my back any day over the stress of watching her realize what these supposed friends are all about.

I have a lot of regrets spinning through my head right now. Not going to her directly is at the top of the list, but I underestimated her powers of observation, and by the time I was ready to make myself known to her, she'd already pegged me as a danger.

And then there's the other small issue of not trusting myself to be alone with her.

I would never hurt her.

Not in a million years.

But I'm not sure I can keep my desire hidden, either. I don't know. I've never felt like this about anyone. Ever.

The urge to fall on my knees and press my face between her thighs is overwhelming, though. Lick her until she understands that all I want is for her to be safe, happy, and pleasured.

God, the way I throb at the *thought* of her scent. Will she be musky? Tangy? Whatever she smells like, it'll be perfect. The spiced honey I've waited my entire life to swallow down.

Fuck.

I need to distract myself.

It's time to go to Ethan's cabin to figure out more about what he has planned for tonight. And then I'll go to the bridge and have a chat with the apparently bribable captain.

———

Lucy's clothes are neatly folded on the end of the bed in Ethan's cabin. Only the fact that I know there are cameras in here keeps me from picking up her little white panties and pressing them to my face. I still trail my fingers across them, my pulse heavy… needy…as the cotton singes my nerve endings.

Ethan brought a duffle bag with him. I expect to find condoms in it, maybe some pot. That's the type of shit he has in his apartment off campus.

I don't find either.

Frowning, I rifle through the spare change of clothes, looking for anything that might provide a clue for what will happen next. Coming up empty, I put the bag down in frustration—and my gaze falls on a jewelry box on the far side of the bed.

Crossing to it, I flip the small velvet square open.

It's empty.

Since I'm on this deck, I check out the other rooms. Whoever is in the cabin next to Ethan has quite a pharmaceutical set up. Boner pills, ecstasy, and a vial of liquid that I'd bet anything is a date rape drug.

Motherfucker.

I pocket that, because central nervous system depressants can be useful in other ways, then carefully crack the door and make sure the coast is clear to make my way up to the bridge.

7
lucy

AFTER HE WINS the first hand of poker, Forrest pops a pill. He makes a big show of it, winking at us girls. "Forty-five minutes until show time," he says, stretching his arms out wide. "Who's going to be Daddy's little virgin tonight?"

Gross.

My skin crawls as he rakes his gaze over all of us, lingering on me.

Ethan snarls at him, which I wish made me feel better, but that just adds another suffocating layer on top.

They play two more hands, the second one taking forever, and Forrest wins that one, too. He's got some cash and jewelry, and because he's loudly keeping us updated on the effects of the pill, we also know he has a big hard-on.

When he stands, I can't really see evidence of that. So big might be a relative term.

"Who wants to put themselves on the auction block first tonight?"

Alyssa is eyeing the stack of money he's got, but it's Hannah who climbs up onto the poker table first.

Well, I can't say they aren't eager participants in this weirdo game.

"I'm Hannah," she says breathlessly. "I'm eighteen years old, and a freshman at Ridge College."

The guys hoot and holler.

And then Gilly opens the bidding at five hundred dollars.

My mouth drops open, which is silly, because that's nothing.

The guys put up eye watering amounts of money. A thousand, two thousand. Forrest finally wins with a bid of ten thousand dollars and the Rolex.

I expect him to pull her into his lap or something. Hold her as a trophy while they play another game.

I'm not prepared for her to lie down on the poker table and for him to peel away her pastel wrapping like he's going to town on a piece of saltwater taffy.

Her matching bikini is flicked away, too, and there's Hannah—a girl from my class, oh my *God*—naked, spread eagle, as Ethan and some of his frat buddies have a front-row seat for Forrest to whip it out and slap his erection between her legs.

Like he actually slaps her with it.

Does that feel good for him? For her?

She makes a gasping sound, but who knows if that's more pretend play or what.

He takes his time between her legs, working his hand over himself and her, making a big deal about how he paid big money to be her first time.

And then when he pushes inside her, she puts on what I hope is a very good show, twisting her face to the side in anguish and writhing on the table as he starts to fuck her.

I've never seen people fuck in real life. I've looked at porn, a little, like anyone with curiosity and privacy. But this is…people I know. Naked. Together. Moving and making sounds.

It doesn't last long.

Forrest pulls out and comes all over Hannah, which is when I realize that he wasn't wearing a condom.

Oh my God.

Someone tosses Hannah a towel, and she slides off the table with a giggle.

Forrest grabs her face, halting her retreat. "I'm not done with you. I want you in my cabin all night."

She nods as much as the firm grip of his fingers allows, and then he lets her cover herself back up again.

He takes his seat again. "Another hand, gentlemen?"

I slug back my Coke.

"I need to pee," I whisper loudly to Gracie.

Ethan notices and watches me head down the hallway to the head I pretended to use before—but that's where Hannah's gone.

"There's another one up the stairs," Ethans says, grinning at me. "Or you can go to our cabin."

Gross gross gross.

I climb the exterior staircase instead. I don't really need to pee, but just anything to get away from people for a minute—and maybe find more out about the boat.

Maybe I can convince the captain to put me in a lifeboat and point me back in the direction of shore. What's the worst that could go wrong? I'd take my chances with an oar right now.

I find the washroom, then quietly tiptoe past it to the bridge. It's dark in there, only a faint red light illuminating the space.

I see the captain leaning over a display, a coffee cup in his hand. It wobbles as he sets it down.

"Hello?" I say quietly. "I'm, uh, one of the guests tonight. Could I, uh..."

He doesn't seem like he hears me. I move a little closer, not wanting to startle him.

"Excuse me, sir?" I lift my voice a little, hoping the raucous laughter from downstairs covers it up.

His hand smacks down onto the counter, his coffee mug tipping over. The liquid inside hits the floor in a wet sound a second before he slumps all the way forward, crashing to his knees.

I jump forward, trying to catch him, but he's heavy, and he falls sideways against me.

I open my mouth to scream for help, but a big, hard hand clamps over my lips before a sound can escape.

gabriel

I YANK Lucy against my chest, pinning her between my body and my arm. Her small breasts mash against my forearm, soft and warm, and the way I've got her up against me, my cock is less than an inch from finding its way between her ass cheeks.

Jesus Christ, she feels good. Smells good, too. I inhale a life-giving lungful as she fights my tight hold, but she's just a little slip of a thing and I'm a trained special warfare operator freshly fuelled by the scent of wildflowers and honey.

I knew she'd smell like honey. My cock thickens even further, straining at the limits of my pants now. Fuck. Fuck.

"Shhh," I whisper in her ear. "I won't hurt you."

She kicks me in the kneecap.

I grin through the deserved pain. "Love your energy, you vicious little bunny, but I need you to calm down. I'm going to take my hand away from your mouth, and you're not going to scream, okay?"

I can feel her pulse going a mile a minute. She doesn't nod, but when I slide my fingers off her soft lips, she's quiet.

Maybe she correctly decided that the morons one deck below wouldn't be able to help her, anyway.

I let her go completely and step back.

She whirls around and shoves her hands at my chest. "Who the fuck are you?"

"It doesn't matter. We don't have a lot of time. Those boys… they aren't stable. I will keep you safe, but I don't want to hurt them if I don't have to. So you should know—"

"Did you kill him?" She's pointing at the captain.

I bend over and check his pulse. "Nope." Then I drag him across the bridge and kick open his cabin door, propping him against it. "He's just going to sleep for a bit."

"What did you give him?"

"GHB, probably."

"Probably?" She looks horrified. I get an overwhelming craving to kiss her. Just stop what I'm fucking doing, fuck everything that's happening around us, and kiss her innocent little face. Her good, sweet mouth, which would never think of casually using a central nervous system depressant to gain the upper hand in a situation.

Which is too bad, because I need her to do exactly that.

I show her the vial. "I found it in one of the cabins below. Don't drink anything anyone gives you down there."

She rolls her eyes at me. "I know better than that."

I raise an eyebrow.

She makes a face. "I know better than to get on this boat, too. Is that what you want to say, you whacko? Or do you have more dad advice for me before you get back to attempted murder?"

I gape at her.

She gasps and claps her hand over her mouth. "Nevermind," she mumbles from behind her fingers. "I didn't mean that."

Slowly, I lean back against the captain's chair and cross my arms over my chest. "Which part didn't you mean?"

Her eyes go wide and she lets out an audible whimper.

"Lucy," I say softly. "It's okay. I'm not a threat to you. Or anyone else on this boat, unless they hurt you."

She drops her hand and looks at the captain. "He didn't hurt me," she whispers, swivelling back to glare at me. "And you know my name."

I know everything about her. Her class schedule, her love of sweet tea, that she needs to untuck the blankets so her toes have room to breathe at night, but she always makes the bed and tucks the blankets under the mattress, military-style, first thing in the morning.

I know that she likes sour candy and YouTube videos about horror movies, but not horror movies themselves.

And she doesn't know anything about me, because the most important fact negates literally everything else.

"I'm Gabriel," I finally say, thickly. "I'm Ethan's dad."

9
lucy

NO. This is not happening.

I laugh. He laughed before, so I guess laughing is okay between us, and it's either that or I cry.

I could definitely go for a good cry right now. That would feel good. But it might also feel like the final breaking point, and I can't handle that yet.

Now, in addition to a boat full of inebriated prep school monsters, I also have to deal with my insane stalker being on board. He thinks he's Ethan's dad?

Well, that explains a lot.

I don't bother to tell him that I've met Ethan's parents. Super awkward moment at a Christmas party that I didn't realize other students brought their family to—and since I'm a foster kid who has no family, it felt like I was the extra-odd chick out.

Ethan tried to get me to stay and talk to them, but he was also doing that super intense staring thing of his, where it feels like he's peeling my skin off millimetre by millimetre for scientific purposes.

Lucy Martin, you should have trusted that instinct more.

Yeah, no shit.

"Okay," I say slowly, drawing the two syllables out. *Ooooohkayyyyyy.*

Understanding dawns in Gabriel's eyes. "You don't believe me."

Nope. I don't believe that his name is Gabriel, or that he's Ethan's dad. But I'd bet anything that he believes both things to be true, so I'm not going to argue with him. "I don't know what to believe at this point," I finally say. It's close to the truth. And while I do worry about this guy for his own sake—he's clearly not completely well, mentally—he doesn't feel nearly as dangerous as the guys downstairs.

Captain drugging aside.

We've been standing here talking for a few minutes, and not once has he made me feel like he wants to peel off my skin layer by layer and then fuck my dead corpse, for example.

Ethan never took it that far, I chide myself.

No, he didn't.

But now I'm getting the feeling like it's possible that he could. It's not one thing specifically. Just a bunch of odd pieces that are fitting together a little too late.

"Look... Gabriel?"

He nods, his attention never leaving my face. That bright blue gaze is something else. Who the fuck knows, maybe he actually is an archangel or something.

I suck in a breath. "Whatever you think is happening tonight, it's not...they're just idiots. I'm fine. I can handle myself. Maybe you should, uh..." I glance at the captain again.

"I'll make sure he's fine," Gabriel says, his voice low and steady. He holds out his hand, showing me the vial again. "Take this."

"I don't want my fingerprints on that!"

"I'll make sure it's disposed of. Take it, just in case. A drop of this in anyone's drink will knock them out pretty fast. Don't use it on the girls, but if any guy gets too handsy with you..."

"I know how to defend myself."

He doesn't point out that I was pretty defenceless in his arms. "They think they're all getting laid tonight, Lucy. Is that what you want?"

I ignore the way his voice tightens, and the corresponding deep tug in my belly. "I'm not sleeping with any of them," I say firmly. "Ethan knows I'm a virgin."

10
gabriel

LUCY'S WORDS hit me like a lightning bolt. "You're a virgin?"

Her soft, pink lips form a surprised O and her eyes go wide. "Yes?"

God damn it. I need to get her off this boat immediately. "Lucy…"

"Don't lecture me," she whispers, her voice cracking.

I push off the chair, advancing on her. Needing to touch her, to show her it's okay.

She backs up, bumping against the bulkhead, and I stop just short of crowding right up against her. Every cell in my body yells at me to take her into my arms. "It's not a lecture. I don't want to boss you around. I just want—"

She lifts her chin defiantly. "What? What do you want?"

I want to strip her bare and worship her virgin body like it deserves. I want to kiss her and taste her and make her need more, wait until she begs for more, and then give it to her. Only what she asks for, only what she needs.

I want her first time to be magical.

And yes, I want it to be mine.

I'm a virgin.

If it were up to me, Lucy would never know anything but mind-blowing pleasure.

Heat makes my arms heavy, but I still lift them and press them against the bulkhead on either side of her. My innocent little bunny. Her breath hitches, catching in her throat, and I'm painfully aware she feels like trapped prey.

"I only want you to be safe," I growl.

"Liar," she whispers back.

I jerk, the unexpected verbal attack electrocuting my senses.

She glares at me, bold and unafraid. "That's a story you tell yourself, *Gabriel*. I don't want you to do that anymore."

"What…?" The word tumbles out of me, thick and confused.

She arches in the confines of my arms, coming off the wall enough to press her barely covered breasts against my chest. "Do you want me, Gabriel?"

Blood roars in my ears. No. *No*….

"I think you tell yourself that you're my guardian angel," she whispers. "But that's not real life, is it? You don't know anything about me. So let me tell you that I've been keeping myself safe in dangerous situations since I was twelve years old. That made me extra vigilant when I started to notice you, and I thought you were a threat. But I can smell danger, Gabriel. You don't smell dangerous to me."

"I'm a different kind of dangerous," I mutter, tensing every muscle as she winds her arms around my neck.

"I want you to do what I ask," she whispers. "Can you do that for me, Gabriel?"

God fucking damn it all to hell. I grunt and sweep my arms off the bulkhead, down her back, scooping her up against me and then thudding her back into the wall. Pinning her there, as if I could maybe pin down my racing heart and make it listen to reason at the same time. "I see what you're doing."

"Do you?"

She pets me, completely unafraid now. No, no, no. I press my head into her touch, hating how good it feels, how right and electric her simple stroke is after all these months of being completely alone.

"What am I doing?"

Her voice is like silk.

I could close my eyes and give in to her manipulation any other day, any other moment but this.

"My little bunny," I rumble. "That soft voice trick is a good one. So is using my name repeatedly. And at some point once we're on the other side of tonight, you can tell me all about the fucked up reasons why you know how to do that to men old enough to be your father. But right now, *I* am in charge. Do you understand me?"

She thunks her head back in frustration. "Argh. No!"

That makes me laugh, which reverberates through her little body.

She snaps her head forward again and glares at me. "Who are you?"

The man who wants to get lost in your pretty grey eyes forever.

If only this were a universe where I could say something like that to her.

Instead of answering, I shift against her and she slides down a hair—bringing her right down onto the aching ridge of my cock. Which is the opposite of the right answer for this moment.

She gasps, her eyes turning stormy in an instant.

"Ignore that."

She huffs a sweet, exasperated breath that feels like a ghosted kiss against my mouth. "Hard to ignore *that*. Ummm…"

I try to hoist her up again, because I'm not ready to let her out of my arms, but I really shouldn't be holding her tight against my erection, either. It's wrong. Very, very wrong.

But she resists my efforts to lift her off. She wriggles her hips, sinking back against my needy fucking shaft, that doesn't care that I'm her classmate's father, that doesn't care that she was scared of me until a few minutes ago, and has been trying to manipulate me ever since she realized I wasn't going to hurt her.

No, my dick only cares that Lucy is finally rocking her sweet virgin pussy up and down against it. My dick is very fucking happy with her current plan, whatever it is.

"Lucy," I say, trying to protest, but it comes out like a plea.

She works her hips faster, her breath puffing erratically against my mouth. I slant my head to the side unconsciously, and then her lips are touching mine, and we both go still.

For three pounding heartbeats, neither of us move.

And then she parts her lips for me, and I'm lost.

I take my first taste of her lips, licking into her plump mouth until I find her tongue and she squeaks.

Holding still again, my soul leaves my body, prepared to die if she bites me or cries out in protest.

But then she licks me back, curious and uncertain, and I take it, I take her little licks and I give her another of my own. Back and forth we taste and kiss and figure out a rhythm that works for her, that teaches her how to make out.

She's the world's fastest learner, taking her trembling first kiss to a deep, searing claim of my mouth, where her hands are tightly pressed to my face and her tongue is all the way in my throat it fucking feels like.

"Lucy?" Her name is called from somewhere in the distance.

She stiffens in my arms.

"Shhh…" I press my mouth to her cheek and drag in a fresh breath. "It's okay. Nobody knows I'm here. You're alone in here."

Her name is repeated, and it sounds like Ethan. Fuck. He's climbing the stairs.

I want to roar. I want to drag her off this boat immediately.

But I've incapacitated the captain and my son is on board— no matter what he's done, I can't just point him and his friends out to sea and abandon them.

I need to adjust our course and get us back to shore without anyone noticing.

I set Lucy down and pick up the vial she's dropped. Pressing it into her hands, I make eye contact with her. "Be a good girl and use this if you can, okay? I'll get us out of here as soon as I can."

11
lucy

GABRIEL KISSES my forehead just before Ethan calls for me again. "Lucy?"

"I'm in here," I say, my voice shaking. I shove the vial into my bikini top. Gabriel's gaze tracks what I'm doing, and having his eyes locked onto my little tits as I shift the fabric around makes me all hot and achy.

But too quickly, he gives me a firm nod, then disappears into the captain's cabin, the door clicking shut quietly behind him and the body at his feet.

Ethan steps into view, blocking the light from outside. "What are you doing in here?"

I put as much dumb girl confusion into my voice as I possibly can. "The captain isn't here…I was waiting for him to come back because it didn't seem safe."

Water turns on in the cabin behind us.

Ethan jerks his thumb in that direction. "He's in his room. I'm sure it's fine. Come back to the party."

He holds out his hand.

I wipe my palm on my translucent white gown, then take his extended fingers in mine.

"Don't be nervous," he whispers as he leads me back downstairs. "I won't let anyone else bid on you when it's your turn."

"I don't want—"

"Ethan! Get your ass down here! Alyssa's on the auction block!" one of his buddies hollers.

He tugs me along faster. We stumble at the top of the stairs and his grip tightens.

I cross my free arm over my chest, terrified the vial will fall out.

He doesn't let go of me until after Alyssa's been "deflowered" by one of the frat boys. Which means I have a front-row seat for the whole—quick—event, which only makes me want to stay a virgin forever.

But when they start the next round of poker, and Alyssa joins Hannah in the "taken" puddle, I manage to slide free and go to the bar. I open a can of Coke for myself, and only pretend to add booze this time.

"Sexy little Lucy," one of the frat boys says, waving at me. "Make me a drink!"

Here goes nothing. When his attention turns back to the table, I put a tiny drop of the clear liquid into his cup.

Heart pounding, I carry it back to the table, set it front of him, then brightly ask the group if anyone else wants something.

To my chagrin, they all say no.

Ethan tugs me back into his side. As soon as his arm slides around my waist, the boat veers sharply to the left. The naked girls scream and the drunk guys laugh.

"The captain might be drunk," someone says with a chortle as water slaps against the hull below us.

Heat rises to my cheeks. The captain is unconscious, and the helm has been commandeered by a man I kissed—who clearly doesn't like someone else touching me. Especially because he thinks that someone else is his son.

You kissed someone who is clearly deranged, Lucy Martin. You're hardly one to judge.

The guy I handed the drink to leans forward on the table, starting to look a little disoriented.

I hold my breath, wondering if anyone else will notice.

Abruptly, he stands up, staggering back, and points at Gracie. "Come suck my dick."

Gilly rolls his eyes. "That's not how we do it, Colin. Sit your ass down and finish this hand."

Colin grabs the cup I gave him and swallows another big slug. "Don't care. I'm fucking horny, man."

Oh shit. Can the drops make someone hyper-aroused, or an asshole, instead of putting them to sleep? Colin is younger and more fit than the captain upstairs. What did Gabriel give me?

Gracie flutters her eyes at him. "What will you bid for me?"

"Anything you want, princess. Come put your mouth on it. Give me some relief."

She glances at Gilly and Forrest, who look like they're in charge. And I guess maybe she's dealt with this before, because she leaps onto an empty chair, then up onto the table, giving them the show they want. "Shortest virgin auction ever, fellows?"

Forrest grunts and waves her over to Colin, who stumbles to a sun bed, unzips, flops onto his back...and immediately starts snoring.

Like, spontaneously. Dick out and everything.

Gracie deftly removes the watch from his wrist and twirls around, curtsying for everyone else. "You guys can bid on me again if you want," she says. "I don't think he's waking up for me to do anything with that."

Forrest shakes his head. "It's the new girl's turn."

No. I shake my head.

Ethan shakes his head.

Gilly laughs. "Oh yeah. Definitely. I want her up on the table. She looks terrified."

Yeah, no shit I'm terrified. "Uhh…" I bite my lip and try to act like Gracie. "How about I start us off with a round of drinks?"

"No," Ethan snarls. "I told you, she's mine."

"Depends how much you put up, asshole." Gilly's voice is harder than before. "She's real pretty. Tiny, too. Bet she's super fucking tight. You said you wanted to bring your tutor out for one of these sails. You didn't say anything about how fucking hot she was."

"Leave her alone." Ethan sounds manic, and I wonder how much of this Gabriel is catching.

Still wish he was your son, you crazy hot angel?

"Get on the table," Forrest says to me at the same time as Ethan says, "Get the captain."

Gilly pulls out a gun. "Shut the fuck up, Ethan."

Gracie screams.

There's a painful beat of panicked silence, then Hannah and Alyssa realize a gun has been pulled, and they scream, too.

My first thought is, *What now, Gabriel? Should I throw the stupid vial at him?*

Which is horrible, because my second thought is, *Seriously, Lucy? You thought you could handle yourself alone here?*

We were both wrong.

Gilly waves the gun at Ethan. "Get her on the table. We're doing this right."

That's when I realize I'm shaking my head. *No no no no no.*

I go still. Try to channel some of the bravado I had before, but I've never been threatened with a gun before. That has a way of profoundly changing a girl. Turning her into a scaredy cat with very good reason.

Gilly turns to Forrest. "You do it. Give her a little taste of what it's like to be manhandled by someone who isn't chickenshit."

"I'm not fucking chicken sh—"

"What the hell do you think you're doing?" Gabriel's voice

booms down the staircase, preceding the first view of long legs clad in captain's whites.

I guess he found a spare uniform in the captain's quarters.

He's pulling on a jacket and he has a hat tugged low over his eyes, and he stops a few steps short of the deck we're on. He's obscuring himself, I realize. But nobody is really looking at him except me.

They all see the uniform and don't notice that he's taller, younger, and fitter than the guy who was captaining this boat an hour ago.

"Just a misunderstanding," Gilly says easily. He puts his hand behind his back, hiding the gun.

But that doesn't make me feel any better. I will Gabriel not to come any closer, even though I desperately want him to pull some angel shit and smite them all.

Can angels smite frat boys? Probably not. Also, he's not an angel. He's someone who's not right in the head.

"It's good the captain is here," Ethan says wildly. He grins. "Let's do this for real."

"Do what for real?" That's Hannah. She gasps. "Oh my *God*, Ethan. The outfit wasn't just a joke?"

I glance down at myself. "What?"

Ethan takes my hands. "I know your virginity is important to you, Lucy." His eyes are bright. Wild.

A tremor ripples through my belly. "That's none of your business," I whisper.

"I told myself I wasn't gonna take it, you know. I just wanted to get you comfortable with the idea of being mine. I'd have made you feel so good. But now we can make it real."

"Make. What. Real?" That's Gabriel.

No, no, no...

Ethan twists us around, so he's got me in front of him, and he's presenting me to them all. "I promise in front of you all that I won't take Lucy's virginity until she's my wife."

This time, I say it out loud. "No."

He kisses the side of my face, making my skin crawl. "Shhh. Be a good girl."

I gag. I can't help it. It's not hot at all when he says it.

He groans. "I'm doing this wrong."

"Yeah, you think?"

Forrest laughs at my outburst, which makes the girls giggle, too.

Ethan glares at them all. "Shut up!"

Gilly rolls his eyes. "No, man. I think it's you who needs to shut up." Then he swings the gun back into view and points it right at Ethan. Which is basically pointing it also at me, and I can't help it. I start to cry.

"Take. Her. Fucking. Virginity."

Ethan shoves me to the ground and lunges at Gilly.

Sobbing, I cover my head as a gunshot snaps in the air, startlingly loud.

It's followed by a series of curses and a lot of fighting as bodies smash into furniture.

"You fucking shot me," Ethan finally snaps, his voice cutting through the chaos.

Everyone goes quiet.

I lift my head just enough to see what's going on.

Gabriel has two of the frat boys tied up, back to back. Which would be more impressive if Ethan's arm wasn't bleeding—and if he wasn't holding the gun now.

"Turn around slowly, captain," he snarls. "We're in international waters. Time for you to do as we agreed and make this girl my wife."

12
gabriel

ANY MINOR PANG of guilt I might have had about drugging the captain and taking his place disappears in an instant as what Ethan says sinks in.

The bribable captain was going to pretend to marry Lucy off to Ethan, huh? Might just fucking murder the asshole before I get off this ship. For sport. For vengeance. For the innocent girl dragged into a game that is getting deadlier by the second.

"I can't do that," I say slowly. I need more time to assess the situation.

I used the cover of chaos to immobilize a couple of the beefier guys. Now there are three left to deal with. Gilly, whose parents own the boat. Forrest, who looks like he mainlined an unhealthy amount of cocaine and Viagra.

And my fucking asshole kid.

The good news is that his injury seems to be a flesh wound, a nick on the arm that'll be sore tomorrow, but probably doesn't even need medical attention.

Which is good. It means I can kick his ass, something I should have done a month ago.

But he's got a gun—fuck—and I'd really rather he not die tonight.

I wasn't there for the first nineteen years of his life. I can't be the reason it ends at twenty.

On the other hand, Lucy is trembling on the deck, and I can't let anything bad happen to her. I just can't. The protective fire I feel inside when someone touches her, and she doesn't like it, is nothing I've ever experienced before.

Ethan doesn't really know how to move and keep a gun trained on someone, let alone multiple someones. He's waving it back and forth between his friend Gilly and me, and looking over at Lucy, too.

I force my voice out in the low, raspy way that sounds like the captain they know. "You kids are acting out of your depth. I'm gonna turn this boat around. We're going back to shore. You don't touch that girl and nothing will happen to the rest of you."

Ethan swings the gun around kind of wildly. "You're not the boss of me. You do what I say."

"What's your plan, son?"

"I told you. I paid you. You're going to marry us."

This clash was inevitable. I didn't see it happening on the deck of a yacht, at the barrel end of a gun, but from the moment I discovered he was stalking an innocent classmate, Lucy, I knew I would have to stop him.

I've done everything in my power to have a good relationship with Ethan. It broke my heart to realize that my own flesh and blood was a truly bad man. And for a while, I tried to excuse some of his choices as youthful stupidity.

But as my attention shifted to figuring out who this young woman was that my son was obsessed with, the worst thing possible happened.

I, too, became obsessed with her.

The fruit doesn't fall far from the tree after all.

It doesn't feel like the worst thing now, though. Not if I can prevent him from forcing her to give him her virginity.

The thought of not knowing she was desperately in need of help tonight…that drives me a little mad.

I drop the rough, low growl. My natural voice carries further and has more command. And Ethan will recognize the sharp, disappointed tone immediately. "I'm not going to do that. You're going to leave the girl alone, you hear me?"

His whole body snaps back as I take off the hat and glare at him. "What are you doing here?"

"Stopping you from making a terrible mistake. Lucy, go up the stairs."

"No!" Ethan swings the gun toward her.

In an instant, I'm between them. "Let the girl go, son."

"Don't call me that."

"Ethan, I—"

"You're not my dad! Stop pretending that you are!"

"I know I wasn't there when you—"

"Wait, is he really your dad?" Lucy only got as far as the stairs before turning around.

God. Damn. It.

Ethan swings around to look at her. "What did you say?"

Her eyes go wide. "Nothing."

"Why do you want to know if he's really my dad?"

"It's just very confusing," she says with a dumb trill.

And that's enough cover for me to snap my body into the air and kick the gun from his hands.

It arcs into the air, then comes down on the railing, bouncing once before sliding overboard and disappearing into the ocean.

"Fuck," he screams. "You fucking asshole."

"Takes one to know one," I snarl, shoving him further away from Lucy. "Don't. Play. With. Guns."

"You broke my hand."

"Turns out if you kidnap a girl, you end up having a bad night. Life lesson for you, kid. Now sit the fuck down with your meathead friends."

"Wow," one of the girls says in awe. "Is your dad a commando?"

Lucy's attention flies to my face. Time slows as her gaze locks on my mouth.

The mouth that kissed her up on the bridge.

She only kissed me because she didn't believe that I was Ethan's father. She thought I was…well, I'm not sure. But she was sure I was lying about the situation.

And I took advantage of that. I told her the truth, and then I let her do with that information what she wanted, even though I knew she wanted to pretend it wasn't true.

I am not a good man.

Now her alarm is palpable. It's clear that she wouldn't have kissed me if she knew there was an actual real connection between me and my son. The boy who invited her here tonight. The boy she now knows has a sick and twisted obsession with her—just like his father.

As Ethan slumps down, not with the two assholes I tied up, but the mostly naked girls wrapped in gauzy fabric, I take stock of the situation again.

His two remaining friends are looking at us from the poker table still. It's hard to read them, but I can grab Lucy and take her up to the bridge. Barricade us in there until the Coast Guard arrives.

She moves away from the stairs, though. Drifting closer to me, but—

"I've met your parents," she says, the silly dumb girl voice back in full effect. "So like, do you have two dads or what?"

The naked, freshly fucked girl in the peach wrap makes an exaggerated dawning of understanding look in Ethan's direction. "Oooh, is it like a threesome thing?"

"Shut the fuck up, Gracie," Ethan snarls. "He's not my dad. He's just some sucker my mom put on the birth certificate."

13
lucy

I'M STILL REELING from the fact that Ethan knows Gabriel after all...but now I see there's a lot more complicated layers to their relationship, or non-relationship, than I ever could have guessed.

Gabriel covers it well, but Ethan's cruel line hits him like a bomb.

I can't breathe.

What is happening? How did these two men get to this place, where one is shot and the other is trying to save me from his son, who might not be his son.

I thought my life was kind of tragic. But it's not the stuff of Lifetime movies.

"I don't fucking care," Forrest sighs. "This is all so exhausting. I want to see someone fuck someone."

"Nobody is fucking anyone else," Gabriel snaps.

Forrest laughs. Then he pulls out a gun, so casually I have to do a double take. "You sure about that, old man?"

Oh my God, how many guns do these idiots have?

Gabriel sighs. Like he's genuinely exhausted by all of this, and boy, do I share that feeling.

"Stand up, Ethan," Forrest drawls. "You're going to get to fuck your virgin bride, after all."

"Touch her and die," Gabriel snarls at his son. Or…not son. I don't know.

"But if he doesn't touch her, everyone dies," Forrest says in a singsong voice. "Starting with the bride."

A sob tears out of me. It sounds so foreign, it takes a second to recognize it as my own sound.

Ethan stands up. Blood drips down his arm.

"No," Gabriel snarls. "Not him. Give her the choice, at least."

Then he gives me a look that says, *work with me here*. He's trying to buy time, but now that they know he's a badass, it's going to be harder to gain the upper hand.

Also, I have no idea what his plan might be.

"Don't you fucking think about it, Forrest," Ethan warns, his voice whiny and panicked. "She's mine."

"I'm not yours," I gasp. "I'm not anyone's."

Forrest gives me an appraising look. "Are you really a virgin?"

"Fuck you." The words tear out of me, shaky but emphatic.

He makes a wounded face. "That's not nice talk from someone dressed like a slut."

"Right back at you," I mutter.

Forrest jerks the gun at Gilly. "Go untie our friends."

Gabriel immediately gets between Gilly and the bound frat boys. "Not going to happen, son."

Gilly smirks. "Last I heard, nobody on this boat was your son."

I don't hear Gabriel's response, but Gilly backs off.

Forrest hisses at his friend.

"What? That guy's scary."

"I have a gun!"

"Then shoot him!" Gilly throws his hands in the air. "Or shoot Ethan. This is all his fault."

"No!" That's me.

Everyone turns my way. "Nobody shoot anyone," I beg. "Please."

The boat is rocked by a rough wave, and Forrest stumbles.

Gabriel moves again, but it's clearly not Forrest's—or Gilly's—first day on a boat. They both get on the other side of the table from Gabriel, and while Forrest points his gun angrily at Gabriel, Gilly opens a cabinet I didn't notice before.

Well, I guess that's where the first two guns came from.

He takes a third weapon from it and points it at my would-be savior. "You heard what she said, man. The pretty virgin doesn't want anyone to get shot, right? So back the fuck up and stop acting like a hero."

Slowly, Gabriel lifts his hands in the air. "All right. Be cool."

My heart pounds in my chest and there's a dull roar in my ears. But I manage to get out, "They want to see me lose my virginity, right?"

Gabriel turns slowly, shaking his head. Like he doesn't even care that there are now two guns pointed at his back. "Lucy, no."

But I can't stop thinking about how he just doesn't feel dangerous to me. Not anymore. I think about the photo. How he's had every opportunity to hurt me and he never did.

"They're crazy," I whisper. It's so quiet I'm sure I'm the only one who can hear it, but he gives me a tight nod.

Well, then I just need to be crazier.

I throw my shoulders back and give everyone on board an even look. Trying to match their rich, stupid vibes. "I choose him, then. Ethan's dad."

As expected, those words are a direct hit on the person who lured me onto this boat. He goes white—but then he sways on his feet.

Maybe he's lost just enough blood now to render him useless.

Good, I think savagely.

I look at Forrest again, who seems like he's in charge now. "Will that satisfy you? Can we get this party started again?"

"He didn't win her," Gilly says. "If he gets to fuck her for free, we all should get a turn."

"What part of touch her and die didn't you understand?" Gabriel snarls.

Gilly blanches, but doesn't back down. "We should at least make him pay for her virginity, then."

"What's her price?" Gabriel doesn't hesitate. He turns to Ethan. "What were you willing to pay?"

He doesn't answer.

"Thousands?" Gabriel's voice is clipped. "You think you're a big man? Tricking a girl into a twisted game, and then it's only a few thousand dollars that you scrape up?" He looks at Gilly, then pauses. "Send a girl up to the bridge. I've brought what I'm willing to bid for the virgin girl."

Hannah wobbles to her feet, shooting me a triumphant look. "I'll go."

Gabriel doesn't even look at her. "There's a black duffle bag on the captain's chair. Bring it down."

I go cold.

How could he have money for this if he didn't know it was going to happen?

Hannah returns in the blink of an eye, dragging a heavy bag.

Oh. Shit.

Gabriel yanks it out of her hands, barely acknowledging her before he unzips it and tosses it on the poker table. Bundles of bills tumble out, many more visible in the open bag.

"Shit," Gilly says. "No way Ethan can beat that. How much is it?"

"It's enough," Gabriel grinds out.

Forrest twirls his gun in an alarmingly casual way. "Then on the condition that you fucking take her in front of us, you win the virgin bride, Daddy."

14
gabriel

IF ANYONE HAD EVER ASKED me if I could get hard while a gun was pointed at me, I'd have laughed. No. Fuck, no.

I've been in a lot of hot spots in my life, and I'm pretty sure my balls lived inside my body until the firefight was over every fucking time. If my cock could retract itself inside, too, it would.

But right now? As Lucy warily, carefully makes her way toward me?

God fucking damn, I want her.

And I cannot have her. Not like that. Not really.

But I can put on a show. Because that's what these little shit-heads want. This isn't about Lucy. This is about them getting their jollies off, projecting their fantasies onto girls. Ethan is the only one dangerously obsessed with Lucy's actual virginity, so he's the only real threat to her.

The others I can manage by keeping them enthralled until the boat's autopilot gets us close to shore again.

And then what, genius?

And then I'll figure out the next step of the plan.

Her footsteps falter as she nears me. She's looking down, her dark red curls spilling forward. The confident girl who confronted me on the bridge is gone now, replaced by someone timid and uncertain. Is that an act like her playing dumb?

Of course it's not an act, she's petrified.

I reach out and hook my fingers in the blue satin ribbon around her waist and tug her right against me.

She starts to cry. "He dressed me up like a bride. I didn't see it, I didn't know—"

I cover her mouth with my thumb. Silence is protection, because they can't know she trusts me. They can't know I'm the best of the worst options in front of her.

"I know," I rasp quietly. I give her a fierce look to say the rest. *I missed it, too. This is on us both.* "Ignore them," I say louder. "You're mine tonight. That's all that matters."

I lift her up onto the table. The gauzy fabric rides up her legs, revealing smooth, soft thighs.

They're going to want to see her naked. There's no way around that, but I can distract them by being even more naked than her.

I strip my clothes off, not caring who sees the big, hard planes of my body, or the jut of my cock. It's important for them to see it, feel small and insignificant next to it, so they let me climb on top of her and have my way with her uninterrupted.

They need to know they will never match up to me in every way. That is how I keep Lucy safe.

But it means when I step between her thighs and hook my fingers into the waistband of her bikini bottoms, there's no hiding how much my body likes being in this position. That there is no level of violence or depravity that would stop me from wanting her.

"You're hard," she whispers, her voice catching. "Why are you hard?"

That uncertain hitch to her words should make me soft. She's asking if I like it. *Do you like violating my sweet, innocent body in front of these monsters?*

"Because you're beautiful," I admit, my voice rough and raw. "Because I know you'll feel like heaven. I'm so sorry."

I try to shift back, pulling my traitorous erection away from the soft cradle of her thighs, but her fingers wrap around my length and squeeze.

"Don't touch me," I rasp. "Jesus, please don't..."

She lifts her hips, squirming beneath me, rubbing her soft inner thigh against the rock hard length of my cock.

"Show me," she whispers. Her eyes shimmer with unshed tears as she blinks up at me. "Show me how beautiful you think I am. Please. Please show me—"

I dip my head and cover her mouth with mine, kissing her to shut her up, to distract her. But it backfires on me, because her mouth is as heavenly soft and warm and wet and hot as my body thinks her tight little virgin cunt will be.

And her tongue is as curious and questing as her clever fingers.

Fuck.

Oh, *fuck*.

"Fuck her," one of the lunatics with a gun snarls.

It takes everything in me to break off the kiss.

I shoot them both a quelling look over my shoulder. "I paid for her. I want to thoroughly enjoy my prize."

Beyond them, I catch a glimpse of Ethan staring murderously at me.

There will be time later to think about the why of it all. Why his mother lied—either to me, or him, or both of us.

But I'm done protecting him from the consequences of his own actions.

I turn my attention back to Lucy and they all fade into the background. Her mouth is wet and her eyes are bright.

Without a word, I peel her bikini bottoms off, revealing her soft, perfect pussy. Puffy and framed with a dusting of wispy reddish brown hair, it's innocently beautiful, just like the rest of her.

My cock throbs in her hand.

She tugs me toward the center of her, that tempting pink seam, and I shake my head.

"You don't need to do that," I growl under my breath. "Pull it up on your belly and they'll think I'm inside you. They'll never know. I'm big enough to hide you."

Something flickers in her eyes and her expression shifts. I'm so fucking twisted, I want to imagine it's disappointment, but I know better.

I stroke my hand up her calf to her knee, then scoop my hand around to the back of her thigh and press that leg up, opening her for me.

She presses my cock against her sex, and the warmth of her is so shocking, so fucking good.

I jerk forward, thrusting against her. Feeling her cunt slide beneath me is unbelievable.

"Lucy..." I groan.

I hate that she can feel how much I like this. I shouldn't be showing her this side of me. This is the worst kind of violation.

But then her trembling beneath me shifts, changing. And, with a small whimper, she lifts her hips to meet mine.

My gaze jerks to her face.

She's staring up at me, wide-eyed.

"You like that, bunny?"

She nods warily.

Relief floods through me. I can make it good for her. I lean over her more, bracing my forearm beside her so I can hold her shoulder, give her something to push against. "That's it, then. Rub yourself on me."

She rocks her hips, and on the second slide, a hint of slickness coats the underside of my cock.

"Good girl. Get wet for me," I breathe. Then I lift my voice enough that the others can hear. "This is what I'm paying for. Gonna take my time with this sweet virgin pussy."

That flicker of uncertainty is back in her eyes. Fuck me.

Every time the reality of us being watched intrudes, she retreats from me.

No more of that. No more of them.

Until someone fucking shoots me, this is just her and me and whatever we can make of this.

"It's been a long time for me, sweetheart," I mutter under my breath. "And you feel incredible. If I explode all over you, it isn't personal."

Her wary expression immediately turns to delight, and the corners of her mouth twist up as she laughs quietly. "Pretty sure this is as personal as it gets."

"Yeah." I shift my grip on her shoulder, my thumb curling around the side of her neck, and I hunch myself over her even more, shielding her completely from their view.

Her breath is uneven now, hitching every time her clit rubs against the tip of my cock.

I drag my gaze down her body, over the fluffy white fabric and the blue bikini top underneath it, to where the costume gives way to bare skin. To where my cock is pressed hard between her pussy lips.

Her pulse jumps against my touch.

The longer I stare at where we're joined, the faster that flutter at the base of her throat races.

"Gabriel," she whispers. Her hips are moving frantically now.

I don't look away.

"Show me how you come," I growl.

The hot slide of her cunt against my cock will haunt me until the day I die. After this electric moment, I will never take another woman in my bed. I won't be able to. All I will have is this incomplete moment and the tight squeeze of my fist, and that will be enough. Lucy is all I need.

"I can't..." she twists her face.

My pretty little bunny is so close, but she can't get there.

I push up enough to slide my hand down from her neck,

over her small breasts and quivering belly, to where she's wet for me.

My fingers find her clit.

Her body goes taut, swirling a dark mix of desire and need straight up my arm and into my brain.

Make her come.

Make her come.

Make her—

She jolts, and then her clit throbs, a hard, unmistakable pulse that triggers another and another. Slick spills out of her, coating my cock, and she cries out.

Loud.

A desperate need to keep that stunning, beautiful sound all to myself rises. I gather her into my arms and crush her mouth against mine.

She kisses me in a hitching, out-of-control way.

I tear at her gown, shredding it to her waist. Her bikini top follows, then I arch her back and fall on her tits.

Her nipples are so fucking hard. I drag my mouth back and forth, kissing and then licking. The tight bumps taste bright, like freshly picked berries bursting on my tongue.

Her thighs grip my hips, and my cock—still hard, thank Christ I didn't embarrass myself—presses in against her at a new angle. This time when she rocks against me, my heavy crown slips and fits itself right at her entrance.

We both go still.

I'm breathing so fucking hard.

"Lucy..."

"If I'm not a virgin, he won't be obsessed with me," she whispers. "Maybe he'll even hate me, and leave me alone."

My heart breaks.

It's a good plan.

But it also means this doesn't mean the same thing to her that it does to me.

I drop a featherlight kiss to the base of her throat, then nod as I lift my head.

I hold her gaze as I reach between us and replace my cock with my fingers. I ease one into her, then a second. She holds her breath as I get her used to being fucked.

"Relax," I whisper. "You have to want it."

She squirms, then exhales, and her body softens around me.

"Good. That's it. You're taking my fingers like a very good girl."

I add another, stretching her as much as possible, then I replace my hand with my cock.

Somewhere just behind us, there's an angry yell and a scuffle.

I don't care. I hinge my hips and push.

She's impossibly tight. I don't get very far before I need to ease off, the tip of my cock working in and out, just at her entrance. Gathering more of her slick so I can push in again, deeper this time.

Her eyes flare and her lips part.

Shock.

Inch by inch, I give her the last cock she ever imagined she might find herself on. Her stalker's father. Her secret second stalker.

I'm old enough to have raised her myself.

I've watched her sleep.

She has no idea the depths my obsession tumbled to over the last month.

That was before I knew how good she would feel wrapped around me. Well, except I did know. I took one look at her and instantly understood that if I ever had the chance to lose myself in her innocent body, I'd do whatever it took.

And I have.

I sink the last inch into her, my balls coming to rest right against her ass.

"Good girl." I exhale roughly. "That's it. You did it. You took me."

"Don't move," she whimpers. "Please."

"I won't," I promise.

I have never felt as close to anyone as I do to Lucy in this moment. She's mine. She saved herself for me. Not her intention, but the truth of this moment. And that knowledge grips me in a way I cannot escape. I am already possessed by the possibility of getting inside her again, being inside her constantly.

"You're so big." She pants. "You're too big."

Her words have the terrible opposite effect they should. I swell at the mental image of filling her to her limits.

She grips my shoulders, her fingers tight on my skin. "Gabriel!"

"You're so beautiful," I murmur. It's all I can say. It's true.

"Ethan, your dad fucks like a girl. All full of feelings," someone says in the distance.

Lucy's brows pull tight. Worried.

No, no, no.

I snap my hips, driving her against the table. Fuck, I don't want her to hurt. But she can't think I'm overcome with feelings here, either.

We're fucking for a reason. We're fucking to distract them.

I can't have her know that it doesn't feel like fucking at all. It feels like making love, like staking a claim. It feels like coming home and leaving on an adventure all at once.

The cock of a gun is an unmistakable sound, though. And it's followed by a curt order. "Move!"

Lucy gasps, trembling anew.

"Together," I tell her, gathering her in my arms. "Hold on tight."

She winds herself around me, clinging as I find a rhythm that feels good but not too good, that I can keep going without losing my mind. I'm holding back, not because I want to, but because I need to, and I'm not pushing all the way inside her, not taking up residence at the entrance to her womb the way I need.

Her impossible tightness eases to a slick, hot snug I glide in and out of with relative ease. At first, all I can hear is the slap of our bodies and her tiny, contained reactions. But then the rest comes back into focus. The waves slapping at the boat. The roll of the ocean beneath us.

And beneath that, the awed, stunned audience. Two of them armed, but there are no more threats. Just hushed and guttural observations. Crude words. Jealous noises.

Every single person on this boat wants to have this. And they don't. We do.

As public and humiliating as this, there's a certain twisted pleasure in knowing something so intense, so right, is being witnessed.

Especially by Ethan.

I don't stop when someone notices that we're returning to the marina.

I know where the dinghy is. I'm even prepared to pull out and carry Lucy over the side with me if need be.

There's shouting, and cursing, and then Gilly races past us, up the stairs to the bridge.

I guess he's not interested in wrecking his parent's million dollar yacht tonight.

Which only leaves one gun trained on us.

I stroke one hand down to her tits, cupping her flesh. "Come for me, bunny. Be a good girl for Daddy."

Lucy sucks in a breath as I duck my head, pulling her nipple into my mouth. Her back arches and I let myself go, giving her every inch of my cock. I fuck her fast and hard and deep, over and over again, until I feel her tighten around me.

I suck and fuck her through her climax, then I cradle her in my arms again, needing to see her face as I let go.

"God, that felt good. Did it feel good for you? You take me

perfectly, Lucy. My Lucy. Daddy's hot little secret, aren't you? Keeping all this pent-up need tight inside you. My. Little. Virgin."

I will forever cherish the memory of her shocked expression as she feels my release throb deep inside her. The moment my cock starts to pulse, her eyes flare wide, feeling my hot seed pump inside her.

It's too powerful to ignore.

She presses her lips together, holding in a scream, and her legs wrap around my hips.

Holding me deep inside her.

Taking every drop Daddy has to give.

And then she collapses on the table beneath me.

15
lucy

I'M in a daze as Gabriel pulls out. He yanks my gown up, covering me, then leans over to grab his clothes.

The next thing I know, Forrest is slammed onto the edge of the table beside me, the gun clattering to the deck as something gives a sickening snap.

I let out a watery scream.

Gabriel, cool as a cucumber, like he didn't just fuck a virgin in front of his son and his son's insane friends, picks up the gun and sweeps it over everyone in a commanding *stay where you fucking are* gesture.

He pulls on his pants with alarming speed and throws me over his shoulder.

"Hold on," he snaps out, only pausing long enough to grab his bag of money.

My bag of money?

Did I just sell him my virginity, or am I being kidnapped for the second time tonight?

I hold on anyway, because the alternatives seem to be falling overboard or being left behind with the frat savages.

He's so big everywhere, my hands find it hard to get

purchase. Of course he's big everywhere. Big shoulders, big arms.

Big cock.

On the lowest deck, he dumps me into a dinghy, then leaps in after me and starts an outboard motor.

"Where are we—" I cut off my own question when I realize we're approaching the marina.

We're back in Conception Ridge.

The nightmare is over.

Instead of pulling in where the big yacht motored out, he steers the dinghy to a smaller, shadowed dock, closer to the surface of the water that has stairs leading up to what I discover is a parking lot.

Because he carries me up them.

He grunts when he takes his first step into the lot.

"What?"

"I left my shoes on the boat."

I start laughing and I don't stop.

"That's funny?"

"Yeah." I wipe my eyes.

He grins at me. "Okay. Good. They were nice shoes, too."

I laugh harder.

He leans in, nuzzling my cheek, his breath warm on my skin. "Not really. They were shitty old shoes, and I'd lose them a hundred times to get you to safety."

"Okay." I drag in a rough breath. "Well, thank you. For rescuing me. I can call an Uber, I guess?"

"Do you have your phone?"

I wince. "No. It's on the boat. In Ethan's stateroom."

He growls. "We'll get you a new phone. Is that one locked?"

My heart plummets. I can't afford a new phone. "Yes, but—"

He opens the passenger door of a pickup truck and deposits me on the seat. "Do up your seatbelt, bunny."

"Where—"

He closes the door on me.

I try again once he's behind the wheel. "Which way are you heading?"

He pauses. Turns to me. Frowns. "I'm taking you to my cabin."

"No, wait." I wave my hands. "Gabriel, this is insane. I need to go back to my dorm."

"That's not safe." He looks me over. "And you need clothes before you go back there, anyway. Once it's safe."

I press the gauzy dress to me. I lost the bikini top somewhere, too. He's not wrong. "Umm… Where is your cabin?"

It's half an hour on the other side of the highway, it turns out. Up the road toward Virgin Peak, which is so on-the-nose not funny it makes me laugh anyway.

For the short drive through Conception Ridge to the highway, Gabriel is quiet. Vigilant, I realize. But once we're across the highway and climbing into the mountains, he relaxes and looks across at me. "How are you feeling?"

I blush, grateful that the cab of the truck is pretty dark. What's the right answer here? There's a mess between my legs. My body thinks I rode a wild stallion through ocean surf at top speed. I have no idea how I'm going to face my classmates next week. And underlying all of that, there's a painful awareness zapping through me.

So, that's sex.

"I feel a bit empty," I confess.

His mouth firms up and he nods. "You've been through a lot."

I didn't mean it like that. But that's true, too. I feel drained, emotionally. But I also feel like he made a Gabriel-shaped space where nothing existed before.

And part of me wants to know when it will be filled again.

After I have a bath or a shower, I might just ask him if we can do it again. He didn't seem to hate it. He's even calling me bunny now, which is nice.

I look at his profile as he drives.

I'm glad he isn't what I thought he was. I'm going to have to get that photo back from Dr. Adler somehow, I think idly as I start to drift off, the warmth of the truck cab and the soothing road noise lulling me to an exhausted sleep.

———

I wake up as he carries me into his cabin. Cling to him as he pulls a warm, clean t-shirt over my head, then puts me in his bed.

"I need to go do something, Lucy," he protests.

I hold on tight, and he gives in, folding in around me.

I fall asleep again listening to his heartbeat.

———

When I wake up again, it's very dark.

Gabriel's arm is thrown over me, but I slide out from the heavy weight without disturbing him.

I go to the bathroom and clean up. He has a small laundry room right next to it, and I dig through the clothes in the dryer until I find something that I can make work for me—a pair of long johns that must stretch like crazy on him, because they stay up on me, just loose in the waist.

It's a small cabin. One bedroom, a bathroom with that laundry space, a kitchen and a big living room curving around it. I'm smiling as I round the corner and discover a pretty high-tech looking computer set up in a nook.

But the smile fades when I see a wall of photos and notes.

It's me.

Over and over again.

My stomach flips over and plummets to the floor as I move closer.

It's me *sleeping*.

Gabriel has been in my dorm room.

He's taken pictures of me eating, studying...

My entire life has been documented. My class schedule, my bus routes.

And sitting on the chair is the black duffel bag of money he bought me with.

Heart pounding, I turn around and look for anything that could possibly go on my feet. There's a pair of socks hanging on a drying rack by a wood stove. I yank those on, then shove my feet into a pair of much-too-big rubber boots at the back door.

I know he saved me from something awful tonight, and damaged his own relationship with Ethan in the process. But this... This isn't right. All this time, he *was* my stalker. It's so creepy.

Shoving the back door open, I take off at a run. I have no idea where I am or where I'm going, but anywhere is better than being barefoot and freshly fucked in a cabin with the man who is obsessed with me.

<h1 style="text-align:center">16
gabriel</h1>

I WAKE UP, disoriented, to the sound of a thump—and an empty bed where Lucy should be.

Stumbling into the living room, I see that my back door is ajar.

"Lucy!" I bellow.

Adrenaline drives me out the door, past the wall of Lucy I should have taken down before she pulled me into bed next to her, and out into the night.

In the distance, I hear her crashing through the forest.

She is a clever young woman.

But she is no match for a trained SEAL.

I'll fix this. I have to. And once I have her back in my bed, I will do whatever it takes to replace the wariness in her eyes with trust.

But first I need to find my bunny girl again.

17
lucy

MY LUNGS ARE KILLING ME. I don't think I've ever run this far before, definitely not in too-big rubber boots, and I really want to stop. But I also want to get as far away from Gabriel's cabin as I can before I slow down.

I trip over something and stumble, biting back a sob.

As I right myself, I hear something behind me.

Whirling around, all I can see is darkness.

Then Gabriel's voice comes out of nowhere. "Lucy, stop running."

I turn and take off again, terrified at how close he must have been.

Now I can hear him behind me, his footsteps suddenly loud, so loud, crashing through the dry twigs and leaves on the ground. Chasing me. Hunting me.

There's no chance I actually get away from him now. Maybe I need to try to attack him. That would at least have the element of surprise on my side.

My legs burn as I pick up speed, trying to gain just a little more ground…

Then I pull up quickly and pick up the pointiest, most jagged stick I can find on the ground. I don't turn around.

He thunders to a stop behind me, and I wait for him to tackle me, pinning me to the ground and attempting to do whatever horrible thing he wants to do with his prey.

That's when I'll stab the most tender parts of his body that I can reach with the stick.

But he doesn't grab me.

He doesn't take me down to the ground and press his weight on top of me.

Shaking like a leaf, I hide the stick behind my back as I slowly turn.

He's standing ten feet back, his bare chest heaving, his hands in loose fists at his side. A stricken expression on his face is the last thing I expect to see. "Don't run," he grinds out. "Please don't run."

"Don't chase me," I gasp.

"I'm not. Not exactly. I'm just…following."

"That's the same thing!"

"They might be looking for you."

"Here?" Desperation claws inside my chest and climbs up my throat. "The only threat to me here is *you*."

"There are other dangers. You could hurt yourself running through the woods."

"Will I hurt myself more than you will?" I shake my head at him. "Why?" The question rips out of me on a sob. "Why did you stalk me?"

"I'm sorry," he says, his voice cracking. And then he sinks to his knees, putting himself down on my level. "I failed you."

"You took photos of me!"

"I was keeping an eye on you."

"In my dorm?"

"I've never…I couldn't trust…" He punches his fist against the nearest tree. "Fuck!"

"Don't!" I scramble toward him before I remember he's a dangerous stalker, and then I do remember just as I wrap my fingers around his muscled forearm. The same arm that he pushed between my virgin thighs a few hours ago.

Now the fingers that he used to work me open are bleeding, torn open from his violent slam against the bark.

He makes a wounded sound as I trace the side of his index finger.

"You need antiseptic," I whisper.

He flicks his hand, lightning fast, and now he's holding my wrist. "I need you to listen to me."

My pulse races under my skin. "Your cabin is full of photos of me."

"Because you're beautiful. Because you're precious. Because I took one look at my son's obsession and knew as wrong as it was that I'd found my obsession, too. Because I have loved you from the first moment I laid eyes on you, and I couldn't help myself."

"I gave you my virginity." My voice cracks. "You bought my innocence. That was your plan all along, wasn't it?"

Shock rolls over his face. "No. Lucy, no."

"Then why did you bring so much money?"

"That's—" He laughs hoarsely. "Lucy, I stole that for you. From the boat. I thought it was the least those asshole kids owed you for the trauma."

"But you're like a trained killer, aren't you? That thing you did on the boat, kicking the gun out of Ethan's hands. You could have done that to the others, couldn't you?"

He doesn't answer. He's not denying it.

"You wanted me to think that you had no choice."

"I gave you a choice," he grinds out. "I will always give you a choice."

"But you wanted it. You wanted to take my virginity."

And he doesn't deny that, either.

"You didn't give me a choice about coming here."

"Because you were naked." The words snap out of him. "God damn it, Lucy. Wrestling for guns is rarely successful. I couldn't take that risk again. Not once they knew what I was capable of. As soon as Gilly went to the bridge, I took care of Forrest and I got you out of there."

"When did Gilly go to the bridge?"

His brow furrows. "What do you want, a time stamp?"

"Was it before or after you came in my unprotected pussy?" I shove at him. "You big jerk."

And then I start crying.

He pulls me into his arms and we sink down. He twists around, putting his back to the tree, and I melt into his chest, all out of fight.

"We'll get you the morning after pill tomorrow," he finally chokes out. "I'm sorry."

I don't say anything.

"I'm sorry about all of it," he adds quietly. "I'm so fucking sorry I didn't talk to you then. I didn't want to scare you, and now look at you." His thumb slowly rubs across the inside of my forearm. "My innocent little bunny."

I press my face into his chest as he curls his thumb around my elbow, then works it up my arm.

He tells me about watching me, and then, haltingly, he tells me about the night he came into my room. He thought I was at a party. He wanted to check to see if Ethan had left any listening devices in my room.

"Did you find any?" I mumble.

"No."

"Did you leave any of your own?"

A beat. "No."

I lift my head. "Did you think about it?"

He doesn't answer that.

"Gabriel!" I plant my hands on his shoulders.

He settles his hands on my hips and turns me so I'm straddling him. "Yes?"

"You cannot spy on me."

He starts to say something, then stops. "Why not?"

"It's wrong."

"But you're precious to me." He shrugs under my hands. "I won't apologize for that. I'm only sorry for scaring you. I won't do that again."

"What will you do?"

"I'll let you know that I'm watching when you're at the library." His thumbs begin making circles on my hips, and the loose waistband on the pants I pulled on gives way. His fingers find my bare skin. "I'll show you the photos I take, the ones I have to take because you're so beautiful it hurts to look at you and not capture the moment."

I blink at him.

Even in the dim moonlight, his expression is clear as day. And it's not at all what I expect.

"Gabriel," I whisper. I cup his face in my hands.

He holds my gaze, raw and vulnerable. "I won't hurt you. Ever. But I am obsessed with you, and I can't be sorry about that. Not when it lands you on my lap in the middle of the forest."

I lean in and press my forehead against his. He tugs my hips forward and the sensitive, aching spot between my legs is brought right up against the growing ridge in his jeans.

"Feel what you do to me?"

"Uh huh."

"I'll always give you a choice. If you want to leave, I'll let you go. I'll drive you back to school and let you live your life. But I'm never going to be far, just in case you change your mind." His cock throbs, heavy and alive between my legs. "I will always be ready for you when you need me."

I whimper. How does he know I need him?

His tongue sweeps into my mouth, hot and claiming. One of his hands skates up my back and sinks into my hair, closing tight. Holding on, holding me still so he can kiss me even harder, put me where he wants me, which is right against his big, hard body.

I grind against him, my thighs shaking now. "Please," I whimper. "Gabriel…"

"Shhh, baby." He groans. "Let's go back to the cabin."

"No. Here."

"You'll be sore."

"I don't care."

"I care."

"Then make it better after." I tear at the clothes I'm wearing. "Make me feel good now. Take care of me now."

"Demanding little thing."

"You did this to me. You set me on fire."

"You're on fire?"

"Burning up."

"Poor baby."

"Your baby," I whisper. "Please, Daddy."

"Jesus." But even as he curses, his cock throbs against me.

"You said it first." I nip at his lower lip. "You called me Daddy's good little girl."

He goes still. "And did you like it?"

I grab his hand and pull it to my bare chest. "So much it scares me."

"No, don't be scared."

"Make it better, Daddy."

He closes his fingers on my nipple and tugs. "I will, bunny. Hold still."

Gabriel rolls us over and puts me on all fours, only pulling the leggings I stole from him down my hips, which traps my knees together.

He gets behind me and releases his cock, then notches it between my ass cheeks.

"Head down, bunny," he growls. He plants his hand in the middle of my back and pushes me down. My face meets my hands on the ground, and I breathe in the scent of the earth and grass as he tilts my hips up. "That's it. Show me where you need me."

I cry out as he slides into that empty space he made, filling it again. Make me whole again.

It hurts, but it's wonderful, and when he's all the way buried, he holds still and soothes me with his words and his touch.

"My precious bunny needs my cock," he murmurs. "I will always give you what you need. That's my vow to you."

The word vow is like a lightning bolt.

He's never going to give me up. He might let me go, but he will always be close by. And he will always give me what I need.

It might have been his son who dressed me up like a virgin bride, but it was Gabriel who turned tonight into a twisted but wonderful wedding night.

I wiggle my hips back, taking a little bit more of him.

What would it be like to have Gabriel forever? To finally have a family of my own. To be…

I choke up thinking about the possibility of love.

"It's okay," he groans. "If you're too sore, we can—"

"Love me," I burst out. I blink back tears. "Please, Gabriel. I need you to love me."

He wraps his arms around me and starts moving. "I do, Lucy. I will, always."

He finds my clit and pins me between his hand and his body, fucking me and rubbing me until I explode for him.

And then he follows, filling me up for the second time tonight.

18
gabriel

IT'S mid-morning the next time I wake up, and Lucy is safely in my arms. Her warm, naked body is all I need in this world.

But my phone is ringing somewhere, and whoever is calling isn't accepting that they're being sent to voicemail.

As I swing my feet out of bed, there's a pounding at the front door, too.

Fuck.

I yank on my jeans, leaving my chest bare to give the intruder a clear hint that I want to go back to bed, then cross the cabin.

"What is it?" I bark as I wrench the door open.

A good friend, a fellow veteran I met through some charity work I signed up for when I moved to Conception Ridge, is standing on my doorstep.

"Gabe," Nolan Adler says with a careful tightness. "You're here."

"Of course I'm here. I live here."

"Are you alone?" He glances past me, but I'm filling enough of the doorway that I know he can only see the raw beams of the cabin ceiling.

I'm not about to lie regarding Lucy, but I'm not offering

information before we've had a chance to really talk about what forever is going to look like, either. "Why are you asking?"

He holds up a basic white piece of printer paper, folded into many parts. My face stares back, a photocopy of a photograph. And above it, in bold black writing, is Lucy's handwriting. *If I disappear, find this man.*

I grin.

What a good girl she is.

"You want to tell me why my student left this for me? And how nobody at her dorm has seen her since yesterday?"

I scrub my hand over my jaw. "You went to her dorm?"

He lunges forward, shoving at my chest, pushing me a foot back into the cabin. The door swings open, and he follows me inside, but he doesn't get very far before a sweet voice asks us to stop.

I pivot, and then stumble, my always sure-footedness failing me at the angelic sight of Lucy wrapped in a bedsheet and nothing else, biting her bottom lip.

"Lucy?" Nolan says, an urgent question in his voice. *Are you okay? Did he hurt you?*

"I didn't go missing, Dr. Adler," she says. "Gabriel saved me from them."

"From who?" Nolan's not backing down.

The weight of what happened last night crushes my heart all over again. "My son and his fraternity brothers. I should have intervened sooner."

Nolan gives me a wary look. "I think someone needs to start at the beginning."

"Yeah. Okay." I point Lucy to the bedroom. "After we get dressed."

When we return, Lucy wearing a pair of my sweatpants with the waistband rolled up a few times, Nolan has made himself comfortable on my sofa.

So I sit in the arm chair. And Lucy curls up on my lap.

Nolan's eyebrows go up, but all he says is, "What happened?"

I let Lucy take the lead. She explains about the invitation to the party, and some things that she thinks she should have realized in hindsight.

That's where I interrupt. "You couldn't have known."

"I was basically invited to a sex party," she says. "And had I known the details, I would have just declined the invite."

"And then Ethan would have kidnapped you," I grind out.

"Maybe." She bites her lip. "He really did want to pick me up for the party. But everyone else knew what was going on."

"That's called a conspiracy to commit a crime," Nolan interjects gently. "That's not a point in their favor."

"I'm just saying I don't want to sex shame anyone." She blushes. "I was more innocent two days ago."

My cock pulses to life.

Fucking not the time, champ.

And then I realize what she said. "They kidnapped you, Lucy. It's okay to sex-shame kidnappers."

She nibbles on her lip again. "I went willingly."

I grunt. "You didn't know what you were agreeing to."

"Okay." Nolan nods. "I've got a clearer picture now. Lucy, you're okay staying here with Gabriel for the weekend?"

"Yes," she whispers.

He looks at me. "You've got a good security system here?"

"The best."

Another nod. "All right." He stands. "Will I see you in class on Monday, Lucy?"

"She'll be there," I promise.

And I won't be very far away the whole time.

19
lucy

AS SOON AS Dr. Adler leaves, Gabriel pins me down on the couch. Hands above my head, lower body pinned in place by his heavy weight.

"Stop taking out your worry on your lower lip," he says, frowning.

Then he kisses me there.

"What's going to happen?" I ask.

"Dunno. That's not for you to worry about. Your job is to stay here and stay safe. And then go to school on Monday with your head held high."

I want to bite my lip so bad.

I don't.

After a beat, Gabriel lets me up, and I scramble into his lap.

"You're going to be okay, baby." He kisses my forehead. "And don't worry about those shitheads. They got themselves into trouble. They can deal with the consequences."

I wrap my arms around his neck. "And what about you? We haven't even talked about the shitty things Ethan said to you."

He clears his throat. "Yeah. Well, that'll work itself out one way or another, too. I'm not really sure what to do, to be honest.

When I found out I had a kid, I planned to love him forever, you know?"

"I don't know." I shrug and hug him tighter, bringing my face to press to his. "Foster kid. I've never had a parent who could love me forever."

Something ticks in his jaw so hard I feel it against my cheek.

"Want to adopt me?" I say it lightly. A joke, the way I've always used humor to protect me from the sadness.

"I would."

Shocked, I yank back and stare at him.

A dark shadow passes behind his eyes. "If you need that. I'll be whatever you need."

"Pretty sure you can't fuck me if you adopt me." More humor. Armor armor armor.

He strokes his fingers over my cheek. "I told myself last night that if all I got was a single, perfect memory of rubbing against your sweet pussy, that would be enough to keep me warm for the rest of my life. If you need us to stop that so I can be something else to you, I would do that in a heartbeat."

Heat swarms inside me. *A single, perfect memory.* "Would you think about it, then? Think about and stroke yourself? Get off to your memory of fucking your adopted—"

He tosses me on my back and starts tickling me. "Don't finish that question."

I laugh out loud. I laugh until I cry, and then he kisses me, and we make out in a desperate, clinging kind of way that promises we aren't going to be changing our relationship like that.

When he finally lets me up for air, it's only to peel off my pants and crawl between my thighs. "I need to know what you taste like."

My head tips back as he presses his face to my belly first, then to the top of my bare thigh.

"Oh baby. You smell so fucking good."

He goes slowly from there, his hands pushing my legs apart.

Looking at me.

Just…looking.

Then he falls into me, kissing me, pressing his face to my mound. And lower, aligning his mouth to my body. His tongue opens me up, tasting me, and he groans so loud it makes me spill arousal straight into his mouth.

"Yes," he says, low and growly. "Give it to me."

My thighs shake as he teases my clit with the tip of his tongue, then they clamp tight around his head when he starts sucking.

I can't breathe.

I can't think.

I can only feel, and I feel perfect. It's like he's sucking my soul out between my legs, pulling it into his body, and returning it in a new form.

"I love you," I whisper.

He sucks harder.

"I love you," I sob.

He makes me come.

And then I'm chanting it as he rises up to kiss me, and I taste myself on his lips, on his tongue. I whisper and sob it again and again as he holds me. *I love you.*

He doesn't say it back until after I've jerked him off on my belly, five fast strokes that make a big pool of seed that I immediately wish was inside me.

And then, after he's mopped up his mess with a shirt and he's holding me again, he looks me in the eye and says, very calmly, "I love you, too. I have from the moment I first saw you in a photograph, and I had to accept that get to be your person."

"You're my person," I promise.

I don't know how I know, but I know it in my soul.

I know that on Monday, and two years from now, and thirty years from now, Gabriel will be the love of my life.

epilogue

Gabriel

Two years later

SHE'S IN THE STACKS, looking for a book.

I'm two stacks over, watching her. Getting hard, because she's worrying her bottom lip, and she knows if she does that she's going to get a spanking tonight.

But God damn it, I don't think I can wait until I get her back to my cabin in the woods.

I'm going to need to take her here in the library.

Silently I leave the stacks and do a quick reconnaissance of the area. There's nobody on this floor right now. Two cameras cover the public study area, but there are dead zones in the stacks.

She's in one right now.

I wonder if she's been checking out the detailed notes I take on the campus security system. Even though Ethan and his whole crew were expelled over their actions that night, I'll never be too careful when it comes to my sweet, innocent bunny.

I step into the aisle she's in, blocking the light that drifts in from the common area.

It takes her a beat to look up, and when she does, her eyes go wide.

I prowl toward her. "You're all alone up here, bunny."

"I just needed a book," she squeaks. "I'll go downstairs—"

"It's too late for that." I growl and catch her by the wrist, spinning her around.

"Careful," she whispers as I press her back against the fixed wooden shelf.

"I remember," I whisper back, holding myself off her enough so her swollen, aching breasts aren't crushed by my chest.

She slides her hands over my shoulders and lets me hoist her up, her sundress falling away so her bare legs are wrapped around me and her wet little cunt, bare under the flowing skirt, is pressed hard against my erection. Once she's braced and pinned in place, I let go of her and curve my hand over the slight swell of her belly.

"Pregnant little bunnies are my favourite prey," I growl. "Can't go an hour without needing to find one and have a little taste."

She smacks my chest. "Bunnies plural?"

I laugh and kiss her mouth. "One bunny. For life."

"That's better." She kisses me and wiggles. Horny little bunny.

I set her down and turn her around, then crouch behind her. I flip her skirt up, my hands huge on her hips. I curve my fingers over her soft, jiggly, perfect bottom. It only takes the lightest pressure to tip her hips up so I can see more of her slit, her beautiful, pretty little pussy looking right back at me.

"That's it, bunny. Show Daddy your pretty little holes. Show me where you're needy."

She arches her back more, her ass cheeks pulling apart, and I lean in to take a complete taste of my girl.

My A-student.

My mate.

The mother-to-be of my baby. Our baby.

She pulses against my tongue, her pussy swelling, her clit getting hard, and fuck it.

A taste is not enough.

I stand and unzip.

"Daddy," she gasps, faking shock at my choice.

It's hardly a surprise that I like to be in my bestest girl.

I thrust into her and groan in satisfaction. "That's it. That's the good stuff."

"You're incorrigible," she says happily, wiggling onto my cock. Taking what we both need. "I love you."

"I love you more."

"I love you the most—Ah!" She sucks in a gasp at the hard thrust. "Okay, you love me the most."

"Gotta fill you up before your next class," I mutter. "Three hours is too long. No more of those next term."

She giggles. "I'm going online next term, remember? You put in a baby in me?"

I sigh happily. Right.

She pushes back, urging me on, and we're quiet but for the wet slap of our bodies together as she takes her pleasure on my cock and milks mine at the same time.

"There, there, right there," she pants. I pin her in place and work that spot until she bites her own hand and goes stiff.

I follow, spurting my release into her, then I slump forward and kiss the back of her neck. "Good girl." I drag in a breath. "That was very fast."

She squirms off my cock.

I pull the supplies to clean up out of one of my pockets, and then her panties from another. I crouch at her feet and help her step into them.

"Find the book you want to check out, bunny," I say after I stand. "You don't want to be late for class."

Do you want a bonus story about Gabriel and Lucy, where they go to a party and everyone is watching but it's totally different than the first time that happened? And Dr. Nolan Adler is there with his own little girl? Sign up on my website to get it delivered straight to your inbox: https://chloemaine.com/her-wedding-night-bonus-content/

BRINGING
Home
TROUBLE
UNWRAPPING HIS
NAUGHTY
Secret
CHLOE MAINE

When my new best friend begs me to come home with her for Christmas, I think I'm doing her a favor—but as soon as her father answers the door, I know I've made a big mistake.

All I want for the holidays is to get over the hot older guy who gave me my first kiss, ever, and then ghosted me.

Turns out, the off-limits hottie who deleted his profile after our first date is…my lab partner's dad. Hunter Dane: silver-haired DILF, gifted artist, and talented cook. Also, not willing to date someone half his age, apparently.

So now we're standing on his doorstep, pretending that we didn't practically get to second base on Main Street a week ago. And I'm trying to figure out how I'm going to survive dinner, a very long night just down the hall from my one-sided crush, and Christmas morning in matching jammies, when all I really want is to steal another kiss under the mistletoe.

Unwrapping His Naughty Secret is a spicy age gap instalove romance about being very, very quiet in the middle of the night. And then trying not to blush too much over pancakes in the morning.

1
cara

"I NEED you to come to Christmas Eve at my house," my lab partner Hannah says in a rush as she throws herself into the chair across from me in the Ridge College library.

"First things first," I mutter, not taking my eyes off my biology worksheet I'm labelling. "We have ninety minutes until this group project is due, and you were late."

"Because I'm having a legitimate crisis."

I sigh and put down my pen. If Hannah is having a crisis, legitimate or not, no homework will get done. "What's wrong?"

"My uncle is bringing his wife and his husband to Christmas Eve dinner."

My eyebrows shoot up. "His wife *and* his husband?"

"Yep." She pops the p, as if that's enough said.

I shrug. "Lucky him?"

"It's going to be so awkward, Care Bear. Please come with me."

"To your family dinner?"

"It's just me and my dad and my uncle Wyatt and his two *lovers*. You'll balance us out. Six is a better number than five. Plus, then we'll have something to talk about besides all the sex they're having."

"Hannah!" My cheeks are flaming hot. I glance around, but nobody in the library heard her. "Please don't say things like that here." I lower my voice. "Do they really talk about…"

"It just sort of slips out because they love each other so much. And my uncle is a bit of an idiot. I mean, I'm happy for him, don't get me wrong. And his spouses are actually great. But it's a lot, and also, I just like the number six. Even numbers are important to me."

"So important you need me to listen to your family accidentally discuss their sex life?"

"Don't be such a virgin, Cara Michaels."

I count backwards from five. It's not enough. I repeat the countdown from ten, and then I smile. "Does your dad know you're inviting a stray from school?"

"He won't mind. He's Mr. Homemaker. We always have way too much food, and our dining room table seats twelve."

Hannah is rich.

And spoiled.

I'm sure her dad isn't Mr. Homemaker, and I'm equally sure that he doesn't want me crashing his Christmas Eve dinner, but right now I'll say just about anything to get Hannah to focus on our final assignment of the term.

Being lab partners with her has been a trip. A wild, chaotic trip. What I imagine collaborating with a very excitable toddler on their first time baking chocolate chip cookies might be like. And I can't wait for it to be over in ninety minutes.

"Sure," I say easily, lying through my teeth. "I'll come to your house on Christmas Eve. I'd love to meet your dad. And your uncle, and his wife and their husband. That sounds amazing. Now proofread this diagram, okay?"

She rolls her eyes and smiles. "Yes, Mom."

I shove a page across the table at her and get back to work.

———

Don't be such a virgin.

Hannah's accidental taunt stays with me long after we leave our biology lab together for the last time.

It's not like I set out to be an almost twenty-year-old virgin. It just…happened. Or rather, it just didn't happen. And actually, there are a lot of virgins my age, according to the internet. None of the people around me at college seem to share my late bloomer status, though, and it's getting awkward.

As soon as I'm alone in the safety of my dorm room, I pull up the dating app profile I've been working on all term. It's time to go live, and try to find a date for the holidays. Not even Christmas Eve. I know that's not likely, but if I have *anything* booked over the holidays, then I won't feel like a complete loser for ducking out on the only offer I currently have.

I read it over one last time. I'm not using my real name, of course. I'm not a dummy. And I'm aging myself up because I've heard too many horror stories about creeps who only want to perv on college coeds. If anyone asks, I'll morph my part-time job in the Admissions office into my actual career or something.

Nobody will ask. You're overthinking this.

Which is how I handle everything in my life. I did extensive research dives on every college I considered. I picked Ridge College because Conception Ridge has a growing tech sector, but it's an affordable town, so if I meet the right person and want to settle down and have kids, I'll be able to do that without breaking the bank.

Definitely *not* putting that in my dating bio, though.

First things first. Cara needs a kiss.

Kira, age 25

I like ice cream, preferably with all the toppings, and waking up early enough to see the sunrise (because dawn is pretty cool, but also because it's extra quiet then and I'm a bit of an introvert). Looking for someone with experience to make my first kiss really, really good. No creeps need apply.

I tap the submit button. An icon flips on the screen, and then there's a green button next to my inbox. Time to see if anyone is interested in helping me out.

———

Twelve hours later, I'm shocked at how many creeps replied.

> Eager to become a slut, huh?

> I'd make you wait for your first kiss until you've taken me bareback to the root, bitch

> Horny bio, I like it. Do you like to get on your knees, honey?

Delete, delete, delete. Twenty-seven responses, and none of them are what I was expecting. I edit my profile to be clear that I'm not interested in sex, just a first kiss. That doesn't slow the creeps down, and by lunch, I've turned off notifications.

I still check every few hours, but I don't need to know when another perv has dropped into my inbox.

It's late that night when I get my first reasonable reply.

> HUNTER
>
> Did you get a deluge of weird replies? Because I posted something similar a few months ago, an eager/honest profile, and it was like waving a red flag for perverts. I'm still getting them.

He attaches a photo of his own bio.

Hunter, age 43

Haven't dated in twenty-two years and I'm not really sure where to start again. We didn't have apps "back in my day" so I could use a tutor for this space. All interested instructors will be wined and dined like a queen. Or a princess. Whatever you like. Delete this, Hunter. You aren't ready for the internet.

I giggle and press my hand to my face before replying. My cheeks are burning.

KIRA

Is Hunter your real name?

HUNTER

Yes? The app said we had to match our government ID

KIRA

They don't check that

HUNTER

groan

KIRA

This isn't my real name

HUNTER

That's smart

You're a good girl for protecting your identity

KIRA

Thanks

HUNTER

Be careful replying to your DMs, okay?

KIRA

I've deleted all of them without reply (except you)

HUNTER

That bad, huh?

KIRA

Pretty brutal

HUNTER

Nothing wrong with waiting for the right guy...I had a kid way too young and it scared me off dating for two decades

KIRA

I'm done waiting

HUNTER

Okay... well, good luck

KIRA

Wait

HUNTER

What?

KIRA

Aren't you... Don't you...

HUNTER

Oh, fuck me

KIRA

I thought we could start with a kiss?

HUNTER

Fuck

KIRA

Is that a no?

HUNTER

That's a... "I'm too old for you, kid"

KIRA

Not the dreaded *kid*

HUNTER

I didn't reach out to you to be a creep

KIRA

If anything, I'm the creep here!

HUNTER

Universally, everyone would agree that the 42-year-old man trying to get a date with a 25-year-old girl is the creep

KIRA

But it's not a date, it's just a kiss! It's a two-minute good deed

HUNTER

I promise, you don't want me to kiss you

KIRA

Do you have bad breath?

HUNTER

No

KIRA

Would you call me a bitch or a slut or threaten me with unprotected sex?

HUNTER

Jesus

No. Also, I want you to get off this app immediately

KIRA

Okay, Daddy

HUNTER

I'm not joking, give me names and I'll make them disappear

KIRA

Let's focus on the mission here: would you make my first kiss good?

HUNTER

Kira...

KIRA

That's not even my name

It'll just be our secret, forever

All I want for Christmas is a good first kiss, and
I think you're the man for the job

HUNTER

I'm old

KIRA

I promise I don't care as long as you're nice

2
hunter

KIRA—OR whatever this girl's name is—wants to meet me right then and there. Since it's late and I'm in the middle of a project, I ask her if she can wait until the morning.

We exchange seventy-three text messages before she falls asleep.

KIRA

There's a nice big parking lot just off campus

HUNTER

Campus?

There's a long pause before she writes back.

KIRA

Ridge College

HUNTER

Do you work there?

If the answer is no, I know I need to find a way out of this. I have no business kissing a college student.

KIRA

Yeah in the Admissions office

I let out a huge sigh of relief and shake my head. She's still too young for me, but I can give her a really good date before making it clear I'd prefer to date in my own age range.

HUNTER

You should have higher standards for your first kiss than a parking lot

Let me take you out for breakfast

KIRA

Kissing after eating food? Sounds risky

HUNTER

Coffee, then

KIRA

Same question... would you want to kiss a coffee-flavoured mouth?

HUNTER

How do you take your coffee?

KIRA

I like sweet lattes, vanilla, hazelnut, that sort of thing

HUNTER

Yes, I want to kiss your vanilla-flavoured mouth

Would you rather I not drink coffee? I can have hot chocolate or tea instead

KIRA

No, if you like it...I think coffee is fine

HUNTER

Getting to know someone a little first is nice, and there's something extra sweet about having to wait for a kiss

When I wake up in the morning, I fully expect to find a message from her to cancel.

She doesn't.

I get to Wake Up Call, the coffee shop she picked, a few minutes early. This early in the morning, Main Street isn't busy. It's a cold, rainy winter morning, and everyone who doesn't have a reason to be out is staying tucked in bed.

I'm too big for the little table and chairs along the wall, so after I order my coffee and leave them fifty bucks for the next few customers—which I hope will include Kira—I sit on the sofa in front of the window.

She's going to take one look at me and decide she doesn't want a kiss after all. That's the most likely outcome.

My phone vibrates and my fingers shake as I swipe in to see the message.

But it's not her. It's my younger half-brother, Wyatt.

> **WYATT**
>
> Emily wants to know if you have dessert planned for Christmas Eve, or if she can make a trifle (we're introducing her to Friends)

> **WYATT**
>
> she promises not to put peas in it

> **HUNTER**
>
> A trifle would be great, thanks

If his wife wants to bring trifle that had peas in it, I wouldn't fucking care. That would be hilarious, actually.

The door opens, the bell above it chiming, and I drop my phone on the coffee table as I catch sight of dark, glossy waves framing a soft, round face.

She's looking straight ahead, scanning the coffee shop. My

chest tightens as I realize she doesn't clock me at all. No instinctive glance in my direction.

I brace myself for a look of disappointment when she finally turns around.

She goes to the counter, slowly unzipping her coat as she orders a vanilla latte. Her hand pauses as the barista explains it's paid for already. A gesture in my direction. Her head turns and—

Fuck. Me.

Her eyes widen as our gazes connect. I stand, rising to my full height, and I have to brush my big hands on my jeans, they're suddenly sweaty and damp.

She's at least a foot shorter than me, and so damn pretty the force of looking at her nearly rips out my throat.

Hi, I mouth, pointing at my chest. *Hunter*.

She smiles.

Thank. Fuck.

She comes over and I start to hold out my hand before I remembered it was sweaty and also, who shakes hands with the girl they're going to kiss? So I convert that to an arm pat that makes her laugh nervously.

Great.

So far, not starting out well.

"You're here," she says as I sit down on the couch again. "Thanks for the, umm, coffee. And the, you know…"

"My pleasure on both counts. Good morning. It's nice to meet you in person."

As I string together that barely coherent response, it takes me a minute to realize she's looking down at the narrow space left on the couch beside me, and then my brain flat lines because I didn't think about where she could sit.

On Daddy's lap would be nice.

Not happening, Hunter.

I move over after an awkward beat, and she sets her latte down, then shrugs out of her coat. Underneath, she's wearing jeans and a cream-colored turtleneck sweater that floats over full breasts and a soft little belly.

She's perfectly ripe, my filthiest dreams come to life, and my cock throbs to life. Which makes it even harder to think when she finally joins me on the sofa, bringing with her a sweet vanilla and brown sugar scent that makes my mouth water.

"It's so quiet this early in the morning." She takes a deep breath. "This is nice. Thanks for suggesting this. I mean, it's nice to have a…"

"Prelude to a kiss?"

She gives me a blank look, not getting the reference to the 1990s rom com at all. Right. She wasn't even born then. "Yes, I guess that's one way to describe it." She grabs her latte. "How's your coffee?"

"Great." I haven't even tasted it yet. I follow suit, and it is, in fact, excellent.

She lets out a nervous laugh. "I bet you think it's silly that I'm this worked up over a kiss."

"Not at all. I'm nervous, too. This is my first date in a very long time." I shift myself sideways so I can better look at her. My knee bumps her thigh, and she sucks in a tiny little inhale before glancing at me from under her lashes. Then she presses back, increasing the contact there. Leg against knee. Warm, unexpected contact that feels really fucking right, at least for me.

We might be strangers, but I'm already game for whatever she needs from me.

I want to wrap my hand around her inside thigh and squeeze. I want to slide my arm around her shoulders and pull her close so I can breathe in more of her scent. I want to turn her nervous laughs into breathless sighs so fucking badly.

Instead, I ask her what else we have in common. "We were up late, but you made it here okay. Are you a morning person?"

She shakes her head vigorously. "Night owl."

"Me, too." I exhale. "I'm an illustrator. I used to draw comic strips, and now I illustrate graphic novels. When my daughter was little, the middle of the night was the best time to work."

"Right, you're a dad," she says, her eyes wide. Like she'd forgotten that, but I know I told her when we were texting.

I'd never hide that fact from anyone. Even a girl I probably won't ever see again.

"Is that a problem?"

"No." She rakes her teeth over her lower lip, her cheeks staining pink. "I love kids. Which is irrelevant for the whole helping me out with a kiss thing, I guess. But yeah, that you're a dad...that's cool. Maybe that explains why you were the nicest DM I got yesterday."

I growl, surprising both of us. My nose flares as I force myself to politely say, "Tell me you deleted all of those disgusting replies without answering."

Her eyes go impossibly big, so bright and shiny like the midnight sea that I could drown in them. "Yes, I deleted them."

I take her hand in my mine, shocked at the visceral relief I feel when she squeezes my fingers back. "Good girl. I wasn't sure if you were being sarcastic when you said yes, Daddy."

She laughs. "Not sarcastic, exactly? Maybe a little teasing. But I agree with you, those messages aren't the vibe."

"You're smart." She smiles at the praise, which feeds a long ignored part of me that pushes to the fore. "And, uh, you can tease me about being a Daddy as much as you want."

Her eyes light up. "Nice."

And if this were more than just a kiss, I'd take that deeper, because yes, it is nice. Very fucking nice. But this is not a date, *not a fucking date, Hunter,* so I leave it there and focus on the task at hand. My gaze drifts to her soft, plush lips.

"It's hard to believe you haven't been kissed yet," I admit. "You're beautiful."

"I've been focused on— other things." She bites her lip. "And maybe my standards are too high?"

Good.

Fuck yes. "Keep them sky high."

Another pleased smile.

This girl makes all of my dirtiest instincts roar to life. I want to pet her and make her glow. I want to strip her bare and make her scream for Daddy.

I'm not going to do any of that. I'm going to make her first kiss magical, though, and set that bar as high as humanly possible so every person who follows has to treat her like a princess.

Taking a deep breath, I ease back, putting a bit of space between us. "Do you have any requests?"

"For…the kiss?" That pink in her cheeks intensifies. "Umm… I'm not sure."

"You must have imagined what it would be like."

"Oh. Yes." She sucks in a little breath. "I want…if you are interested…I want it to be open-mouthed. With tongue."

My fly suddenly feels like an iron bar holding my cock back from taking flight. "That can be arranged."

"I want a full kiss, you know? Nothing too…virginal. Although I don't think I have to worry about that with you." She roves her gaze over me. "You don't look like the soft and light kind of guy."

Jesus, what kind of looks have I been giving her?

"I can be gentle," I promise her. "I do careful, precise work every day."

"Don't be too careful with me." She licks her lips, leaving them shiny and perfect. Her eyelashes flutter against her cheeks, then blink open again.

She's like an honest to God real life doll, and I want her so much it fucking hurts.

I have never had this kind of response to a woman. Ever.

It's dangerous.

"Drink your coffee, sweet girl," I manage to say. "And then we'll go for a walk and I'll give you the first kiss you deserve."

3
cara

WHEN WE LEAVE the coffee shop, Hunter takes my hand in his. It's stopped raining outside, so it's cool and damp, but his hand is warm and strong around my fingers.

I look sideways at him, taking in his strong profile, his heavy jaw and his silver-streaked hair, and I marvel at how and why he ever swiped on me in the first place. A Christmas miracle, maybe.

"Did you drive or walk?"

"I…" I have to swallow around a lump in my throat, that's how nervous I am. "I walked. I live near campus."

Dark red slashes across his cheekbones. Not a blush, exactly. Something much more mature and responsible than a blush. He glances sideways, and smiles slightly at my wide-eyed, unvarnished observation of him. "Would you trust me to drive you home?"

"I…" Again with that lump. "I'm actually expected at the library soon. Just…over there." I point across Main Street. "I'm a community tutor. Every weekend, I set up at a table and school kids can come and do their homework with me."

Something flickers in his gaze. "That's admirable."

I duck my head, hiding a smile. "Thank you. It looks good on the resume."

He stops walking and lifts my face with the slightest of pressure, his fingertips under my chin. "It is. But it's also a considerable investment of time in your community. Take the compliment, sweetness."

I blush. It's not mature or responsible. It's girlish and silly to let the compliment and the endearment work their way under my skin like this.

He strokes his thumb across my bottom lip, his eyes darkening as I sway toward him. "Not here," he murmurs. "Let's keep walking."

He takes my hand again, tugging me against him. Even though he's taller than me, we fall into a natural pace, and before long we've circled the block and we've arrived at the wide alley between the library and the community theater.

Picnic tables dot the space, and overhead there are strings of white lights, although this early in the morning, they aren't turned on yet.

Right now, we have the whole space to ourselves.

Main Street is just steps away, but Hunter has found me a private little nook for my first kiss.

Slowly, he backs me up against the brick wall, his gaze searching my face the whole time.

"Hunter," I breathe.

He strokes his knuckles along my jaw, then brushes his fingertips over my hair. Soft. And then his hand pushes into my hair, his hand closing around the loose strands, his fingers caressing my scalp before he closes them in a gentle fist. "Hold still, Kira."

"Cara," I whisper, but I don't think he hears me before his mouth descends on mine.

His lips are so warm in the cool misty morning, so strong and sure against my mouth that my heart leaps at the contact, flinging itself at this solid oak tree of a man who is giving me the soft, careful first kiss he promised.

Oh, how I love it.

He caresses my mouth with his, making me melt, and then he pauses. "More?"

The question is felt as much as it is heard.

"More," I whisper back, and I barely get it out before he tilts my head to the side, slants his lips over mine, and licks into my mouth.

Wild, glorious heat sparks inside me at the first stroke, shooting dizzying fireworks throughout my whole body.

I don't know what I was thinking someone else's tongue would feel like against my own, but this is better than anything I could have imagined. This is…incredible.

Panting, I clutch at him and kiss him back, licking deeply into his mouth, swallowing his groans.

He releases my hair, his hands sliding down my body and into my open coat and under my shirt.

At the first delicate swipe of his fingers on my waist, I gasp and then giggle.

"Ticklish?" he asks.

"I guess so," I breathe.

"Is this okay?" He firms up his touch, his thumb dragging against the bottom of my rib cage. This time, the reaction isn't that fluttery panic, but a deep, warm sizzle.

Oh. Oh yes.

"Mm-mmm," I say as I catch his lip between my teeth.

He groans.

And when he slides a thick, muscular thigh between my legs, I take it that he likes the biting, so I do it again.

He pushes his tongue into my mouth, down my throat, and I get it now. I get why people make out in the library stacks and on the couches in the common rooms.

I get why people abandon their studies to do nothing but

kiss, because I want to kiss this man forever and ever, and then at least a dozen times more after that.

His leg feels so good between my thighs. So very, very good.

I tip my head back, almost slamming into the brick wall, but he's got me. One of his hands immediately snaps up to cradle my head.

Plus, he tells me he does, and I believe him.

"I've got you. Daddy's got you," he breathes against my neck, and that's so electrically perfect I know it's okay that his other hand is moving up under my shirt, his thumb tracing small circles on the underside of my breast.

I tremble at the exploration, straddling the line between tickling and caressing.

My nipples pull tight, aching for that touch to be a little higher, a little harder.

His kisses trail down my neck to where my pulse is going a million miles an hour at the hollow of my collarbone, and then he groans into that spot and I feel it, I feel it in the matching throb against my hip.

He wants me.

He's not just giving me a kiss. This man…this man…he's *hard* for me.

And I'm riding his thigh like a cowgirl.

We've gone right past kissing to…

Is this second base?

I don't even know, but I like it, whatever it is.

"More," I beg. "Please, Daddy."

His hand goes firm on my ribcage. He groans, low and dark, and his hips jerk, pushing his thick cock harder against my body.

Just for a second.

But then, as if he's gone right to the edge of something dangerous, he freezes.

He inhales slowly, dragging in air as he presses his face into my neck.

And then his touch slides away from my breasts, his fingers trailing back down to my waist. They catch on the waistband of my jeans, and there's a deep tug inside my belly, shooting want straight between my legs, straight to where I'm pressed against his thigh. I rock my hips. Even as I know he's putting a stop to this, I can't stop myself from taking a final desperate bit of pleasure.

"Sweetness…" He drags in another, rougher breath and braces himself against the wall, his hands on either side of me now. His whole body shudders. "We have to stop."

"I'm sorry." I scramble to the side, under his arm and away from him. And somehow I manage to pace down the alley, even though my legs feel like they're made of jelly right now.

"Don't be sorry." He comes up behind me and sets his hands on my shoulders. Squeezes. Kisses the top of my head. "It's just that we're in public, and…"

"I got carried away."

"We both did. That was…" He curses under his breath. "I wasn't expecting that. You are incredible. That was, without a doubt, the best kiss of my entire life. I had no right enjoying it as much as I did."

"Really?" I turn around.

He looks down at me with a surprised expression that turns guarded as he searches my face. "Was it not good for you?"

"Oh. No, it was *so* good for me. You are…" I puff out my cheeks and laugh. "So fucking hot, pardon my French."

He laughs, too. "Okay. Good. I wanted it to be good for you. I… You…" He strokes my cheek with his knuckles.

A car horn on the street interrupts whatever he was going to say next.

He steps back and holds out his hand. "Can I walk you to the library front door?"

I slide my fingers through his. "I would love that. Thank you."

4
hunter

I'VE FUCKED UP. As I watch her walk into the library, I know without a shadow of a doubt that if I see this girl again, I'm putting a ring on her too-young, too-sweet, too-perfect finger. Fuck, I'm already picturing putting babies in her soft little belly.

I want all of her firsts. I want to be all of her onlys.

I'm almost twenty years older than her, and if I steal the best years of her life by keeping her for myself, I'll never forgive myself later on, when she regrets not having a very different life a younger man could give her.

There is only one option in front of me, and I fucking hate it.

5

cara

I FLOAT through my three hours of tutoring. I'm so tempted to pull out my phone and fire off a quick thank-you message to Hunter, but the flow of kids is non-stop, and I figure it's probably good not to be *that* eager.

Plus, just in case he's online when I message him, I'd rather be alone in my dorm room if we end up exchanging dozens of messages the way we did last night.

My cheeks feel like they're on fire by the time I get back to campus.

I called him *Daddy.* And he *liked it.*

I race up the stairs and throw myself through my door, locking it behind me for good measure.

Grinning like an idiot, I open the app and tap into my DMs.

And then my grin falls away.

Idiot is right, though.

Where Hunter's profile picture had been last night, now there's just a gray, anonymous illustration. A generic profile "picture".

Fingers shaking, I click on it to see our messages, but the chat thread won't even open. All I get is an error message pop up instead: this user cannot be found.

The best kiss of his life?
I don't think so.
But that jerk stole *my* first kiss and then ghosted me.
And right before Christmas, too.

6
hunter

Deleted accounts cannot be restored. Continue?

THOSE WORDS HAUNT ME NOW. I created another account almost immediately, regret pulsing through my veins, but I couldn't find her anywhere.

The app wasn't going to match us twice, because I'm not the right man for her.

It's been a week since our kiss, and Kira has snuck into my work—apple-cheeked beauties with dark, glossy hair suddenly the only characters I want to draw—and everywhere I go in town, I see couples with obvious, visible age gaps.

The barber has a young wife with a baby on the way. The lighthouse keeper, too—his young wife works at the retirement home where I volunteer a few times a month, drawing pictures of the residents.

And once the feverish guilt over how far I'd taken the kiss had passed, I'd realized that even in my own family, Wyatt and Heath are both older than their wife Emily—the gap between Heath and Emily even larger than my seventeen years on Kira.

All of them, men who are bolder and braver than I am.

As I'm waiting for my family to arrive on Christmas Eve, I

look up the tutoring sessions at the library. There isn't one this week, but they'll resume in the new year, and when they do, I'll be the first dummy to show up at her table and ask for help.

After the holiday break, I'm going to go there in person and explain why I went dark. And then ask her out on a real date. Not coffee and a dry hump in an alley. A proper, keep-my-hands-off-her date where I find out more about her and show her more about me and do whatever it takes to get a second chance.

Muscle memory has me swiping to the dating app, even though I know I won't find her. Frustration churns as I swipe through faces I'm not interested in. Mouths I don't want to kiss. Bodies I don't want to cradle in my arms, because they aren't the unique soft, lush shape I can still feel trapped against my chest if I close my eyes.

A text message to the family group chat slides down at the top of the screen, interrupting my pity party.

WYATT

On our way

And then another, not a surprise.

HANNAH

Running late, just picking up Cara now

My daughter is always running late.

I'm not sure what to make of this last-minute addition to our little family gathering. Hannah insists this friend is just that, a friend from school. A new bestie, she said, and not a date. Although she also insisted that this friend stay over and participate in all of the holiday moments with us, so I'm not sure I believe her denial.

My daughter is a chaotic energy demon of the best sort, and I've learned it's best to just roll with her ideas.

As a single dad who is a bit of a chaotic energy demon

himself—although I try to keep that locked down these days—I get it.

My brother arrives first, swinging a sprig of mistletoe. Right behind him is his husband Heath, who is laden down with bags of presents, and their wife Emily, who is carrying a trifle bowl bigger than her head.

I'd forgotten that she was going to make that. It slipped my mind in the Kira-obsession of the past week, which isn't like me. I've been completely family-focused for so long. To have this quiet distraction under my skin is very unlike me.

Wyatt is the reason Hannah and I settled just outside Conception Ridge a decade ago. Back then, it was just the three of us. Once I sold syndication and print rights of my most popular cartoon strip, I knew I wanted to use that once-in-a-lifetime advance to put down roots, and the Pacific Northwest now feels like home.

And then last year, Wyatt went and fell in love, not once but twice, in a wonderful surprise that almost doubled the size of our little family.

"Come on in," I say, take the monster-sized trifle. "What kind of gravy did you use?"

Emily rolls her eyes, but that joke slays with Heath. I know my audience.

"Tree is in the same place it was last year." I jerk my head toward the library.

Heath and Emily head that way. Wyatt hangs the mistletoe on a hook in the archway separating the foyer and the rest of the ground floor before he follows me into the kitchen.

The whole main floor of the split level rambling house is open, with a kitchen at one end and a library at the other, and in between a sunken family room.

It's a mid-century modern retro throwback to another time, an era I draw a lot in my comics, and I love it.

But it's too big for just me now that Hannah has moved into town for college.

That's partly why I demand to host the holiday get togethers.

The other reason is that I miss what we once had.

My kid is busy with her own life.

My brother is busy with his own family.

And I'm…alone.

Which might be too obvious today, or something, because Wyatt is looking at me carefully. "You okay, bro?"

"I'm fine," I snap, not prepared to tell my younger brother that I'm fucking lonely.

"Festive lying, I like it," he says with a grin.

Despite myself, I laugh. "Okay, I'm not…fine. But I will be."

"Work trouble?"

"No."

"Woman trouble."

I don't answer him.

His eyes light up. "Yessss. It's woman trouble!" He dances around in a circle, his arms raised over his head victoriously. "I can help with that. I'm so good at women now. Have you tried going down on her again after sex? Like, of course you go down on her before sex, right? But if you do it again *after*, she will love you forever."

"It's not—"

He gives me a pitying look. "Oh my God, are you not going down on her first, bro? Because—"

I slap my hand over his mouth. "There's no sex. Not…yet? I don't know."

His eyes bug out behind my hand. "Blue balls?" He whispers around my fingers.

Somehow, those two words carry all the way across the main floor to where Emily and Heath are putting presents under the tree in the library.

All of his cavorting around about oral sex didn't catch their attention, but the murmur of blue balls…now I have three pairs of eyeballs staring at me in concern.

"I—"

The doorbell rings.

I exhale in relief. "I'll get that."

My brother isn't wrong. He *is* good with women, or at least, he's great with Emily. All three of them are a relationship gold standard, and I could learn from them, although I didn't need the specifics. Like rubbing salt in a wound, because I'm so far from being able to bury my face between a lush pair of thighs, it's not funny.

First step is finding Kira again and apologizing.

Through the glass panel beside the front door, I see a blur of a person, and the color of the jacket pricks at my brain, like it's familiar, but I don't have time to process why that is before I pull the door open—

Shocked hazel eyes stare back at me.

Hannah tries to push her forward, but Kira doesn't move.

"Hi," I say hoarsely.

Hannah doesn't notice that we're both stunned. "Merry Christmas, Dad! We made it."

"You made it," I repeat dumbly.

"This is Cara." When I don't react, Hannah adds, "My lab partner and the smartest person on campus."

Her friend's pink cheeks go pale.

Her lab partner. I try to remember anything Hannah said about the girl she was bringing home for Christmas. I draw a complete blank. All my brain can remember right now is eager vanilla licks and gasping little pants that made my cock so hard I couldn't think straight. Friend. Friend. Daughter's friend. What the fuck.

"Cara?" I repeat her name like it's a question.

"Cara," she whispers, and I think she did that when we were kissing, too.

Is Hunter your real name?

She'd told me Kira wasn't her real name, but it was so damn close.

I nod, blood pounding in my veins, loud as a winter storm on the ocean in my ears. "Come on in, Cara. It's nice to meet you."

The words sound inauthentic and harsh, even to my own ears.

"I—" She takes a tiny step in, but no further than that.

Hannah rolls her eyes. "Dad, you're *looming*. Can you give my guest some space, please?"

Yes, space. That's what her friend needs. Space from Hannah's pervert dad, who was just thinking about how he'd stalk his daughter's friend in the new year and try to force a second date on a girl he didn't even know.

A girl who lied about her name, and probably her age, for sane security reasons. I'm not so far spun that I can't see that.

But at the same time, I thought she was twenty-five. And now, looking at her next to my nineteen-year-old daughter, I'm really fucking sure she isn't twenty-five at all.

"Don't worry, Care Bear, he's very nice and usually more talkative than this." Hannah glances past me as I take a giant stride back. "Uncle Wyatt is here?"

"Yeah," I say, distractedly. All I can see is Cara's panicked expression. "Sorry. I'm sorry, Cara." I hold her gaze and remember my fucking manners. And I do the right thing. "You are very welcome here. Any friend of Hannah is a part of our family."

As I step back, the damn mistletoe catches my eye. I'm going to have to take that down before she steps through the archway. "Hannah, why don't you take her upstairs and show her to her room? And then you can join us in the great room. We'd all like to get to know you better."

7
cara

HANNAH CHATTERS the whole way up the angular staircase. Apologizing for her dad, which is hilarious. She doesn't have any reason to apologize.

I'm the one who practically got to second base with him on Main Street a week ago.

"That's my dad's room down there," she says when we get to the top of the stairs. "He's in a wing of his own, basically. And then this used to be my room, but now we let Wyatt use it because it has a huge bed."

Right.

"So now my room is at the far end of the hall, which I don't really mind, actually, because I get my own en suite that way. Which leaves these two little rooms here as the random guest rooms. Not that you're random, Care Bear."

I'm not sure when Hannah decided I was nickname worthy. Maybe around midterms? Feels like a lifetime ago. We stayed up studying, and got a little punch drunk and silly. I called her Hannah Banana, and she laughed and laughed, rolling around on the floor, and then called me Care Bear.

I haven't called her the nickname again, but mine stuck.

She pushes open a door, revealing a truly small room, with a tiny twin bed on one wall and a dresser on the other. At the far end of the room is a mirror, leaning against brick, and above that is a wide transom window that runs the width of the room. Right now it's dark outside, but I imagine that in the morning, it will flood the room with light.

"I'll leave you to unpack." She hands me a gift bag. "And you don't need to wear them tonight. It's more of a morning thing, but…we do matching PJs."

"Pardon?"

"Christmas PJs. I bought you a pair, too."

"They match yours?"

"We all wear them. My dad, my uncle. His partners."

My head is spinning. "I… Where is a washroom?"

"Just down the hall," she says, stepping back into the hall. "Next to my dad's bedroom."

———

By the time I return downstairs, there's a lot of raucous laughter guiding me to the great room.

The stairs go back to the foyer, and from there, I turn the corner and find myself in an incredible living room that looks like it hasn't been updated since the 1960s. Okay, maybe the kitchen has been renovated, but very carefully.

Hunter is standing at a brass and glass drink cart, shaking a drink in a large silver container. He's wearing faded blue jeans that cling to thick thighs and a gray buttoned down shirt, rolled up to reveal thick forearms.

Behind him is a framed print of a goblin-like cartoon character wearing a little Santa hat.

Merry Fecking Christmas, it says in a speech bubble. *Fecking.* That's the favorite curse word of that character. What is its name?

I feel Hunter's gaze on my face, and my attention is dragged back to him. I try to smile, but I can't.

I'm sorry, I try to convey with my eyes. *I didn't know.*

He said sorry, too. At the door.

This is so awkward.

Everyone else is oblivious, at least for now, so that's some small comfort.

"Everyone, this is Cara," Hannah says loudly. "Cara, this is everyone."

I tear my attention away from him and wave nervously. "Hi. Thanks for inviting me."

"This is my Uncle Wyatt," she says, gesturing at a blonder, younger version of Hunter, sprawled on the longest part of a low sectional with a muscular older man, and a young woman sandwiched between them. "And Heath and Emily."

"Do you go to Ridge, too?" Emily asks.

I can feel Hunter staring at me, and my stomach drops. "Yes," I manage to whisper.

"I just graduated," she says. She brushes a dark curl off her cheek, and I notice she's wearing two matching rings in a stack on her left hand. "It's great, isn't it?"

I nod. That's all I can manage.

"Drink, Cara?" Hunter finishes pouring whatever he's just made, and hands it to Heath. But his attention is locked on my face, his expression hard and piercing. "I'm making hot chocolate martinis. Or maybe you're not old enough for that, yet?"

"Dad!" Hannah jumps up. "I'm going to make real hot chocolate for us kids."

Kill me now.

She drags me into the kitchen.

"Sorry about my dad," she whispers as she slams cabinets.

I need her to stop mentioning the fact that Hunter is her father every two seconds. It's making me die a little inside every time. *I called your dad Daddy, and he pushed his cock against my body because he wanted to fuck me! Merry Christmas!*

From across the room, he shoots a glower this way. As if it's my fault he has a daughter my age! What a jerk.

"My uncle says he's getting over a girl." Hannah shakes her head. "I didn't even know he was dating someone. But something must have happened in the last week, because now he's moody as fuck and he's got woman troubles." She does air quotes around the last two words.

My insides flip over. "Oh?"

"I swear, he's never like this." She slams a pot down on the stove.

Out of the corner of my eye, I see him pour another drink, then square his shoulders and head our way.

"Incoming," I whisper.

She giggles, which makes me smile despite myself.

As he strides across the great room and bounds up the three steps to the kitchen level, I can't help myself from looking. Staring, really. He's...massive. Tall, with big arms and even bigger legs, and a thick torso that I can still feel against my fingertips from when I curled my fists into his shirt.

"Hannah, stop being so theatrical," he says as he joins us, carefully not making eye contact with me. "Your guest is going to get the wrong impression."

"Oh no, Cara," she says in a pseudo-whisper. "You might figure out that I'm *dramatic*."

I press my lips together.

"She *knows*, Dad. She's put up with me all term. Got me a B+, too." She taps her temple. "Smart."

Now his attention snaps to me, and it's like all the air in the entire house is sucked out in a powerful vacuum.

Hannah stirs the milk she's heated on the stove. "This needs a splash of something. *Just a splash*, Father. Like a cooking ingredient. Don't say no, I won't even listen to you."

She darts past him, taking a running leap into the living room, heading for the liquor cart.

"How many broken bones did she have as a kid?" I ask.

"Three, all well-earned," he mutters. "Cara, we need to talk."

"Nothing to talk about." I feel like I might spontaneously combust. He made it clear he didn't want to date someone as young as *twenty-five*, so to find out that I'm not even twenty must be killing him. "Mistakes were made. Consequences are being felt. We'll survive."

Startled surprise slashes across his face, softening his hard mouth at the corners. "Will we?"

I take a deep breath and nod. "Yes." I'm going to will myself to not give in to the embarrassment of this moment. "But if this is too weird, I can go."

"God, no." He reaches out and curls his hand around my elbow. Unwelcome heat slams into me, and matching sparks light up his gaze. His fingers press into my flesh, caressing the inside of my upper arm for a second before Hannah returns, waving a bottle of Amaretto, and he drops his hand. "I don't want you to go anywhere," he says under his breath. "Please stay. I... I want you to stay. I need to explain why I—"

"How much, Care Bear?" Hannah pulls me away from her dad before he can finish.

"Just a splash." I swallow hard. "I don't really drink much."

She laughs.

I don't laugh.

And from his careful, watching perch just down the counter, Hunter doesn't laugh, either.

8
hunter

HANNAH DOESN'T LEAVE Cara's side again. They pour their hot chocolate into mugs, and then we rejoin Wyatt's family in the living room.

It turns out that Cara's career focus is environmental science, and Heath co-owns a construction company that specializes in passive solar design, so it doesn't take long before they're deep in discussion.

Which leaves me to sip my drink and watch her be beautiful and smart and fascinating.

She's wearing a silky black top with little slitted cap sleeves that curve over her shoulders and leave the rest of her soft arms bare. If I stare hard enough, I think I can see the imprint of my fingers where I grabbed her and begged her not to leave.

"Dinner won't be much longer," I say abruptly, interrupting everyone's conversation.

I'm unsettled. I'm restless.

I need to drag Cara off to my den so we can talk, but I can't. Not without raising Hannah's suspicions, and once I do that, she'll be like a dog with a bone—and once she finds out I kissed her classmate, I'll never hear the end of it.

And I don't know how Cara will be treated, either.

That has to be my top priority: making sure she is our guest of honor tonight. Nothing else.

"What are we having for dinner?" Cara asks.

"Italian," I say. "Lasagna, specifically. But I have lots of other options if you don't like—"

"Lasagna is great," she says quickly.

"He's being modest," Wyatt says. My brother never misses an opportunity to be anyone's hype guy. "He'll have so much food the table will groan. Did you make those yummy little roaches this year?"

Even if the hype involves unnecessary insect mentions. "Goat-cheese stuffed dates wrapped in prosciutto," I translate for Cara, heat racing up the back of my neck at her wide-eyed confusion.

"They look like bugs," Hannah offers, trying to help.

Cara's expression turns to outright distress.

Fuck. Me.

"There's also prosciutto-wrapped melon, and some tomato and mozzarella appetizers, too," I say desperately. "I'm going to work on those."

While I'm putting out the appetizer trays, and trying to make the dates look less bug-like, Hannah comes in and refills her hot chocolate mug.

I don't bother pointing out that she's probably ruining her appetite for dinner.

The sooner dinner is over, the better. Then the Christmas movie watching can begin and I can disassociate until midnight.

Maybe we'll make it through this night without my filthy fantasies about her lab partner being revealed.

But nobody in my family understands that I want dinner to be over quickly. Hell, they won't even let it begin.

They all take their sweet time coming to the table. They

linger in the kitchen, admiring the two lasagnas I made, nibbling at the appetizers, and pouring another round of drinks.

"These really do look like bugs," Cara says suspiciously, looking at the wrapped dates. She's switched to water, smart girl.

"You have to try one," Wyatt urges, popping one in his own mouth. "Fuuuuuccck."

Emily giggles.

Heath grunts.

Hannah narrows her eyes. "Don't make sex noises, Uncle Wyatt."

Cara's cheeks turn scarlet and she stuffs a date in her mouth. Her eyes flare wide and her lips purse in a way that makes me lean in. "Oh," she moans softly around it. The bright red cheeks soften to a pleased pink. "Ohhh…"

Hannah throws her hands in the air. "Et tu, Cara?"

"So good," our guest mumbles, grabbing another one. "Why are they so good?"

I'm gripping the island so hard I'm surprised the granite doesn't crack.

She likes the sweet and salty combination. I'll remember that. I'm going to remember every single second of this night. Even the awkward parts where she won't look at me. Those drive a dark, possessive part of my inner beast, who knows she's scared and just wants to soothe her.

Emily pours a glass of Prosecco and hands one to Cara as well.

I make a strangled sound before I can stop myself.

"I don't need that," she says in a hurry, putting it down.

Hannah glares at me.

So I'm forced to circle around to Cara and pick it up, press it back into her hand, and ignore the way my heart twists when her fingers graze mine. "Please," I grind out. "We're all having a bit."

"Thank you," she whispers.

I watch as she takes a careful sip, her lips touching the flute nervously.

There was nothing nervous about the way she kissed me. Her hot-blooded reaction to our kiss stunned me, and I ran scared.

And then she showed up on my doorstop, sending me spinning for a second time because she's not a twenty-five-year-old college employee. She's a student, an undergrad like Hannah, and I'm a lot older than her than I originally thought.

That's not scaring me away, though.

It fucking should.

I shouldn't be imagining those perfect plush lips kissing their way down my chest and teasing me until she wraps them around my cock.

"Dad!"

"What?" I drag my attention to Hannah.

"Should I put the lasagnas on the table?"

"They're heavy. Wyatt, put them on the table. Hannah, grab the salad."

She rolls her eyes.

I'm brooding as I take my usual seat. Hannah puts Cara at the opposite end of the table, and I fucking hate it.

I want her beside me.

Hell, I want everyone else gone, and I want her on top of the table.

Need to give her a Christmas kiss on all her festive parts.

What you need to do is talk to her, you idiot. Apologize for putting her in this position and then swear you'll never touch her again.

Maybe when we get into the movie watching, I can give her a tour of the house. Show her my studio and barricade us in there until she accepts my apology.

Except if I do that, I'll definitely pull her into my arms. Wedge my leg between her thighs and make her ride me again, like she did in that alley.

I can't tear my eyes from her as I pass the salad and bread

past me. Wyatt puts a piece of lasagna on my plate, but I barely touch it.

"This is delicious," Cara says.

Wyatt grins at her and tops up her glass of Prosecco. "Hunter takes good care of us."

Her gaze flits my way for a second, then drifts away. Comes back, searching. Then gone again.

Don't look away, I want to demand. *Look at me. Ask the question that's on the tip of your tongue. Ask it here, and now. In front of my family. Ask me why I dirty deleted my account. Make me admit I was scared.*

And making me admit shit isn't what she needs. That's what I want.

It's what I've wanted since I swiped across her profile, impressed and more than a little worried about her guileless honesty.

I never drop into anyone's DMs. In two years of trying to date, I've had nothing but dud experiences, and I'd basically given up. But this girl needed to know that her bio needed a bit more…cynicism.

Instead, she talked me into being her first kiss.

Her first fucking kiss, Hunter. You really believed she was twenty-five?

Fuuuuuck.

If I'm being honest with myself, I was a goner when she called me Daddy in the text message chain.

What did she say to me in the kitchen? Now we're experiencing the consequences of our choices?

Yeah.

Fuck indeed.

Cara takes another small sip of wine, her tongue swiping against her bottom lip after she drinks, and my cock goes so hard under the table I swear my face must drain of blood because it's all needed elsewhere.

She is a stunningly beautiful woman, and under any under

any other circumstances I would be falling over myself to kneel at her feet. *Tell Daddy what you need, sweet girl.* It would be a fucking honor to take care of her. Except for two inconvenient facts: she is my daughter's friend and classmate; and I am, without a doubt, not worthy of her. She's out of my league. I mean, she's *really* out of my league, because she's too young for me, but also smarter than me, and has her whole life ahead of her.

I'm just a middle-aged guy who draws sarcastic comics.

"That's it. That's our Christmas tradition!" Hannah claps her hands. "Dad feeds us far too much food."

A middle-aged guy who draws sarcastic comics and gives his family stomachaches.

"And then Wyatt and I insist on decorating the house a bit more than the nothing that he has already done."

Oh come on. I have to protest that. "What? I got a Christmas tree! And I put up Hannibal's Christmas portrait!"

Hannah shakes her head. "Dad, for someone who cares so much about Christmas, you don't have any outdoor lights. You don't even have any mistletoe."

An electric spark zaps up my spine and I look at Cara, watching our exchange with wide eyes. There has never been any need for mistletoe in this house before tonight.

Kiss Daddy goodnight.

I could use some mistletoe.

"It's okay, bud, I've got you," Heath says. "I brought back the lights that we bought last year, that you very helpfully took down for us and returned."

I glance over at Heath. "You didn't want those lights up at your house?"

Heath grins. "I bought him a separate set of matching lights for our house, man. Love makes the grumpiest of us do fun things."

Hannah gives Cara a pointed look. "So we'll eat dinner, and then Wyatt and I are going to put up those Christmas lights."

Emily and Heath exchange a knowing look. "We'll supervise the Christmas lights."

"Oh, thank God," I say with a smile.

Hannah rolls her eyes and continues, undeterred in her mission to fully explain the evening to her friend. "And then we usually watch Christmas movies and have some fun dessert. What is it this year, Dad? An affogato cart?"

Wyatt looks at me, confused.

"An ice cream sundae bar," I translate for him.

He pumps his fist. "Aww, yeah. Love that. But um, what about Emily's trifle?"

"Fuck," I growl.

I forgot about the trifle when I bought the ice cream and toppings. And then I forgot about it a second time after Cara arrived on my doorstep.

Hannah sighs.

Emily laughs.

Wyatt looks genuinely confused.

From the other end of the table, Cara is now giggling openly at all of us. Her laugh is better than the gleeful rustling of paper on Christmas morning. And hearing it again is suddenly all I can think about.

Getting her alone so I can hear it privately is my top priority.

"We do have two dessert options tonight, that's true. Emily made a gorgeous-looking trifle," I say. "But I forgot about that, so I also got the supplies for an affogato cart."

"That sounds really specific," Heath says. "Inspired by something?"

Oh, if he only knew. I stare at Cara until she gives me her gaze, and then I say, "I guess I've been craving the combination of sweet vanilla and dark coffee all week. I had that specific combination last weekend for the first time ever, and it's all I can think about now."

9
cara

I CAN'T BREATHE.

Hunter is staring at my mouth. Hannah is staring at her dad. Wyatt is whispering something to Emily that is making her blush, and Heath is doing a slow, analytical look around the table that feels like we're about to be revealed in some terrible way.

"That just sounds so…weird," Hannah pronounces. "Vanilla ice cream and *coffee*?"

"It's a thing," Heath says dryly. "Maybe not for you, though."

"Definitely not," she agrees. "I'll have Emily's trifle. But maybe not just yet. Is anyone else stuffed?"

"I've always got room for something delicious," Wyatt drawls.

He's got his hand tangled in Emily's hair now, and his thumb is stroking along her jaw.

Heath clears his throat.

Wyatt looks at him, and they exchange something wordless. "Or maybe we should wait for dessert," he finally says slowly, letting go of his wife.

"If you're going to insist on decorating my house, you might want to do it before Hannah's hot chocolate really kicks in," Hunter says.

Hannah and her Uncle Wyatt swiftly agree that the affogato sundae bar and trifle dessert extravaganza would be better *after* hanging Christmas lights, so before I know it, they're bundling up to go outside and Heath and Emily are gamely following suit.

"Dad, do you have any snow pants that Cara could borrow?" Hannah asks.

"No. Go outside," he barks in her direction, but his eyes are locked on me, his gaze a hot warning to stay inside with him.

I can't really argue. I didn't dress for hanging Christmas lights in the wet Christmas Eve sleet. And I don't want to go outside with the others. I feel compelled to stay inside with Hunter, even as I'm afraid of what he's going to say.

So while they clamour about at the front door, I busy myself with the dishes.

"You don't have to do those," Hunter says as he brings the leftover lasagna into the kitchen.

"I don't mind. I'm happy to chip in." Plus, it gives me something to do with my hands.

"Please stop."

I stop. But I don't look at him. With how quiet the house suddenly is, that feels…risky.

"Cara." He says my name with a confused kind of wonder that slides under my skin and takes hold. A promise that maybe, actually, he's not mad at me for being Hannah's classmate.

He exhales, low and slow, and it's a sound I never want to forget. It's steady and careful, just like the way he made our kiss happen. This is who I want to remember Hunter as, this kind of man. Someone…affected by me. Someone raw and human. "You need to know that I wanted to see you again."

I can't hold in my disbelief. "Is that why you deleted your profile?"

"Yes."

Startled, I lift my head and find Hunter glaring.

Not at me. There's nothing sharp in his gaze pointed in my direction. His glare feels...protective. Stern. And he's obviously aware that it's not how he should be looking right now. But frustration still ticks in his jaw even as his expression softens. "I don't know how to say this now that you're here, because I don't want you to leave. I really, really don't want you to leave."

"Why?"

He shakes his head. "Don't make me lead with that. That's not... It's not... logical."

I laugh again, unexpectedly delighted at how wound tight he seems. "Not logical?"

"It makes no sense. I mean, other than you're fucking beautiful and I have eyes."

"Oh." I swipe the tip of my tongue across my lower lip, processing the raw confession. He thinks I'm beautiful. "And you were like, I can't kiss her again, she's too nice to look at?"

He groans and shoves his hands into his hair. "Yes. And also that you were too young."

"Ah." That hurts. Because if he thought I was too young when my dating profile said I was twenty-five, then he can't be a fan of how old I really am.

"I wanted you more than I should. I wanted you so much it felt wrong."

That hurts even more. Numbly, I nod, then look away from him, seeking anything else to focus on.

Outside the floor to ceiling windows, four people are arguing over light strands. That should be funny, probably. But it just feels surreal.

"But the second I deleted the account, it felt way more wrong. I created a new one that night, but I couldn't find you again."

"I, uh..." I wave my hand. "Removed myself. When I went

to send you another message and I saw the message about the account being deleted, I knew it wasn't the app for me."

Because the whole thing had been humiliating.

"Shit. Cara, I'm sorry."

I shrug. "I'll get over it."

"I won't. I should have thought about how it would feel to you. I'm sorry that I didn't." His voice gets even deeper, and he comes around the island. Suddenly very close. Very big. "I wish like hell I'd still been online when you got back that afternoon. I want to know what you'd have said."

"I don't know anymore. I can't remember." I lift my chin. Defiance feels safer than vulnerability.

Regret slashes across his face.

From outside, there's a shriek.

He pauses, closes his eyes, and mutters under his breath.

I smile slightly, but swipe it away before he blinks and twists to look out at the progress. "They're fine," he says.

"So am I," I manage to say. "You don't need to be sorry anymore. It's fine."

"But I want more for you than just fine." He closes the gap between us and plants one hand on the counter beside me, and brings the other one up to ghost beside my upper arm. Not quite touching me, but almost.

Heat radiates between us, and my breathing goes shallow.

"Hunter," I whisper.

"What would make you happy, Cara? What do you need?"

10
hunter

CARA PARTS HER LIPS, and my gut pulls tight in anticipation of whatever she's going to say, but at that exact moment, my dumb-ass brother falls off a ladder with a loud clattering thud, and this time the shrieks are urgent.

A tap on the window is next, as Heath alerts me that he needs a hand helping Wyatt inside.

"I'm fine," my brother protests as he hops between us, his arms slung over our shoulders.

I'm this close to banning the word *fine* from Christmas Eve.

"Stand on your left foot then, you idiot," I snap.

"I mean, I will be fine." He sighs. "I might need to sleep on the couch, though."

"We can make that happen."

"I'll sleep down there with you," Emily says, hurrying along beside us.

"But then who will keep Heath warm?" Wyatt worries.

"All three of you can sleep downstairs," Hannah suggests. "But remember, there's no door."

"Hannah," I bark.

"What?"

"Stop it. They're grownups."

"But I'm not," she pouts. "And I don't—"

"You are a grownup, actually," Wyatt points out. "You can vote and everything."

"Not everything. I can't drink yet."

"Your spiked hot chocolate suggests otherwise." I gesture at the front door. "Now open—"

But it swings wide just as I say that, Cara apparently at the ready.

"I brought a chair to the foyer in case he wants to sit for a minute," she says sweetly.

"Oh, bless you." Wyatt sinks into it and exhales dramatically.

Danes are nothing if not dramatic at every turn.

"What would help?" Emily frets, worried about her man.

He catches her hand and pulls her close. "A kiss. And some trifle."

"He's going to be fine," I say. "Everybody inside. Let's go."

Hannah goes ahead to the living room and cues up *Home Alone*, the first Christmas movie of the evening.

Cara and I follow, leaving the threesome alone in the foyer for a few minutes. Cara sits next to Hannah, and I take the opposite couch, but I ache to have her curl up next to me.

Also, I feel like my thoughts are written all over my face, and it's fucking uncomfortable.

When Wyatt hobbles into view, it's a relief. "Told you I'm fine," he says cheerfully. "And I put up the mistletoe again, Hunter. Don't be such a Scrooge. Is it trifle time?"

He carefully makes it to the couch, then Emily brings the trifle into the living room. "Who wants some?"

Heath does.

Hannah does.

But when Emily asks Cara, her gaze slides over to me. "I might just want some vanilla ice cream," she says softly, hazel eyes glittering. "If that offer still stands?"

It stands forever and ever, amen.

"I've got a few options for you," I manage to say calmly, off-limits desire surging. "They're in the freezer in the garage. It might be better if I showed you?"

We both stand, and nobody is watching us as I lead her from the room—they're all focused on the trifle—but I still feel like there's a spotlight on us.

The college coed and her lab partner's dad.

Heart pounding, I cross the foyer and hold the door to the garage open for her. She steps through, brushing right past me. She smells so good it makes my mouth water, and if she really only wants ice cream, I'm going to have to crawl into the deep freeze myself.

"You've got your choice of—" I start to say as the door swings shut.

But the second it's closed, she takes my hand, pulling me right up against her, and *thank Christ.*

I wrap my free arm around her waist, savouring the soft press of her curves against me. Holding her tight, because she's mine. Mine mine mine.

My secret need.

She tips her face up to meet mine as I curve over her. "You owe me a really good kiss for Christmas," she whispers. "You ruined the first one by ghosting me. And you just led me under the mistletoe without kissing me there, too."

"I'm so fucking sorry." I slant my mouth across hers, eager to make this right. She moans as I find her tongue, soft lips opening wide. She presses up into our embrace, surging to me, making my head spin. Her need is just as strong as mine, and she twines her arms around my neck, arching her back. Pushing her soft, full tits into my chest.

I want to squeeze and grope and explore every last inch of her, but—

The door squeaks open.

Cara spins away from me so fast I'm basically making out with mid air when Heath steps into the garage.

He takes one look at me, then a quick glance at Cara, then clears his throat. "Can you bring in chocolate ice cream?"

"Yep," Cara says brightly.

I can't form words. There's no blood in my brain, it's all below my belt.

He steps back into the house, the door swinging shut.

Cara presses her lips together and gives me a helpless look. "Oops," she whispers.

I'm not sure how to read her reaction. Heart pounding, I pull her back against me. Even with the risk of being caught, it feels better to have her in my arms than not. "Are you okay with them knowing? Because Heath and Wyatt and Emily don't have any secrets from each other. Their relationship is so honest it's frankly awkward for anyone else around them."

"I know. That's why I'm here." Cara grimaces and pats my chest, her fingertips curling instinctively like she wants to sink her claws into me. I wonder if she knows she's doing that. "Hannah thought it would be less awkward if there was someone else for balance here. Little did she know, she invited someone who had kissed her dad."

"Technically, her dad kissed you," I say. I don't want my active part in this to be minimized. I kissed her behind the library. I kissed her here in the garage. I'm going to kiss her a lot of places, and my daughter just needs to deal with it.

"Probably isn't going to make her Christmas better if you put it that way." Cara shakes her head. Her eyes sparkle as she slowly backs away from me, heading for the garage door.

"Hang on." I wave at the freezer. "We can't forget the ice cream."

Her cheeks flame. "Right."

I cross to her and kiss her again, then murmur, "Stop blushing. I'm not going to be able to keep my hands off you."

She sucks in an eager little breath. "I don't want you to."

God damn it. I cup her cheek and brush my thumb over her

sweet lower lip. "Can you be a good girl for me tonight and stay up?"

She exhales, her breath warm against my thumb, and electricity arcs between us. "Yes," she whispers, her glittering gaze turning to pure fire. "I'll wait up for you, Daddy."

11
cara

IT IS AGONIZING to go back to the living room and watch holiday movies after the too brief, interrupted kiss.

I need more. I feel like I'm on fire.

And Hunter's gaze is always, always on me.

All of my most secret fantasies feel fully on display for him, as if *Daddy's horny girl* is tattooed on my bare skin.

Two movies and three dessert breaks later, Hannah finally yawns and announces it is bedtime.

"Santa will be coming soon," she says happily.

I wonder if I should feel some kind of shame for the wicked thrill that goes through me as she says that.

I don't. At all.

I follow her upstairs, and promise to wear my matching PJs in the morning. I go into the little spare bedroom and lay down on the bed, heart galloping a mile a minute. There's no way I'm wearing the PJs she picked out to secretly meet up with Hunter tonight, so I leave my regular clothes on. Then I listen to the house settle, to Hunter going up and down the stairs a few times, bringing bedding down to Wyatt and crew in the living room.

Doors open and close. Water runs.

And then silence falls over the house like a cozy down blanket.

According to my phone, it's only been about fifteen minutes since Hannah went to bed, which isn't nearly enough time, but my body is aching to go to Hunter now.

I play a puzzle game on my phone. Lose badly.

Listen to the quiet nothing of the house.

Try to play again. Give up.

Finally, when it's been twenty-three minutes and also a lifetime, I ease the door open, step into the dark hallway, and run smack into Hunter at the top of the stairs. He's taken off his buttoned-down shirt, and is now just wearing a t-shirt over jeans. He's also carrying a giant sack.

He gives me a wide grin. "Hi," he whispers.

"What are you doing?" I whisper back.

"Playing Santa."

That's freaking adorable. And it feels maybe a decade late. "I hate to break it to you, but Hannah knows that the North Pole isn't a real place."

"I mostly do it for Wyatt."

I giggle. That's fair.

He jerks his head. "Can you find my room?"

Heat races through me and I nod.

"Go on then." His gaze slides over my body, and he smiles in a deeply satisfied way that turns that rioting heat into something even more intense. "I'll be right there."

I walk past the bathroom at the end of the hallway and turn into the wing Hannah pointed to earlier.

Hunter's private space.

A light was left on inside, a warm glow that pulls me deeper into the room. There's a bed at the far end, but before that is a sitting area with an oversized reading chair, a large full-length mirror next to a door that looks like it goes to a walk-in closet, and on the other wall, a lot of framed art. In the centre of the sprawling display is a large illustration that catches my eye, of the same cartoon character in the framed print downstairs, but this sketch is rougher. And he's sitting next to a little girl.

"Hannibal the Unterrible's ignoble beginning," Hunter says quietly from behind me. "Hannah always wanted a brother. But he morphed into a grumpy little tyrant. Which maybe would have happened with an actual sibling, too."

I turn around. "Hannibal the Unterrible," I repeat, looking at my first kiss in a whole new light. "I couldn't remember his name. He was a big deal."

Hunter shrugs a little, but he looks proud.

"So when you said you're an illustrator…"

"You might be familiar with some of my work."

"They made this into a *movie*."

"They sure did."

"That's…" Well, that explains why Hannah drives a nice car. "Very cool."

He puts his hand on the door. "Can I close this?"

A tremor of anticipation ripples through me and I nod. "How did the Santa Claus mission go?"

"They all pretended to be asleep downstairs."

I smile. "That's cute."

"Wyatt likes you, you know. And my brother is an excellent judge of character." Hunter's gaze searches my face. "My daughter likes you, too."

"I know." I worry my bottom lip. "The nickname was a strong clue."

"Practically kidnapping you and demanding you attend her family holiday gathering was another one?"

"Yeah." I nod. "Is she always that…forceful?"

"Only if she loves you."

"I…" I don't know how to tell Hunter that my relationship with Hannah is a bit lopsided.

He smiles softly. "It's okay if you don't love her back in the same way."

"She's just a lot."

"She is."

"Raising her must have been hell."

"No." He shakes his head. "I mean, yes. To the outside observer, that's a likely guess. But no. I love being Hannah's dad. I love how willful she is. It's going to take her far in life, even if it does sometimes knock the wind out of anyone trying to make her slow down."

I blink in surprise. It's not what I expected him to say. It's... better.

And the guilt that missed me earlier now floods my chest like a dam burst.

I have been a horrible friend to Hannah. "She really is remarkable." A lump forms in my throat. "And, um... I should go back to my room."

"Why?" He frowns. "Cara, wait—"

"I can't get between you and Hannah." I shake my head and go to step around him. "She might not believe in Santa anymore, but she still believes you are the world's greatest dad, and I can't be a part of ruining that for her. Or for you, for that matter. If we do anything more than what we've already done, I think you'll regret it in the morning."

12

hunter

OH, fuck no.

I catch Cara's wrist as she tries to slip by. "Wait. Don't go back to bed just yet. I'm not going to regret anything, I swear."

She glances at the closed door. Down the hall, my daughter is sleeping.

And fuck, I know she thinks it's wrong, but the jolt of off-limits temptation doesn't stop me. If anything, it fires me up. It just underlines how right our connection is.

"Cara, I'm a grown man. I won't deny that I was shocked to see *you* when I opened the door, because for the last week, *you* have been wholly separate from the rest of my life. A fantasy. But that was just a stupid, immediate reaction. I've spent the rest of the night thinking about you. All of you. Not a fantasy, not my daughter's friend, but the very real woman in front of me. And I've been looking at you in this silky top, wanting to unwrap you. It can't be a coincidence that you show up on my doorstep on Christmas Eve. Even if you had to be delivered here by my daughter."

Cara huffs a little protesting breath. "Then maybe it's just me who has a problem with looking her in the eye, knowing that I've called her dad Daddy."

I laugh. God, that's funny. Genuinely. "Okay, fair deal. Call me Hunter if you'd rather."

Her lower lip plumps out in a pout.

I lean in, heart pounding with confident anticipation. "You don't want to, do you?"

She shakes her head a little. "No," she admits.

"Then we have a little secret to keep, don't we?"

Desire wars with the duty of friendship, and she twists her face.

I keep pressing my case. "Cara, I don't deserve you as my Christmas present, but I won't deny that I want you anyway. I want to unwrap every inch of you and give you more kisses to make up for the fact that I disappeared. And as for my daughter… Don't you think I should teach Hannah that love is worth waiting for?"

Cara's eyes widen. "What are you—"

"I told you it was illogical." I circle my thumb on the inside of her wrist, feeling her delicate pulse flutter against my touch. "But the reason I backed off after our first kiss is that I knew I was already a goner. I knew if I kissed you a second time, I'd want forever, and that wasn't fair to put on you at such a young age."

She stares at me as she brings her free hand to her lips. Remembering how insanely good that kiss was, I hope.

"That was something special. Something worth holding on to. Kisses are never like that, Cara. You have to take my word for that, because I'm not letting you kiss a bunch of creepy toads to find out for yourself."

She giggles despite her shock.

I lift her other hand and press it to my chest, right over my heart. "This isn't the setting I pictured for this conversation. I swear. I planned to come and find you at the library at your next tutoring session. Ask for help with an apology letter, but I'd already have it written."

She turns a little, enough to take in my bed in the shadows of the room. "This is a lot more private than the library."

"You can go back to your room if you want," I say hoarsely. "But I'll come find you at the library, then. And it'll get awkward there, too."

"Awkward is sort of our thing, apparently?" She frowns. I take her face in my hand and soothe her furrowed brow. She bites her lower lip again, her gaze locked on my face, and I ease it out from between her teeth with my thumb.

"I don't think awkward is that bad," I murmur before I kiss that wounded flesh. So gently. "If we can survive Christmas with the whole Dane clan, that's a pretty good start to forever, don't you think?"

She gasps against my mouth.

I take that as a yes, and turn her around so we're facing the full-length mirror where most days, I just check to make sure I'm basically presentable for the world.

Tonight, for the first time ever, I'm not alone in this reflection.

"Do we look awkward together?"

A gorgeous smile blooms across her face. "No."

I press my lips to her temple, heart pounding. "Do I look too old for you?"

Slowly, she shakes her head. "No."

"Do I look like a man who wants to give you the entire world at your feet?"

She laughs.

"I'm serious."

She studies our reflections.

I'm taller than her, and wider, too. But she's no little slip of a thing. She's a solid stack of curves. My cock thickens as my hands graze down her bare arms, my fingers itching to touch more of her.

Her shoulders roll back and her head tilts to the side. She's really thinking about this, really watching us as I caress her arms. I drop my hands to her hips, touching, squeezing…

Her breathing changes.

Still watching.

I sweep my touch to her belly, filling my hands with her silky shirt and the soft flesh beneath it. Up, up, up, until my hands are just beneath her breasts, both of them, my fingers aching to curve over her tits.

"Hunter," she whispers. "I don't understand."

I'm not surprised by her uncertainty. I, on the other hand, have the context of a lifetime without her, so I have more bone-deep confidence in this rightness.

"Oh, sweet girl." I press my face into her hair. "Don't you? Can't you feel what you do to Daddy?"

She moans, which I'll take as a yes.

"You know when I knew you were mine?" I kiss her temple, her cheek, nosing at her until she tips her head all the way to the side so I can kiss her neck. "The moment I saw your profile as you strode past me up to the counter in the coffee shop. I was so fucking nervous you wouldn't give me a second glance. I thought for sure you'd come over and realize immediately you'd made a huge mistake."

"That's not at all what I was thinking." She shakes her head a little, her aroused gaze tracking my touch in the mirror.

I slide my hand under her shirt, remembering where she is ticklish, and being careful as I fill my palm with her warm flesh. "What did you think?"

"I thought, *thank God I lied about my age.*"

I half-laugh, half-groan. "Fuck."

"And I still wasn't old enough for you!" She twists away from me.

But I catch her wrists again.

We can play this game all night.

I'm smiling down at her as I back her up against the mirror. "I don't care about your age now."

She gives me an uncertain look. "Are you absolutely sure?"

I press her hands to my chest. "Feel that?"

"What?"

"My steady heartbeat."

She smiles. "Yes."

"Cara." I hold her gaze. Steady steady steady. "I fucked up our first chance because I cared about the wrong things. I will not make that mistake again, I swear to God. I am deeply attracted to *you*. You are singular and special, and nothing is going to stop me from owning that feeling."

She takes a deep breath. "I have to ask you something."

"Anything."

She swallows hard. "What if Hannah doesn't like us together? Not even *if*. She *won't* like us together."

I lift her hand to my mouth and kiss her palm. "There will be a storm, no doubt. But I will be your shelter from it. She can be mad at *me*, not you. And we'll ride it out together. I'm not letting you go. She'll get over any outrage she feels, and then she'll see how I feel about you."

Her hand curls against my jaw, her fingers stroking my cheek. "Okay."

Now my steady heartbeat takes off at a gallop. "Okay?"

"Oh. Kay." She exhales with wonder. "I guess I'm your Christmas present." Her eyelashes brush her cheek for a moment before she looks up at me again, coyly this time. "If you still want to unwrap me, Daddy?"

My hands are already on her, greedy and demanding. While I kiss her deeply, my fingers find a hidden zipper down the back of her shirt and work it down, down, down, revealing a warm slice of skin bisected by what feels like a lacy bra.

She whimpers into my mouth as I work the loosened satin up over her breasts, and then release her mouth long enough to bring it up over her head.

Then I look down.

"Oh fuck me," I groan, getting my first proper look at Cara's breasts, heavy and full in a black lace bra.

"I will eventually," she says shyly. "Although you might be doing the fucking first?"

I blink in disbelief. At the perfection of her. At the shy sex joke. At the fucking *gift* of her half-naked in my bedroom.

"Marry me," I growl, picking her up.

"Oh God, Hunter, don't—" She flings her arms around my neck as I wrap her thighs around my waist.

"Don't what?" I carry her to my bed and set her down on the edge of the mattress.

She clings to me, shaking her head. "I wasn't sure you could pick me up."

I laugh. "Ah, sweetness. Holding you in my arms is the easiest thing in the world. You make me feel ten feet tall and as strong as—"

"An oak tree?" She squeezes my shoulders. "That's what I thought when you kissed me the first time."

"I'll be your oak tree. I'll be anything you need."

"I need more kisses," she says shyly.

I roll to the side, pulling her with me so we stretch out together on the mattress. "Come here, then."

She gives me her lips, eager and soft, and I pour into this kiss everything I'm feeling, because I can't rush my girl into anything else.

If all we do tonight is make out, I will be the luckiest man in the world.

As our first tastes stretch into breath-stealing deep kisses, I roam my hands over her bare arms and back and tummy, caressing her everywhere her bra isn't covering. Tension radiates through me, and it's so hard to hide from her. She squirms closer, rocking her hips into my obvious erection, even through both of our jeans.

"I thought you were going to unwrap me," she whispers as she pulls my hand to the button on her jeans.

I shudder, need ripping through me. With a flick of my fingers, the button is open and her jeans are unzipped.

She gasps and I kiss her again, holding her against me as I push my hand into the back of her jeans to cup her ripe, lush ass.

"Cara, my Cara," I growl as I roll her onto her back.

I rear up on my knees, looking down at her with unrestrained hunger now. Her chest is rising and falling unevenly, but her gaze is locked on me and her eyes are glittering with desire.

"Hips up, pretty girl," I murmur as I hook my fingers on her jeans and ease them off her. Under the denim, she's wearing blue cotton panties, and once the jeans are flung over my shoulder, I settle my hands on her hips and just....look. "Fuck, you're perfect."

She wriggles in my touch. "I didn't know I'd be getting halfway naked." She blushes. "I do own matching underwear."

I drag in a rough breath and roll my thumbs over the soft padding at her hipbones. "That would be perfect, too."

"And I have ugly underwear," she says slowly.

"Good. Perfect."

"Hunter."

I jerk my eyes up and meet her gaze. "Yes?"

She smiles. "You just said ugly underwear would be perfect."

"Is this a bad time to admit I'm going to be an easy lay for you?" I grin. "I'm...I mean, the joke is that I'm like a kid on Christmas morning, but you're so pretty and soft and sexy, and I can't quite fucking believe that you're in my bed."

"How easy are we talking?" She licks her lips and looks at my cock, bulging at the fly on my jeans.

"Fuck, don't tempt me with that mouth."

Her eyes light up. "Is that tempting?"

I fall forward, bracing my arms on the bed on either side of her.

She bites her lower lip and gives me an innocent look. "Good."

Fuck. Me. My cock is raging now, desperate to get free. Desperate to feel the hot, wet slide of her tongue.

Her pupils are dark, deep pools of seduction as she slowly smiles. "Do you want my mouth, Daddy?"

"You're not completely innocent, are you, sweet girl?"

She shakes her head proudly.

"We'll get there. I want everything you're offering. But first… Daddy wants to unwrap the last parts of his gift." I stroke her silky hair, gathering the glossy strands in my fist. "Are you ready for more kisses?"

13
cara

I NOD eagerly and Hunter tilts my head back, his mouth falling to my neck first, then moving down to my cleavage.

He inhales deeply between my breasts before he works the bra off me and cups my tits in his big hands.

My nipples ache for his mouth. He promised me kisses, and my imagination is working overtime.

"Hello girls." He brushes a light kiss on each of my nipples. "I'm Hunter. Cara might call me Daddy, but you can call me Sir."

I laugh out loud.

He grins. "Too much?"

"Don't make me laugh. We're going to wake the others up."

He surges back up to kiss me on the mouth. "I'll have to swallow all of your giggles," he murmurs. "But don't hold back. I love the sound of your laugh."

I sigh and arch my back as he returns to my breasts, this time sucking one into his mouth with a big, hungry pull. "Yes, Daddy."

He releases that breast with a wet pop and growls in a way that makes my belly pull tight. "I love that even more. Every time you call me Daddy, it makes me want off-limit things."

And *that* makes my thighs shake before he latches on to the other side.

I can't believe he's still fully dressed and I'm down to only my panties.

And he doesn't seem to be in any rush to get naked, which is... I mean, I can't complain (at all) because he's feasting on my tits in a way that feels so good I can't think straight.

But.

I want to see his body.

I need to feel him against me.

"Hunter," I whisper, and it comes out as a moan.

He nods and growls again, pulling at my nipple until the last possible second when he looks up. "Yes, my girl?"

Overwhelmed, I can't speak. I pluck at his t-shirt, stretched tight over his shoulders.

He understands anyway.

With one hand, he reaches behind his head and pulls off his t-shirt in a fluid motion.

And when I can finally see his big, broad chest, dusted with dark hair and packed solid with hefty muscles and a layer of padding, it's like I've been holding my breath all night.

All week.

Maybe my entire life.

I scramble to my knees and reach for him. He pulls me against him, warm skin on warm skin, and it feels like coming home.

"Take off your jeans," I mumble against his mouth.

He can't answer me because he's kissing me back.

I laugh and he swallows that. I sigh happily and he swallows that, too.

Then I'm fumbling with his fly, and I can't get it down because he's huge behind it, his cock thick and straining.

"Help me," I pant when he finally stops kissing me.

"You can do it," he encourages. "If you want to play with Daddy's cock, you need to earn it."

Oh. *Oh.*

Well, that's motivating as heck.

I look down and work his button loose, then tug at the waistband, giving myself a big of slack to unzip him.

Under the jeans, he's wearing soft black boxer briefs, and his cock fills them *completely.*

That's a *bulge.*

I gulp.

Hunter tips my chin up, making me look at his face instead. "One thing at a time, sweet girl."

"I want it," I breathe.

"You'll have everything in good time." He tumbles me onto my back again, then kicks his jeans off with surprising agility for a big guy.

And then he's beside me, curling me against him. The hair on his legs tickles my thighs as he tangles our limbs, but it pales compared to the eager press of his erection against my belly and the raw drag of my nipples against his chest.

My pulse pounds in my ears as I trace the crisp, dark hair in the middle of his chest.

Hunter exhales, long and slow, and we both go quiet.

"We don't have to do anything more tonight," he finally says. "This is wonderful."

"I don't want to stop." I tug at his chest hair. "Do you want to stop?"

"No. But…"

"But?" I tug harder. "What?"

"My thoughts are running like an out-of-control racehorse. Or a whole herd of Clydesdales."

"Something in the horse category?"

"Maybe minotaurs."

I laugh. "I've got racing thoughts, too."

He kisses me, his breath warm, his lips inviting. "This is a lot. I wouldn't let you leave. I talked directly to your tits. I asked you to marry me."

This time, my laugh is louder, and he's forced to kiss me to keep me quiet.

His hand sinks into my hair and he presses his forehead against mine, exhaling. "I've never wanted anyone like this. I want all of you, heart and soul and body, immediately. That's a huge ask of anyone, let anyone a…"

"A virgin?" I offer.

He groans and crushes me to his chest. "Fuck, I'm sorry."

"Why?" I wriggle until my lips are against his neck. I kiss the warm, taut skin there. "You're going to make my first time amazing. No need to be sorry. But maybe that can be a tomorrow thing?"

He smiles into my hair. I don't know how I know that, since I can't see his face, but I can feel it. His whole body feels like he's smiling.

"Do you want a shirt to sleep in?"

I'd honestly forgotten I was naked except for my panties. "Do I need one?"

"God, no. I want to hold you like this all night." He lets go of me long enough to turn off his bedside lamp, plunging the room into darkness.

"Hannah's not an early riser on Christmas. Don't worry," he whispers.

He tugs the covers back and rolls me under the blanket, then slides in with me, spooning around me.

"Hunter?"

"Yeah?" His chest rises and falls against my back.

"I think you're an amazing dad."

He squeezes his arm around me, his hand big and warm across my tummy. "Thanks."

I close my eyes and sink into the lovely heat of his body.

"I'm sorry my family is so bonkers," he murmurs into my hair.

I smile without opening my eyes. "I actually love the chaos."

"You mean that?"

"You sound shocked."

"I am shocked."

"Well, the alternative for me was a very boring, very quiet Christmas alone."

He tenses behind me. "How long have you been alone?"

"Depends who you ask. A few months or my entire life." I roll onto my back so I can look at him now that my eyes have adjusted to the dark. "My parents are both academics. Professors at a university in Washington, D.C., and very active field researchers. Right now they are in Siberia."

"Festive," he says dryly.

"Yeah. Christmas was always pretty quiet at our house."

He brushes a strand of hair off my face. "Did you have to manage that?"

"What do you mean?"

"Well…" He stretches his big body, hunkering down closer to me again. "Tonight I saw you watching everyone and being very thoughtful. I know how much you had to help Hannah in your class together. You tutor at the library. So I'm wondering if that caretaking nature was something you had to do as a kid, too?"

"Maybe. I guess I usually am the responsible one."

"Responsible girls deserve to have someone else taking care of them sometimes, too." His fingers slide down my neck, then around my breast, raising a line of goosebumps.

"I've never had that."

"Now you do." He pinches my nipple, gently tightening his grip and then tugging my breast into the air. Making me arch my back, and sending a spiral of heat through my belly.

"How about you? Who takes care of you?"

He chuckles. "I don't need anyone to take care of me."

"Oh no, that can't possibly be true. Everyone needs a little caretaking." I reach between us and find his erection, hard and ready between us.

He hisses under his breath. "You are trouble."

I smile. "I think for you, I just might be."

"Do you like that? Do you like being trouble for me?"

I squirm, my good girl instincts warring with something deeper and more instinctual to tease and stroke and make him lose control.

He lets out a ragged breath. "You do. Good. Be as much trouble as you want. I can handle it."

I have a wicked, wicked thought. It makes liquid need pool between my legs, and now that the thought is in my head, I can't keep it to myself.

Dragging my fingers up the outside of his underwear, over his jutting erection, I circle the tip of his cock, waiting for him to audibly react—with a delicious grunt—before I innocently ask, "Did you want more children?"

His whole body reacts with a hard shudder. He sucks in a breath. "It wasn't an option."

"That's not an answer." I slide my hand lower again so I can squeeze all of him. Except I can't, because he's too big.

He's breathing so hard as he catches my wrist and pulls my hand off him. "It was lonely. Being a single dad. And I wasn't drawn to anyone before…"

God, I love the sound of how that thought trails off. My breasts feel heavy, my nipples are tight.

Maybe what we needed was just a bit of darkness to shake out all the rioting thoughts we weren't sure we could share.

Except, of course, we *can* share these thoughts with each other.

I think I can tell Hunter literally anything.

But before I can spill my next thought, he's pulling me on top of him. "Cara, you have your whole life ahead of you."

What a noble, lovely, silly man. I nod as I try to arrange myself on top of him. A noble, lovely, silly, giant man. "You don't want to trap me."

He laughs under his breath and settles his hands on my hips, guiding me to straddle him. Teaching me how to rock against his cock. "That's the thing. I want to trap you so hard it scares me. You make me possessive. You make me irrational."

I'm panting now. "Logic and rational thought are important to you."

"Usually. Yes." Even through my underwear, he knows exactly where to give me friction, where to make his hard cock strain up against me.

"So if I told you that I'm not on birth control…"

His hands move to my ass. Squeezing. Pulling. He flexes beneath me. "Cara…"

"I want you inside me, Hunter."

14
hunter

CARA'S VOICE is clear and steady and so fucking sexy. *I want you inside me, Hunter.*

I thought she needed me to back off. I thought if I turned out the lights, she would fall asleep in my arms.

I shouldn't underestimate Cara like that.

Now she's used the cover of darkness to skillfully pull me right to the brink. The combination of her eager, inexperienced stroking of my cock and her confident, bold line of of questions and statements has my balls heavy and my shaft throbbing.

She wants me inside her?

All I can picture now is rolling her beneath me and working my fat, bare cock into her unprotected pussy. The sounds she would make. The heavenly warmth of her body making room for me.

I trace the edge of her cotton panties. Her belly quivers against my touch. Right in the middle of her waistband, there's a small satin bow.

My Christmas present. My naughty secret, at least for tonight. In the morning, I'll claim her under the mistletoe for everyone to see.

Danes are always dramatic, and it's my fucking turn after all these years.

I work my fingers in under the elastic, continuing the back-and-forth stroking. Soft, soft belly. And then the rise of her mound, and soft springy curls. Fucking sexy.

In the dark, I find her mouth with mine, stealing a kiss as I push my hand the rest of the way into her panties and cup her sweet little slit with my big hand.

God, she feels good. Warm and soft, with puffy lips that take the weight of my middle finger, and when I squeeze her possessively, her legs fall wider and those soft lips part perfectly around my finger, giving me access to a slick, hot core.

I trace the shape of her, listening to how her breath catches.Since it's dark and I can't see her clearly, I need to use all my other senses to learn what she likes.

And she likes my fingers. Her slick virgin folds soften and bloom against my touch, a dangerous invitation my primal instinct recognizes with shocking aggression.

I need to bury myself in her.

Need to take.

Need to claim.

Mine.

A low, deep growl rumbles out of me and I climb on top of her, her legs falling open for me.

Immediately, she rocks her hips up, grinding against my cock through the thin layers of cotton separating us.

And the primal need intensifies.

I cradle her in my arms, burying my face in her neck. My breath stutters out, hot and ragged against her shoulder. "Jesus, Cara, you feel good."

"I know," she gasps. "I mean, you too."

"Fuck, I was going to…"

She throws her head back. "Don't stop."

"Need you to be ready. Need to kiss your sweet little pussy and make you soft for Daddy."

"Next time. Hunter, I'm close."

"Can you come like this? Oh sweetheart, that's so good. Yes, work yourself against me. You're going to make me come, too."

She gasps. "Like this?"

"Fuck yeah. Milk my seed, baby. God, I want to pump it into you so damn bad."

That makes her moan.

"Love your fucking sounds. You make me crazy."

"Oh God, same. Hunter, I need you."

"You'll have me. Over and over again. I'm keeping you in this bed for the next week." My head is spinning, electric sparks racing up my spine. My balls have pulled up tight, right on the edge. I need her to come first, though. "Is this good for you? Do you like the feel of my dad cock riding you hard? Not even inside your virgin pussy yet, and you're gonna make me come."

Her breath hitches, panting faster, and her head rolls back and forth, restless beneath the heavy weight of my body now.

I let loose every bit of the unhinged fantasy I have for keeping her under me. "I want to pump you so full of my seed. Over and over again. I want to breed you."

She gasps and I cover her mouth just before she screams. She slams her lips shut, swallowing the reaction as her hips snap up and freeze, pressing her clit against me.

With a roar, I thrust against her one more time and spill my release for her, on top of her, but not yet inside her.

She's shaking as I come down from that startling high. I ease up, shifting my weight to my arms and my knees, and I kiss her quivering mouth.

"I was too loud," she whispers.

"You're perfect," I promise. "Nothing has ever sounded sweeter to me."

All of it. Starting with her intentional dropping of the fact that she's not on birth control. My lush, fertile breeding girl. Ripe for Daddy's seed.

Now that I've nutted out that primal aggression, though, I know that I won't be taking her virginity tonight.

I wouldn't be the safety-minded dad she's been attracted to if I didn't insist on a sober second thought on that delicious idea in the morning.

But I'm also not an idiot. Just because I've had my release, doesn't mean this horny little nineteen-year-old is done for the night. If I'm going to get her to sleep at all, I'm going to need to—get to—take care of her in other ways.

"You know what time it is?"

She glances around, but I don't have a visible alarm clock in my room. One of the perks of having my kid finally out of the house, and working on my own schedule—I can sleep in until I'm ready to wake up.

With a jolt, I realize that those days are numbered one way or another.

"I didn't mean literally," I add with a chuckle, moving past the question. "I meant, it's time for me to unwrap the last part of my present."

She sucks in a breath that could be either excited or nervous. Maybe both. "Oh."

I shift down her body and circle that little bow on the front of her panties with my fingertip before I efficiently peel them down her thighs, finally baring my sweet girl.

"It's not fair that I'm the only one naked," she says quietly.

"I'm a mess."

She wiggles her legs back and forth. "So am I."

"The, uh, volume of mess is different."

"Oh."

"I'll clean up when I'm done with you."

"There's more?"

I shoulder my way between her thighs. "Are you tired yet? Ready for bed?"

"No," she admits.

"Then yes, there's more." I take a long, deep inhale of her

sexy scent. It's been a long time since I've been intimate with another person, but I still know this is different. She smells *right*. She smells like *mine*.

"Are you sensitive?" I ask as I nose along her slick curls. She is a little messy. I love it.

"A little."

"I'll be gentle."

"Not too careful," she says, shifting her legs again. An echo of our first conversation about kissing.

I knew then that she wasn't like anyone else I'd ever met. That she was a bold, fearless woman who knows how to ask for what she wants. I thought it was dangerous.

It's not dangerous at all. It's fucking beautiful.

So I brush my thumbs up her tender pussy lips and ease her cunt open for my kisses. "Not too careful," I promise. "I'll give you the deep kisses you want, sweetness. I promise."

She jerks at the first slide of my tongue up the middle of her pussy, then moans when I do it again.

I grin. Good. She likes me eating her sweet pussy. That makes two of us.

And she makes the best fucking sounds as I dig in and make a meal of her. Delicious little virgin cunt. Tastes fresh. Sounds ready.

I don't wait long before giving her a finger, too, circling her entrance until she trembles, then pushing in to feel the tight squeeze of her pussy from the inside. The way she breathes *Yes, Daddy*, when I add a second finger is the stuff of legends.

Her clit is the most sensitive part, and every time I lick around it, she shakes and pushes on my head. Too much, too soon.

I don't care. I'll settle in for a slow French kiss with her pussy, if that's what she wants. But as I start to fuck her with my fingers, her grip on my hair shifts, and instead of pushing, she starts pulling.

Up, up.

My breath wafts over her clit and she says the magic word.

"Please, Daddy."

"You want me to suck your little clit? Not too sensitive now?"

"I need it," she whines.

Generous, giving Cara, finally hitting her selfish *gimme* point.

Good.

Chest puffing with pride, I give her exactly what she needs.

I close my mouth around her taut clit and I pull her to the heavens. Her thighs tighten up around my head, her hips jerking hard, slapping me in the face.

Making Cara come is a wild fucking ride.

I suck hard, licking and swirling as she goes off, as I feel her body spasm and then give give give.

I keep licking because I'm addicted now.

Panting, pushing, her thighs fall away, off my shoulders, uncovering my ears. "Oh God oh God oh God you monster," she cries out. "Stop kissing me right now!"

Twisting my head, I laugh into her inner thigh. "I stopped."

"That was too good."

Pleased as punch, I roll onto my back. She's all over my face. I can die a happy man now. "How is something too good?"

"It just is." She crawls down the bed and curls up beside me, pulling my hand to her bare breast. To her heart, I realize, as the rapid thud meets my fingertips. "You could give me a heart attack doing that, you know."

"Doubtful. But I do think we should play doctor just as soon as I can kick people out of here tomorrow. I'll give you a thorough check-up before giving you the all clear for another date with my face." My eyes drift shut. I can't fall asleep. I need to wash up. I need to get her some water. I need…

Cara kisses my bare chest and tugs at the hair there. "Do you have a private bathroom?"

I blink my eyes open again.

I need to run my girl a shower. "Yep. Let's go."

15
cara

HUNTER GOES AHEAD, turning on just one dim light in the bathroom. Suddenly I can see him properly—and realize he's about to see me fully naked, too. He's touched me. Licked and sucked at me.

And sure, we were looking at each other up close, but it was basically dark.

Now it's…more real.

Nervously, I go as far as the edge of the bed, and then I wait.

He turns on the water, then strides back into view. Backlit by light behind him, he's extra-giant. Long, thick legs. A heavy core. Big arms that come up and hook on the top of the door frame as he looks right back at me.

"You coming?" he asks.

My heart leaps into my throat and I nod.

Sliding off the bed, I try not to be self-conscious of my body wiggling and wobbling.

But I'm nervous anyway—until I reach him in the doorway and he pulls me against him, dipping his head to kiss me.

When Hunter's kissing me, everything is just fine. Better than fine. Everything is amazing.

"Get in the shower," he murmurs. "I need to put these in the laundry hamper."

He points down at his boxer briefs.

I blush.

I'm under the spray when he returns, the steam swirling around us, but nothing could interfere with my first look at his cock.

It sways like a long, heavy truncheon in front of him.

"He won't bite," Hunter says slowly, smiling cautiously when I jerk my gaze up to meet his eyes.

"I might," I say in a rush. "He looks tasty."

He laughs under his breath. "Pass the soap."

I hand over a nice smelling bar, and he lathers up. Letting me watch, putting on a bit of a show.

He pushes the suds across his meaty chest first, the dark curls there catching the bubbles. Then his hand trails down over his belly to his cock. He circles it in a loose ring of his fingers, working the soap up and down his shaft before cupping his hand over his balls and tugging there, too.

I'm staring. Rudely, probably. Eyes bugging out.

Stop staring, Cara.

The lecture in my head doesn't work.

"Do you want to help?" Hunter's voice is low and silky. "After all, you're the one who made me come in my shorts like a teenage boy."

"I'm sorry," I gasp.

He takes my hand in his, sudsy bubbles transferring. "It's okay, baby. Get me clean."

I feel faint as he guides my hand to grip his cock. It's so firm, with a real weight to it, and it feels alive.

Duh. Obviously.

But like…it *moves.*

That's what it will feel like inside me. Alive and moving and heavy.

Shivering, I slide my wet hand down to the base of him, where thick dark curls have been trimmed short.

And then below his cock, I mimic how he touched himself, curling my fingers around his balls.

He groans and backs me up against the cool tile.

"Come here," he grinds out as he tips my head back, and then we're kissing deeply, a little less uncoordinated than our other kisses. More desperate.

I lift my leg, curling it around his thigh, and he scoops his hands under my ass, lifting me onto my toes. Our wet bodies fit together perfectly.

So perfectly, nothing feels more natural than pulling the head of his cock to my entrance.

"Not here, Cara," he rasps.

I roll my hips, aching for more of the steady, delicious pressure. "Why not?"

"Because…" He exhales roughly and flexes his thighs. Not pushing into me, but not pulling away, either. "Because I don't want to swallow your cries. I want to take my time, stretch you out on my bed, and I want to see your face. Hear your sounds. Because I want this so fucking much, and I don't want to rush to it." He takes another quick breath. "And because it's been a long time and just being pressed up against you is enough to make me come again."

"So?" That sounds amazing. I want to make him come right now. I rub us together again just to see what happens.

"So I'd like to last more than a…" He groans and clutches me tighter against him. "More than a hot fucking second."

"But if this second is really fucking hot," I tease. "Then maybe it's worth it?"

"Oh fuck." He's panting now, his gaze blown out with lust. "You want to make Daddy come like this? Just teasing me? Don't even have the tip inside you?"

"Yes. Yes!" I jerk my hips faster, rocking him against my slick entrance. "Make a mess on me."

"If you make me spill all over your little pussy, I'm going to have to get on my knees and lick you clean."

"You say that like a threat," I gasp, my clit literally pulsing at the notion. "But it really feels like a promise."

He doesn't reply to that, just moans, and I've never felt anything as powerful as reducing this man to simple noises. I hump against his cock faster and faster, until he thrusts against me, his cock shoving up between our bodies, and finds his release, punctuating it with three ragged grunts.

Both of us go silent. His chest heaves. His come-slicked cock slides down my thigh as he pulls away, setting me down on both feet. His gaze is hot and primal, raw and unguarded, and he doesn't break eye contact as he drops to his knees.

"You ever get yourself off in the shower, sweet girl?"

I shiver despite the hot steam and nod. "With the shower head."

"What do you think about?" He lifts my thigh, hooking it over his shoulder the same way I hooked it around his leg when we were both standing.

I close my eyes and remember. "I imagined a man I thought I would never meet in real life. I imagined his fingers on me."

Hunter's thumb grazes my aching, sensitive flesh.

My heart pounds.

"I imagined…his breath."

Hunter presses his face to my belly and exhales.

"Yes…"

"Did you imagine his fingers inside you?"

"Yes…"

Hunter works one big finger in me up to his knuckle, then adds a second. Stretching me for what's going to come tomorrow or the day after.

It's well into Christmas Day, now. In a few short hours, everyone is going to wake up.

How long do I have to wait until everyone leaves?

How long until Hunter tells them how he feels about me?

They'll leave after that.

It'll be awkward.

They might even label me as trouble.

But it'll be worth it, because Hunter will bring me back to his bed and he'll finally make love to me.

"What else, baby girl?"

"I imagined your mouth…licking me…"

He gives me that fantasy, the one that always got me there really fast. The one where licks turn to harder sucks and quick bites and then fluttering passes on my clit, in time with the slow, steady thrusts in and out of me, getting me there, closer closer closer—

"You," I cry out, breaking for him. "I imagined you."

"That's so beautiful," he growls before he latches on to my clit and I fall into fireworks, clutching at his head, holding on for dear life.

Hunter stays on his knees, breathing into my belly and holding me up, until I straighten up and pat his head.

Fatigue rolls through me as I tip my face into the steamy spray.

He waits until I turn back to him, then he takes the shower head wand and uses it to rinse us both off.

He turns the shower off, then grabs an oversized towel and wraps me in it. "Wait here a minute," he murmurs.

He disappears, then returns with a big robe and another towel, which he slings around his waist after putting the robe on me.

"Back to bed for you," he whispers.

I get as far as the foot of his bed, and then I sit down there.

He grins at me as he towels off.

We don't talk.

I just watch him as he finds the silly Christmas PJs Hannah bought everyone. He looks like a candy cane. Like an extra-thick, extra long candy cane.

He doesn't look embarrassed at all.

Once he's dressed, he eases me back to my feet and nudges me through his sitting area and toward his door.

In the hallway, I hold my breath. It's only ten, maybe fifteen feet to the spare room, and the house is entirely still.

We make it to the spare room without detection, and he comes inside with me.

"Do you want to sleep in the robe?" He tugs on the collar, pulling me close so he can kiss me. "Or naked?"

"Or...the candy cane PJs?"

He shrugs. "Tradition."

I nod. "Tradition it is."

He peels his robe off me and hangs it on a hook, then dresses me like a smaller, curvier matching candy cane.

I crawl into bed and he follows. I look at him in surprise.

"I'll go back to my room once you're asleep." He kisses my forehead. "And in the morning, we'll figure out the next steps, because tomorrow night, you're sleeping in there with me."

———

I can't find my phone when I wake up. It's not completely dark out the window, and I hear a bit of movement, so I let myself get out of bed. There's a fine line between being excited about Christmas morning and being too eager to see your friend's dad again. If Hannah's already awake, I need to play it cooler than I probably know how to.

It feels weird to just go downstairs in my PJs without a bra on when I barely know half the people in the house. So I take a minute to put underwear on under the candy cane fright before I step out into the hallway.

Hannah's door is still closed, but there's a light on downstairs. I creep down to the foyer and find Hunter in the kitchen, quietly making coffee.

He lifts his head as I approach, and my breath catches in my throat.

Hi, he mouths.

And it's exactly the same way he did when I saw him in the coffee shop. I was so nervous when I saw him, because he seemed so out of my league, like what was I even doing asking this man for a first kiss?

Now he's slow rolling me through all of my firsts, and I'm nervous for a whole different reason. It feels like everyone is going to know I spent the night in his bed. That I didn't get much sleep because we kept talking and kissing and…

Hunter crooks his finger. *Come here.* I glance sideways, but nobody else is up yet.

"Hi," I whisper as I come to stand right in front of him.

"You're blushing," he murmurs. "That's so beautiful."

That echo of what he said when he was between my thighs in the shower doesn't help the heat rolling through me at *all.*

He ducks his head so his lips brush my ear. "Are you thinking about me eating you out?"

I gasp and press my hands to my cheeks. "Yes."

"Fucking proud of putting that look on your face, I'm not going to lie." Hunter presses a coffee cup into my hand. "Here you go. Vanilla latte for a very yummy girl. Think of passive solar houses or cell division or something else science-y while I get breakfast started."

"Do you need help?"

He takes a deep breath, and a glance down at the candy cane PJ bottoms tells me I'm not the only one affected by our morning reunion.

I lick my lips. "Would it be more help if I go check out the Christmas tree or something?"

"Or something, yeah." He bites his lower lip, his gaze hooded and hot. "Merry Christmas, sweet girl."

"Merry Christmas, Daddy," I whisper before twirling away with my coffee.

In the living room, Wyatt and his partners are still sleeping. I creep past them and go into the library. This part of the house is under the entrance to Hunter's room upstairs. There's a door off it that has glass panels on either side, and through those I can a big desk and an even bigger drafting table.

"That's his den," someone says from behind me.

I glance back.

Wyatt waves sleepily at me from the couch.

"Good morning," I say softly.

Emily raises her head. "Is there coffee?"

"Yep," I say, lifting my mug.

Wyatt swings his legs off the couch, but Emily stops him. "I'll get it."

"Full service at the North Pole. I like it," he teases.

She rolls her eyes. "I'll make myself a useful elf and be right back."

While she heads to the kitchen, I look at the Christmas tree. An absurd number of presents are piled under and around it. I didn't bring anything with me, because I didn't know it would be like this.

I can't even remember clearly what kind of emotionally unavailable mess I thought I was coming into here. The reality has been so far from that, it's silly. The Danes are over the top, but they're so loving.

I wonder if I could sneak out and go to the truck stop at the highway, and what I could buy Hunter there that would show just how special it has been to share his family Christmas. And should I borrow a car or—

"Merry Christmas!" Hannah hollers from the top of the stairs before galloping in to make her grand entrance.

Time's up.

I take a big swallow of coffee and brace myself.

16
hunter

BREAKFAST IS A SLIGHTLY stressful but mostly deeply enjoyable blur. Hannah is genuinely thrilled that everyone is wearing the matching PJs she bought. Wyatt's ankle feels a lot better than it did when he went to sleep. Cara keeps smiling at me from the other end of the table, and my cock manages to behave.

It's after breakfast when Hannah wants to take a group picture that things go off the rails.

She uses my phone, because it has a little attachment for a stick-anywhere tripod that I find useful for sharing art-in-progress videos to my Instagram account.

But once we take a dozen pictures and she swipes in to look at them, she notices the dating app on my Home Screen.

In all of her nineteen years, I've never had to hide what's on my phone before. That's going to have to change now. Should have changed a week ago, but I wasn't thinking.

Damn it.

"Dad, are you dating again?" She taps into it as I lunge for her. Laughing, she rolls away, holding the phone out of reach. "Oh my God, no, these photos are *terrible*. Have you matched with anyone?"

Wyatt snatches the phone from her and tosses it back to me.

"Thanks," I say, out of breath.

She scowls at us. "No tag teaming. But seriously, there are better apps. Cara, tell him."

"Umm…" Cara darts her gaze back and forth between us. "There are better apps," she whispers.

"Oh?" Now she has my full attention. "What other apps do you recommend?"

Red spots burst on her cheeks. "None."

"None *yet*," Hannah says confidently. "Because she had a bad experience—"

"It wasn't that bad," Cara says, giving me a helpless look.

"He *ghosted* you," Hannah says. She gestures to her friend. "Can you imagine kissing this girl and then immediately deleting your account?"

Emily's mouth drops open. "No."

Heath looks at me.

Wyatt looks at Heath, and then, understanding dawning, looks at me with sheer, unadulterated delight. "Really?"

Hannah doesn't notice her uncle's reaction because she's deep into storytelling mode now, relaying to Emily what I did, without any awareness that the "giant idiot" she's talking about is the same guy who made her pancakes this morning.

While dressed as a fucking candy cane.

Time to move the festivities along. "We should open some presents," I say loudly.

"That's a great idea," Cara agrees. She holds my gaze long enough to convey that *she's* not mad at that giant idiot anymore, and then she's whisked to the library by Emily and Hannah.

Heath comes up on my right side.

Wyatt comes up on my left.

"So," Heath says.

"Those woman troubles you're having," Wyatt adds.

"Are none of your business," I say.

Wyatt doesn't agree with me at all. He keeps going. "Did you know she was classmates with Hannah?"

"Of course not," I bite out.

Which is all the admission the two of them need.

Heath grins.

Wyatt cackles.

"We're working it out," I mutter. "And there's a present in that pile for her that might make Hannah lose her shit, so I'd appreciate if you two assholes could have my back when it comes time."

"Of course we will," Heath says sagely.

"After we let a few fireworks fly," Wyatt says honestly.

I wouldn't expect anything less.

————

It takes two hours to open all the presents.

Two hours of exchanging too brief glances with Cara. Two hours of keeping my hands to myself.

I didn't mean for her gift to be the literal last one pulled out from under the tree, but that's how it worked out.

Hannah takes a look at the name on the tag and hands it to her. "This one is for you, Cara. It's from my dad."

My heart in my throat, I watch as Cara nervously takes it from her. I didn't have a lot of options at five in the morning, but I did my best and scoured my den for something that would show her that she has been on my mind all week.

She slides the ribbon free, then rips off the paper, revealing a thick black frame. "What is this?"

Hannah scoots closer to her. "That's...you. My dad drew you."

17
cara

THE FRAMED PENCIL sketch is a drawing of me, smiling shyly, with the Main Street Branch of the Conception Ridge Public Library behind me. To one side of me is the alley where we had our first kiss. Behind me on the other side is Main Street, and in the background is a pickup truck parked on the opposite side of the street.

Hunter has drawn himself standing beside that truck, watching me.

Hannah stares down at the scene in confusion. "This is... Wait a minute. Dad, is that... you?"

I trace a finger over the drawing. It doesn't look like something even a really talented person could do in a hurry.

Lifting my head, I meet his gaze. "When did you draw this?"

"As soon as I got home that afternoon."

"What afternoon?" Hannah shakes her head in confusion.

Hunter doesn't shy away from her question. He looks at her, steady as can be, and he says, "I met Cara last week, sweetie. Neither of us knew about our shared connection to you. We had a coffee date, and it was honestly the best date of my entire life. You know her. I bet that's not a surprise. She's...

incredible. But I did something stupid. I made a bad judgement call, assuming for the both of us that I was too old for her."

"Because *you are*." She glares at him, and they've never looked more alike than in this moment. "Dad! What the fuck? You're the idiot who ghosted her?"

"Which was a mistake."

"And then I brought her to you? Ew, Dad!"

"Some connections transcend—"

"No. No. Nooooo. Not my lab partner. I wanted Cara to be my bestie!"

"She can still—"

She turns on me. "Care Bear. My *dad*?"

"I didn't know," I whisper. "And then when you brought me here…"

"Oh *gross*." She throws her hands in the air. "Well, now Christmas is ruined."

"Not for me," Wyatt says. "Maybe you just need to eat more pancakes."

Hannah stares at him.

And then she bursts into tears and races out of the room.

Emily slowly looks from me to Hunter, and then to Wyatt and Heath. "Hunter is the guy from the dating app? The 'best kiss of your life' liar?"

"It *was* the best kiss of my life," Hunter says steadily as he crosses to stand beside me. He gazes down at me as he adds, "I just didn't handle that well."

"And you two knew about this?" She wags her finger at her husbands.

"I figured out that they were sneaking around last night," Heath says. "I didn't know anything about the app."

"And I just figured it out this morning," Wyatt says. "There wasn't time to tell you."

Emily frowns at Heath. "You could have told us last night."

"It seemed like their private business," he says mildly. "And this was more fun." He glances at the ceiling. "Broken daughter hearts aside."

Hunter shakes his head. "I should go talk to her."

Emily holds up her hand. "I actually think Cara needs to go."

Hunter shakes his head and pulls me right up against him. Sheltering me from the storm, as promised.

"Me?" I shake my head. "I don't—"

"You heard her. She wanted your friendship. That's why she invited you here. She knows her dad will always love her. She can be mad as hell at him, and she knows they'll get past that. Her wound right now is about losing *you*, Cara."

Hunter wraps me in his arms. "If this is too much—"

I squeeze him tightly. "No. It's not." I take a deep breath. "She was dropped into my lap, and my lab, for a reason. I'll go talk to her."

Upstairs, I find Hannah's door ajar, which I think is a good sign.

I knock, then push it open.

Her room is a whole wing, just like her dad's, but where his is dark and masculine and moody, hers is light and airy, a spa-like retreat. She's curled up in a window seat, looking out at the morning mist.

"Can I join you?" I ask.

She makes a face.

But she doesn't say no.

Another door left ajar, I think, and I take the risk, sitting at the opposite end of the same window seat.

"When you think about it, we aren't really best friend material," I say.

She rolls her eyes.

"But we have a connection anyway, don't we?" I gesture at the PJs she picked out for me. "Look at us."

"God, I hate this," she says. But then she slides a glance my way, and smiles a little. "You look cute."

"You do, too."

"We're the same age." She wrinkles her nose. "That's—"

I cut her off. "Can we stop saying that your dad is gross? Because I don't think he is. At all."

She gives me a reproachful look.

I take a deep breath. "I think your dad is incredible. I think the way he devoted himself to raising you, an absolute hellion, is remarkable. And I think his talents—on the page, and in the kitchen, and with his family—are nothing short of amazing. I look at him and I…I'm in wonder, Hannah. It's this very special, very warm, magical kind of wonder. I know he feels the same way. Can you please not ruin this for us by throwing a tantrum?"

She doesn't say anything. But the reproachful expression fades a little.

I press my case. "Was last night terrible? All of us spending time together?"

Hesitantly, she shakes her head. "No."

"We'd already kissed before last night. That so-called *gross* thing had already happened."

She doesn't argue with me.

"And you know who we were both thinking about all night? You. Your dad loves you so much. And I care about you, too. I love your enthusiasm. I love your joy. I didn't want to dim that at all, but the second your dad opened that door, I knew at some point this would spill out into the open, and I wanted to soften that for you as much as possible."

"Why are you so…smart?" She sighs, exasperated now. "Why do you have to be so… mature?"

I laugh. "I don't know. Just your cross to bear, I guess."

Her eyes spark, and she covers her mouth with her hand. "Oh, shit," she mumbles from behind her fingers.

"What?"

"Remember how many times I called you Mom for bossing me around about homework?"

I groan.

"I'm not calling you Mom ever again," she says.

"That's fair."

"But it probably was prophetic."

"That might be putting the cart before the horse."

She shakes her head. "No. I have to be okay with the idea of you having my dad's babies. Oh my God. You'd be such a good mom, too."

"Ummm… thanks. I think."

She jumps up and races out the door. "Dad!" By the time I reach the hall, she's sprinting down the stairs at top speed. "Father!"

Hunter appears in the foyer as she reaches the bottom of the stairs.

She grabs his hand and gestures to me at the top of the stairs. "I got you a Christmas present."

"What?" Hunter and I both say at the same time, equally confused.

She grins broadly. "I knew Cara was special from the second I met her. Maybe I should have invited her over here to study so you could meet her sooner, but… ta da! I got you a girlfriend for Christmas. She likes babies, you know."

He looks up at me, and we exchange a *what the fuck* look, probably not the last when it comes to Hannah.

Then a slow smile spreads across his face. "Well, all right then." He wraps one arm around her and squeezes her tight as he holds out the other hand, gesturing for me to join them. "Thanks for the lovely introduction, Hannah Banana."

Slowly, I descend the stairs.

When I reach them, Hannah slips out from under her dad's arm and marches back into the living room, announcing to her uncle and his spouses that Christmas is not, in fact, ruined, and then she's taking credit for the matchmaking.

"But I am going to have to have a sleepover at your place tonight," she says, projecting her voice loud enough so we can hear it. "Because *some* people just can't keep their hands to themselves."

I giggle. "Remember when she thought inviting me here would put a damper on all the happy sex talk?"

"Whatever gets us to this in the end," Hunter murmurs, cupping my face in his hand. "Merry Christmas, sweetness."

"Merry Christmas," I whisper back as his lips collide with mine.

Right under the mistletoe.

18
hunter

"WE'LL BE BACK tomorrow night for a belated Christmas dinner," Hannah says as she follows Wyatt, Heath, and Emily out the door thirty minutes later. Nobody even changed out of their candy cane PJs. They just grabbed their overnight bags and are hightailing it out of here as fast as they can.

"Sounds great!" I cheerfully wave once more, then decisively close the door with my family on the outside of it.

And my sweet, patient girl alone with me at last.

"Hi," I say, turning around.

Cara beams at me. "Hi."

"I'm Hunter. Nice to meet you. I'm a single dad."

"Cara. Mature-for-my-age college student. It's a pleasure," she says with a laugh. "Are you going to ask me how I want my first time having sex to go, too?"

I groan. "Look, I don't have a lot of slick moves, all right? Nice Dad is my default setting."

"Good thing that Nice Dad really turns me on," she murmurs, crossing to me.

It's so fucking easy to take her into my arms and kiss her. "You feel perfect against me," I say between kisses. "I love how soft you are."

"I'm even softer without clothes on."

Fuck yeah. "Upstairs with you, then."

She races ahead, youthful ass bouncing. I can't believe I thought this was something to be worried about a week ago. Pulse pounding, I follow.

As she reaches the top of the stairs, she turns around to smile breathlessly at me.

An animalistic growl rumbles out of me.

She paces backwards. I prowl forwards. She looks so pretty and innocent. Wide hazel eyes. Pink cheeks. Soft fucking mouth.

My balls are already full for her.

"This isn't very Nice Dad," she breathes.

"No?"

She shakes her head.

"You aren't worried I'm going to be too gentle?"

"Not even a little careful." She bumps into the doorframe to my room, twists around, and runs for my bed.

I catch her before she gets there, wrapping my arms around her waist. Filling my hands with her in that way I've wanted to all morning. "Good. Because holding back last night just about killed me."

"I want Nice Dad and Rough Daddy and everything in between."

"Let's get these ridiculous PJs off."

"I agree. It's kind of hard to take you seriously as Rough Daddy when you're a giant candy cane," she teases.

I tickle her sides. "I'm sorry, what?"

"Nothing!" She waves her hands, laughing, as she twists away from me. Gaze locked on my face, she pushes her pants off, taking her underwear with them. I get a glimpse of her sweet little cunt as she crawls onto the bed and sits like a pinup girl, ass and tits out, as she peels off her top.

Under it, she's wearing a barely there bra made of some kind of translucent fabric that has a glitter to it.

She looks like an erotic, lush Christmas ornament.

"Your turn," she says, breathy and tantalizing.

I yank off my clothes and stand there for her appraisal, cock rising up to point straight at her. I want her to look at me as much as she wants, for as long as she wants. I love her warm, caressing gaze on my body.

And I love how her eyes go comically large when she locks on my cock. "Is it bigger than it was last night?"

Feels like it, yeah. "Ignore him."

"Can't do that."

"Don't worry, he'll fit."

"I didn't even say that I wasn't sure it would!" She bites her lower lip. "But now that you bring it up..."

I step closer.

She shivers.

Fuck me, but I like that more than I should.

I hold out my hand and she comes to the edge of the bed.

"Baby, I'm taking my time with you," I murmur, tracing the line of her pretty bra. "He's not going to try to get inside you until you're begging for it, I promise."

The offending cock in question sways and thumps against her belly, making her squeak prettily.

"Mmm, but he does want inside you."

She squirms. "I want that, too."

"I know you do, sweet girl." I slip her bra strap off her shoulder. "Can you be all the way naked for Daddy?"

She looks up at me, wide-eyed innocence for a second, and a surge of protectiveness rolls through me.

"Cara, I—" Fuck, I'm getting choked up. "You're going to give me everything, though. That's the thing. You already have."

"Not quite everything." Her gaze glitters, innocence dissolving into earnest desire.

I take her hand and press it to my bare chest. "I mean here."

"Oh." She nods, shy again. "Good."

Then, her eyes dancing, she trails her fingers down to circle my erection.

I growl another curse word under my breath and cup her face, crushing my mouth to hers. Kissing her hard enough to make her squeak again, those sounds I can't get enough of.

As we kiss, I peel off her bra, the pretty wrapping around my beautiful doll.

Once she's naked, I cup her breasts, relishing the weight of them in my hands.

In the bright, middle of the day light, she's a winter goddess.

"I'm so fucking lucky to be your first."

"My only," she whispers, arousal darkening her hazel gaze.

"In every way." I sink to my knees at the edge of the bed. "Lean back for me. Show Daddy your pussy."

She shifts back onto her hands, her legs spreading eagerly.

I circle my fingers around her ankles. She's so fucking delicate. Soft little feet. Round, smooth calves. Her knees are dimpled and lovely, deserving of kisses. I drop my head and bite her there gently, then kiss it better before I nose my way up her inner thigh, chasing heaven.

Her hips tilt up as my mouth reaches her pink slit.

It's good that she's eager, but I need her even more than that. I want her writhing with need.

Licking between her folds, I focus on teasing her, getting her worked up. There won't be any relief for my girl until my cock is buried inside her. It's a fine line between being a monster and taking good care of her, and I'm going to walk it carefully.

My cock strains up, brushing my belly.

As I kiss her slowly, I reach down and stroke myself. Pleasure swirls up my spine at the joy of doing this while I have Cara on my tongue, too. There will be many days in our future where I kneel in front of her so we can both get off this way.

Today is not one of those days.

I swipe my tongue against her in a final, hungry pull, then push up to my feet. Rough need courses through me as I scoop my hands under her hips, lifting her and moving her toward the headboard.

"You taste so good," I rasp. I squeeze her tits and taste her there, too. Her nipples bead hard against my tongue as I go back and forth, sucking and licking. Feeling her go molten beneath me.

And when I cup her mound, my fingertips teasing her slit, she's slicker than before. Softer, too.

Blooming.

"Please Hunter," she begs. "I'm ready."

I take her wrists and pin them above her head. "You might be. You want to try to take my cock now?"

"Yes."

"Spread your thighs for me. Show me that you want this."

Her knees curl up and out, her pink slit pulling open to a fucking gorgeous little entrance.

I notch my cock against her—too big, holy shit, I'm never going to fit—and she pushes her hips up.

Eager.

But she's not going to be able to do it herself.

"I'm going to push in, baby. I want you to kiss me. I want you to think of having me deep inside you, and how good it's going to feel to be full, okay?" I brace my legs against the backs of her thighs and curve over her, giving her my mouth and my cock at the same time.

She moans against my lips as I work the head in.

She's so hot and tight, it makes me see stars. I can feel the veins on my cock getting fatter as I hold most of my length still outside her.

"Let me in, sweet girl. Let Daddy in," I breathe.

A lovely whine escapes from her as she tips her head back. My mouth falls to her throat, kissing her there as she swallows hard, trying to catch her breath.

I press my hips against her, testing her, and a bit more of my heavy length finds access to her slickness.

"Oh, fuck, Cara. You feel incredible. Tell me you can take it. Tell me this feels good."

She sobs and nods. "More."

I sink in deeper, and as her walls stretch to take me, I let go of my cock, trusting she's going to take the rest in time. I brace my arms around her and dance butterfly kisses along her jaw. "That's it, baby. Hold on tight. Daddy's almost all the way inside you. You're doing so good. You're so fucking sweet."

It feels like I'm way too big for her tiny hole, but as I talk dirty to her, she takes every inch slowly but surely.

Gasping, she clutches at my shoulders as my girth fills her completely. I bottom out and hold still. Waiting for her to get used to me, waiting for her to catch her breath. As she trembles beneath me, I feel every inch and pound of our size difference, like she's fragile and I could break her if I make a wrong move.

"You did it," I whisper, my heart pounding. "Tell me how it feels, baby."

She stares up at me, but as if from a distance. "Like I've been cleaved in half by the sweetest blade."

"Jesus Christ." My heart stops.

"I mean it in a good way," she adds.

And my heart gallops again. "Well then, fuck, let's get that tattooed on my chest."

She blinks slowly, her gaze still glossy and dazed. "It's…" Tentatively, she shifts beneath me. "I feel like I'll never be the same again."

Knowing I've changed her forever knocks the breath out of me. "Baby…"

"Never stop." She focuses on my face and smiles. "Please, Hunter. Show me everything."

God willing, she will always crave this rough, full stuffing from me. I'll cleave her in two every damn day if she loves it.

I shift my hips, easing out of her just a little, then sliding back home. In and out, in and out. Testing my girl's readiness to be fucked properly. Filling her all the way up, until we're nothing but a thick cock in a tight pussy. Until our souls are tightly focused on this act of mating, and she's moaning and moving with me. Until she's chasing my cock, demanding that fullness over and over again.

I pin her down again.

She wraps her legs around my waist, her skin slipping against mine as sweat slicks down my back. A matching sheen gilds her tits, and I need to get my mouth back on that glistening flesh.

"Hold on tight," I rumble, shifting my grip to hold her against me and roll onto my back. "Hands on the headboard."

She reaches past my head, putting her nipples right over my mouth, and I latch on. The taste and scent of her on top of me is fucking insane, I love it.

My hands find her hips and I drive up into her again, showing her how good it can feel from this angle.

She cries out, her back arching. I open my mouth wide, letting her breasts slide across my tongue, and focus on giving her more of that angle. In and out, in and out. She's so perfectly tight, I could nut at any minute, but there's something else holding me back.

If I'm her Daddy, and this is her first time, it has to be perfect.

Nothing will stop me from giving her that.

My sweet girl is coming first. Twice, three times if she wants. And then, when she's sated, I'll pour my seed into her.

I shift her hips a little, making room to find her clit.

She goes still, shaking on top of me as I roll my thumb across the top of her sensitive bud. "Hunter?"

I stare up at her. "Is that good?"

She nods.

"Then come for me, pretty girl. Come on my cock."

She lifts up a little, then comes back down. Legs shaking, she finds her own rhythm, filling herself with my bare shaft. Driving herself down against my thumb. And it doesn't take long, now that she's found a good combination, for her pleasure to ramp up. Inside, she clenches up around me. Her riding movements become more of a grinding, and then she shudders, her whole body seizing. Her clit throbs, then spasms, and she moans low and long and perfect.

"God you're beautiful," I say, my balls pulling tight.

She falls on top of me, burying her fingers in my hair. "Come in me," she says before kissing me. Hard, desperate kisses that shatter any plan to make her find another release.

We'll have forever for that.

Right now, my girl wants to be filled up, and I want to do that for her so damn much.

Our heady, combined scent swirls around us as I thrust my hips up against her. "You're going to make Daddy cum inside you, aren't you?"

"Yes, Daddy."

"You want me to fill up your unprotected cunt."

She moans and bites my lip. "Yes."

"God damn it, Cara—" I snap my hips, pulling her down with my hands so I spill my load as deep inside her as possible. "I'm going to love you forever, baby. So fucking much."

She giggles against my mouth.

"Don't laugh, it feels too good," I groan.

She kisses the corner of my mouth. "I love you, Hunter."

I smooth my hand over her tumbling hair. "I love you, too. With my whole damn heart."

epilogue

Cara

nine months later

I GET a lot of stares as I walk through the Natural Sciences building on campus on the first day of school. Yes, I look like I'm about to pop. No, I'm not actually going to have a baby any day now.

Hunter just makes big babies.

I actually have another six or eight weeks to go, so I decided to fill this term with classes I can participate in remotely after the baby arrives. I have a two-credit independent study project, a film studies elective that just seemed fun, and a biology lecture that will be the most work, but seems straightforward. Attend the lectures, do the assignments.

Most of the seats in the biology lecture hall have built in desks, and there's no way me and my Dane-sized-baby-belly are fitting behind one of those. I start to climb the stairs at the side when vigorous waving catches my attention.

Hannah is in this class, too.

"I saved you a seat," she says brightly.

"The desk..." I wave at my midsection.

"The desks in this row fold down! And I can take notes for

the both of us." She hides the table part of the chair next to her, creating more than enough space for me and her baby-brother-to-be.

"Thanks," I say gratefully, climbing into the seat beside her. "I didn't know you were taking this class."

"I didn't, either. But when I got to school today, I realized I had to drop a different class, so I went over to student affairs and asked what classes you were in."

That's probably a violation of privacy, but given that I'm her step-mom now, it's fine. Weird, but fine. "I can only help you until the baby comes," I say mildly.

"Bestie!" She presses her hand to her chest in mock shock. "You know that this term, I'm going to be the one helping you."

"Oh?" Now I'm struggling to hold back a laugh.

She nods confidently. "When you need to take notes, I'll hold the baby. And when we have a group assignment, I'll come over and take the baby for walks while you work on it. And—"

"I get the idea." I sigh.

"Don't sigh," she says. "It makes you sound like a mom."

A year ago, she thought I sounded too much like a virgin. Now, I sound too much like a mom.

"Oh, Hannah," I say, handing her a notebook and a pen. "Never change. Now pay attention, the lecture's about to begin."

Her phone lights up. "Oh, my dad says I should find you after your class today?" She holds it up and takes a selfie. I wave at the camera. "This will be a fun surprise for him."

A second later, *my* phone vibrates.

I'm smiling as I swipe in.

HUNTER

Tell me she's not bothering you.

CARA

She's not bothering me.

HUNTER

I think she just wants to be close to you with the baby almost here.

CARA

I think she just wants the easy B.

HUNTER

That's my daughter.

CARA

Am I bringing her home for dinner tonight?

HUNTER

I got a call from an old friend who's driving down the coast, so it's turning into a big dinner party

Wyatt et al are coming, too

CARA

Oh fun!

HUNTER

I love you. And I love that you mean that earnestly. I'm sorry in advance for the cacophony.

CARA

I love you, too. And your cacophony.

———

If you haven't read Emily, Wyatt, and Heath's book, that's available now in ebook, print, and audio: https://chloemaine. com/cabin-mates/

A "why choose" instalove weekend of fun!

My plans for a solitary weekend of hiking and hot tubbing at my family's cabin in the mountains take a turn when I arrive at dusk, only to discover it's been rented out. And the unexpected guests aren't exactly strangers to me. Heath Taylor and Wyatt Dane are construction workers who renovated my college dorm. Who growled at any boy who dared to look in my direction while I was trying to study.

I don't need protection this weekend, though. I'm looking for a sweet kind of oblivion that it turns out only four strong arms can provide. Little do I realize they want a lot more than forty-eight hours of uninhibited bliss. These possessive men want double the happy ever after.

also by chloe maine

Links to all books are on my website at
www.chloemaine.com

operation: wife her up

I have a week off and a leave pass burning a hole in my pocket. I should go home to Conception Ridge. I head there, but when the exit on the highway comes up, I keep on driving to Virgin Peak, and my cabin on a mountain lake.

I don't expect to find a squatter. Or to immediately have a visceral connection to the young woman, who refuses to tell me her name. And despite the fact I'm a big guy, a Navy SEAL, she seems to trust me.

We have five days together. Five nights, too, and I'll use every second to forge a stronger bond between us. Before I leave this island, I will know her name—and give her mine, if she'll have me.

Operation: Wife Her Up is underway, and I never fail in my mission.

father of the bride

She's the maid of honor. He's the father of the bride.

Thanks to a snowstorm on the East Coast, I'm the only member of my best friend's wedding party to actually arrive in Vegas as planned. But she has a plan. . . her father will pick me up at the airport, and we'll take care of any last-minute wedding details together. Not in the plan is the unexpected sizzling chemistry with an older, off-limits man and being talked into sharing his suite.

What happens in Vegas, stays in Vegas? Not if the father of the bride claims you as his own.

before he was her headmaster

My one-night stand? He's sitting behind the headmaster's desk.

We meet at a truck stop. The chemistry is immediate, and we both do something out of character: one night, no explanations. The next day, I arrive at yet another private school. I'm a mature student who just needs three credits before I can graduate. Now I'm the off-limits forbidden temptation Sebastian Craig can't forget, and we both try our best to behave. It works for a few weeks. . .until our secret cravings come tumbling out in the library after hours. How will we keep our private connection hidden until the end of term? I want to be his sweet girl forever, but the age gap and responsibility of his role might be too much to overcome. . .

above the shop

He was my mom's high school boyfriend.

I have seventeen dollars to my name and a one-way bus ticket to my new college town—two months early. Oh, and the name of a man I've never met scrawled on a piece of paper. Henry Wilde.

But when I show up on his doorstep, he has no idea that my mom said I could stay with him. And he only has one bed.

It's eight weeks until I can move onto campus.

Eight weeks of living with him above his barbershop. So I'm going to make myself useful. Help him out, and not try to pester him about what it's going to be like at college. Because this homeschooled girl has a lot of questions, but they're not appropriate for my de facto guardian. Not even if we're both consenting adults…

santa's baby

She calls him Daddy Christmas. . .

Ford Gamble is my dad's best friend. He's also the reclusive keeper of the Conception Ridge lighthouse. I remember a time when he was around more—the perfect, hotter-than-sin fodder for all my teenage fantasies. And if I'm being honest, for most of my fantasies since then too. . .

Now there's just enough silver in his shock of sexy hair and thick beard that he looks a little like a hot forty-year-old Santa with six-pack abs. And that's what has me heading to the lighthouse on a dark, stormy Christmas Eve when the retirement home where I work needs a fill-in Mr. Claus for their annual celebration.

Except I underestimate the bad weather. The next thing I know, I'm waking up in his bed, and I realize I may have revealed my forbidden fantasies to him in my feverish sleep. Can I convince him to finally let me call him Daddy Christmas? Or will he deny he shares my taboo feelings?

Because I know Ford can't stop looking at me with a wild heat in his gaze. And my desperate Christmas wish is that he's thinking about corrupting his little, not-so-innocent angel.

about the author

Chloe Maine has written other books before, but none of them as purely id-driven as her debut, *Before He Was Her Headmaster*. She delights in the fantasy of bending big men to the wicked desires of supposedly innocent women. When she's not writing, she's probably reading. She lives in Canada with her own big man, raising the babies they made together.

facebook.com/chloemainebooks
x.com/chloemainebooks
instagram.com/chloemainebooks
tiktok.com/@chloemainebooks